CREATING
Melody

CREATING
Melody

MEREDITH MADDISON

J. Kenkade
PUBLISHING

Bryant, Arkansas

J. Kenkade Publishing
5920 Highway 5 N. Ste. 7
Bryant, AR 72022
www.jkenkadepublishing.com
Facebook.com/jkenkadepublishing

J. Kenkade Publishing is a registered trademark.

Printed in the United States of America
ISBN 978-1-955186-55-1

CONTENTS

Prologue

The sounds of summertime filled her ears. She was awakened to how exhilarating it was to finally hear them again. The quartet of cicadas that serenaded long crescendos all throughout the days and into the nights were accented by the definitive calls of a lone whippoorwill once the sun began to fade. The intermittent prestissimo of a nearby wasp or yellow jacket added to the overture but was soon taken over by the solos of mourning doves, bluebirds, and the occasional shrill yell from a red-tailed hawk. The distant sound of dogs was hardly an interruption but more of a downbeat to the wild, orchestrated music being conducted by nature itself right outside her bedroom window.

As the newness of this symphony of nature passed through the open windows, so too did the suffocating heat of the Mid-South, but she'd rather endure the malaise of near-heatstroke just to hear this sweet melody than close the windows and have air conditioning. It was a tune that she'd missed copiously for more than a decade. A song that her heart had longed to enjoy. But being locked away in her own mind had kept her from hearing the escapades of these beloved mistrals for too long.

It had been nearly two years since she began to wake from the topor that stole approximately half of her life. Turning forty seemed to be the last ingredient needed for her to escape the lasting effects of a somnolence that had held her mind confined to paralysis. She finally felt alive again.

She had just purchased a small farm in a small town that was hardly a speck on the map. Short of this landmark furniture company that people drove from several states over to come to, Woodland was scarcely heard of and equally populated. She had no neighbors. She'd have to drive half a mile in either direction to come to the next house, and it was just as she liked it. The first thing she had attended to was the fence. She had fenced the yard so well even the FedEx man wouldn't come to her door with a package.

A menagerie of mutts barking in the yard was an excellent deterrent for anyone trying to come too close. This was exactly as she needed it. She'd lost trust in humanity. There seemed to be a serendipitous prerequisite that she had been blind to for the first part of her life but now spotted almost immediately. People lied. They lied about themselves, their intentions, their accolades, and their lives but with such a defiantly innocent specter of indifference that no one seemed to catch on.

She, too, had missed it at first for many years and person after person. It was the very reason she lost half of her life and was just beginning at the age many of her peers were settling into lives of mediocrity. And it was the very reason she knew she could not trust anyone again.

On the other hand – if she kept herself at arm's length from everyone, this town was the best place she'd ever lived. There was a sense of security, peace, reverence, and piety that enveloped her as a new resident. She had already become well-acquainted with the abilities of the local mechanic, as her tires seemed to be a magnet for every stray nail and screw on the gravel country roads. But this, so far, was the only downfall to this precious town. Still, the consistency of the low tire symbol became like a friend calling; she knew it would mean a short visit to a family-run business, which was genuinely nice as long as she didn't ever need to know them for more than patching tires and changing oil. It was almost like a game, if you will, a contrived version of life where she could mingle within society, meet people, make "friends," and still maintain solitude.

CHAPTER 1

They told me I was blessed. The pastor, his wife, and the Elders. They said I was a "blessed wife" and this was my "blessed life." I didn't feel blessed. I felt emptiness, pain, frustration, and I felt lonely. I was a stay-at-home mom, homeschooling teacher, homemaker, and doleful wife. Being a stay-at-home mom had been my life's goal. I had looked forward to those 2.5 children and a picket fence. I would have added a small barn, a few acres, and a couple of horses to that dream – a dream Peter said he wanted, too – but that was now a dream full of empty promises and excuses. At some point, I stopped dreaming, stopped hoping, and had just bunkered down to love my three boys in a house that was falling apart around us, with a multitude of unfinished projects, on a small plot of land within city limits. These boys of ours were the only reason I went on, but somehow, the rest of it wasn't what I'd expected. The rest of my life was manifested with aching so strong my heart literally felt as though it was bleeding.

I lay in bed exhausted and yet unable to sleep. Analyze – rehash - think… I was sure that if I put enough thinking to it, I'd figure it out – be able to fix it. I'd be able to find solace and appreciate the simplicity of simply being alive. That's what they kept telling me.

I had to be grateful God woke me with breath. I had a roof over my head, leaking as it was, still a roof – I was to find my own joy in Jesus, or I wasn't really a believer and the cause of my own problems. That was the summation of counseling with my church Elders and their wives. On top of this disdain for life – caused by details too numerous to count – I needed to take full responsibility for the failure of our marriage, my feelings of desolation and agony, and for all of *his* shortcomings.

"The woman sets the tone of the house," they said. "You must be woman enough to make him want to be home and involved in a godly way. Pray for him instead of nagging at him, and you will wake up to a godly marriage," they promised.

Everything in me had wanted to scream at them and make them live with him, to come there and see what he was like, to know how impossible all of their advice was, and how it wasn't going to work – how it hadn't worked yet. But all my words were met with the preposterous rebuttals from women who did just as they preached against in front of everyone in church and couldn't see for themselves both the hypocrisy in their advice or the fear I had of my own husband, the way I could never nag or speak to my husband in the ways that they did. They couldn't fathom or understand that it was not what they imagined – and that our "marriage problems" were not going to be cured by *my* changes. I couldn't get them to believe that I'd already read all the books they'd given me, silenced my woes, and accused him of nothing but could not feign joy in a torturous life any longer, consumed with frustration and loneliness that surpassed a bad marriage and festered now because of a church family with fellow believers who would neither hear me nor help me and instead lifted the man who made my life miserable onto a higher pedestal. I'm not sure how to explain how I cognitively knew they were wrong – yet accepted it as a challenge to fix something I knew I could not, driven with shame, guilt, and chains that forced me to own this as my "cross to bear for Christ."

I knew his footsteps would soon be heard on the hardwood floors. Just that thought set my heart racing and my stomach in a knot. I rolled over to face the wall. If I could quiet myself before he came in and act as though I was already asleep, he might leave me alone. Focusing on my breathing, I tried to make it sound shallow. To match that of a sleeping woman. I'd been forced to believe that I wasn't allowed to "turn him down."

"To be a good wife, one must not only say "yes" every time but swing from chandeliers and provide such entertainment and extreme pleasure that your man never thinks to stray." I guess I hadn't delivering in that department because I hadn't prevented him from wandering, and now, the thought of "being" with him was almost as nauseating and dehumanizing as it was to actually "be" with him.

I felt the bed move and the mattress creak as he sat undressing for bed. The clunk of his pants on the floor with his belt still threaded through the loops would have woken anyone – but not me; I was not going to budge. I prayed for God to forgive me as I attempted to reject him by pretending to sleep.

He was a tall man but scrawny. His legs were long but entirely too slender for a man of his height, and his chest looked like that of a teen boy beginning puberty. His dark hair was always too long and greasy for lack of being washed even when he showered, but he thought of himself as so handsome. He regularly told me how handsome he was and that he often described himself as such on online dating forums.

His cheekbones were too high, and his skin sagged, creating hollows in his cheeks and jowls at his jaw. He couldn't grow a full beard or mustache, but dark hair and irregular shaving made him look as though he were destitute and unable to care for himself. Poor oral hygiene contributed to both stained, crooked teeth and missing ones as well. His breath was a mix of rotten tooth decay and garlic every day. His eyes were green with flecks of brown. I'd read once that a Chinese proverb warns of such eye color, claiming it a warning for hot tempers, but I'd not heard that before marrying him. Maybe I would have still – because by the time I'd married him, I'd already been told by all his laughing family that he sure had a hot temper, and I must have been something to have changed that. While it made me feel special to think I had such a temperament and way about myself that curtailed a lifelong hot temper in this man, it never occurred to me that this anger would ever erupt on me as long as I kept being sweet enough to keep it in check. It also set me up to blame myself every time his anger surfaced because it naturally meant I was not doing something right and was causing the eruption. He told me so himself... so I accepted my challenge, took the blame, and tried harder from then forward and again the next time and the next time.

"Focus – breath shallowly. Don't move," I told myself. He moved toward me, calling out my name with a voice that shot involuntary trembles through my core.

"Steady, be quiet – breathe," I silently chided myself.

Pretending to be asleep, I ignored his fondling, hoping he'd give up and roll over to his own side of the bed. It was work not to squeeze my eyes in panic and disgust as he reached down the back of my underwear to fondle me. This was my captor, my tormentor. I was trapped in "his" home, raising "his" children, and minding "his" business. I was "the wife."

I hated to hear him tell our church friends about our home. It was entirely in my name because he couldn't get a loan with his poor credit and work history. I'd worked hard tutoring scores of children, working odd jobs, and giving riding lessons, all with our children in tow because I wasn't permitted to have a babysitter. I was called an unloving, abusive mother willing to put the children at risk of predators if I suggested such a thing. So, I could pay the mortgage, electric, water bills, and such, but it was "his house," "his yard," "his roof," and "his shed"... then, when it came to me, I was "the wife." I shuddered as the thoughts running through my mind were interrupted by the pawing of angry hands.

He tore at my pajamas, gruffly removing them and grabbing at my chest with force. He was on top of me and holding my hands above my head with a handful of hair I couldn't be sure whether he held intentionally or not. Spit dripped on my face as he pushed me up against the headboard and whispered in my ear that he knew I was a slut and liked it that way, and he seemed to intentionally miss where he was aiming, instead penetrating me further back…

Silently, I prayed to God, repeating his name because I couldn't think of anything else to think.

"I'm sorry! Forgive me, Father," was my second internal chant as this man used me against my will. I was married to this man but felt as though I was so deeply entrenched in sin for allowing such an atrocity of this sex to occur that I inaudibly pleaded for forgiveness as tears rolled from the corners of my eyes.

He groaned, releasing my wrists and hair, grabbed my body one last time, and then abruptly rolled over, taking the entire comforter from my own body and wrapping himself inside it like a chrysalis.

I would have to lay there motionless and without shivering from the chill of not being covered any longer. I would have to wait until I knew he was sleeping before I moved and could get up to bathe. I could feel dripping down my rear end and wasn't sure if it was from him or if I was bleeding.

Tears threatened to sting my eyes as the details of my life flooded my mind. With a heart so heavy with pain, I squeezed my eyes shut to block out my own emotion. I had to stay quiet even while I pleaded with the Creator of the Universe to take my life and not let me live to see morning. The only prayers I knew to pray anymore were for forgiveness and for my own death. It seemed to me that if He would comply and take my life, it wasn't quite suicide. And if He would take my life, leaving our children without their mother, somehow He would have a plan for keeping them safe from Peter, I rationalized so I could keep praying to die.

Somehow, I had gotten to be 35 years old when I last remembered being 27. Thinking over the past 8 years, one day just seemed to bleed into another, I guess, until all sense of time was lost. I lived, I aged, and I gave birth to two more children during this time. I knew I went through the motions, but I couldn't evoke a single memory from the last 8 years except for the obvious – even those were fuzzy. Those memories were really only recalled as bullet points on a timeline with no detail to go along with them. Eight years had gone by, and all I knew was that I breathed.

I watched the red glow of numbers on the clock across the room. Minute by minute, I wished for sleep to escape from the night. I prayed for death, to escape this life. But I received no answer to either prayer. I lay awake.

Readjusting my long legs, pushing and fluffing the pillow under my head, and wrapping my long brown hair into a loose bun on top of my head, I hoped to find a physical comfort that would relieve me from this insomnia. Morning took too long to come, and yet the new day was beginning too soon.

Soundlessly, I rolled out from under the quilt I'd used to stay warm last night and made my way to the master bathroom as quietly as I could. I could hear the birds chirping outside my windows but couldn't feel the melody anymore. For a brief moment, I paused, listening and trying to capture the sense of delight eavesdropping on the chatter and songs of the birds had given me before, but I couldn't drum up anything. I felt nothing…

I went into the bathroom feeling defeated, reached in behind the plastic shower curtain, turned the hot knob as far as it would turn, pulled the metal lever up on the faucet, and waited for the water to warm up. Careful not to look at the image reflecting from the full-length mirror, I stepped over the height of the clawfoot tub and into the now scalding water.

The hotter, the better. Every morning began with the same ritual. Standing beneath the stream of hot, pulsing water, first, I washed my face. Crying into the pouring water, no one would see any evidence of defeat this way. I rinsed both the soap and anguish down the drain. Leaning forward, I grabbed the bottle of shampoo from the side of the tub, lathered up, and rinsed again under the steamy deluge of water. Methodically, I reached for cream rinse and worked it into the length of my hair. Leaving it piled up on my head, then, I soaped up a wash cloth and washed the rest of my body.

Moving my head under the shower to rinse away the conditioner from my hair and soap from my body, I didn't hear him come in. Somehow, he had gotten into the back of the tub with such stealth swiftness that I didn't realize he'd come to invade my solitude until he was there. Taller than me by three inches, he hovered close, towering over me. The smell of his body gave me an immediate dry heave that I tried to cover with a cloth to my face as if I were washing. I was trapped. Dirty again as he touched me and moved my hands to satisfy his morning desires. Before I knew it, I was being swung around. Trying to stay upright and looking for something to hold for balance, I was bent forward, violated, and held by coarse hands at the hip until he finished. New tears stung my eyes as I washed the filth from my body, trying to act as though I were not bothered by his presence and insistence. I turned the water hotter to burn away the decadence of my husband and resisted the urge to cry again. I tipped my head back, straightened my back, and pulled the curtain back far enough to get out of the shower. I heard him catch his breath as the heat of the shower scalded his body full-on, and I smirked.

"Maybe the heat of the water will burn away some of his indecency," I thought as I moved out of the shower with such prowess and speed I could only find when trying to get away from him. I could hear him chuckle. He had conquered me and knew I was rushing away from him. Before I even dried off, I was wrapped in a towel of protection. The largest, thickest towel that would insolate me from his eyes, his touch, and his tenure. Staring at the toilet, I checked to be sure I could hold back the vomit suddenly trying to escape the pit of my empty stomach and went to the sink to brush my teeth. Needing to leave the bathroom – his sounds, his stench – I pushed the revolt from deep within my heart and mind, forcing me to evacuate the room without drying my hands.

I could feel his gaze piercing me, looking through my towel, and blaming me for his betrayals.

I dressed quickly to be clothed by the time he came out of the shower. A pair of baggy pants, a loose-fitted tee shirt, and a pair of sandals were the usual attire. This day would be no different.

CHAPTER 2

S he dried her freshly-showered body and hurried to dress. Perfectly-proportioned, tan, and eager to get breakfast on the table to please him, she knew she had failed to catch her husband's attention as she pulled a sundress over her taut body, which hugged her in all the right spots.

Utterly unaware of her beauty and yet trying to impress a man who seemed to ignore she existed, Melody glided from the room to begin her day.

Hoping the smell of bacon would stir her sleeping husband, she set to work cooking eggs and pancakes from scratch and putting pure maple syrup on the table.

Instead of hearing her husband rise, she heard their infant son wake up in his room down the hall.

Grabbing a towel to dry her hands and turning the heat down on the frying pan, she briskly walked up the hall to get to her son. Taking him straight to the changing table, she changed his diaper and brought him to the kitchen, placing him in a bouncy chair away from the stove.

Melody finished cooking breakfast and sat at the table with her son, nursing him and staring into the distance through the window overlooking their backyard.

Lost in thought and hopeful her husband would soon join her for breakfast, Melody returned to reality, realized the hot breakfast had grown cold, and carefully got up with her infant still attached to her breast to put his plate in the microwave for easy warming. She knew her husband had come to bed late; she'd stayed awake waiting for him, so she knew it wasn't until 2 a.m. that he'd finally joined her.

"I guess he's tired and won't be up until later," she'd mused to herself, trying not to allow disappointment to cloud her morning. She rechecked his diaper when her son, Joey, finished his meal. She brought him into the living room where she set to work on her undergraduate assignment. With a baby in her lap and a computer open on the coffee table in front of her, she typed up two essays due for the end of the week. She submitted them before closing the top of her laptop and taking her little boy to the family room, where he could lie on the floor with a few toys to look at. Knowing how vital "tummy time" was for a baby, she arranged him on his belly to get the needed opportunity for neck strength. To her surprise, the little two-month-old baby turned over to his back. Overjoyed and enthusiastic, Melody put him back on his tummy for him to do it again, which he did. Breakfast had long since passed, but Melody could not wait for her husband to wake up to see what their son was doing that morning.

Around 11:30 in the morning, he walked into the family room in a pair of freshly-cleaned jeans and a tee shirt. He sat with a pair of socks in hand and bent over to put them on. Melody was glad to see her husband and eagerly looked up toward him to offer breakfast or that she could make him lunch. She was sure that he'd want to see their son could roll over, so she placed him on his belly and excitedly told her husband to watch.

Like a small laugh, she heard a sound come from her husband. Looking up eagerly to see if he was happily enjoying their son's milestone – she was disappointed to see he wasn't even looking at him and had just coughed. She tried drawing his attention to their baby and put him back on his tummy to do it again.

She was sure he'd want to see and be equally excited about it.

As she bent down to adjust the baby, he walked out of the room.

Melody scooped up their little boy and carried him toward the kitchen where she expected her husband to go for food, but he passed the doorway and grabbed his sneakers instead. She cheerfully told him about breakfast and ran to grab it from the microwave in a quick attempt to feed him before he left.

He sat listlessly at the counter. He seemed depressed. Melody worried about him staying in bed so long and how he looked as he sat there staring into space. She felt compelled to cheer him up.

"I hate seeing you so sad," Melody offered.

Her husband looked up at her; his hair was disheveled and greasy like he hadn't washed it in days, although she knew he'd showered the day before.

His eyes looked sunken in and listless. "It's hard to be in a new state. I left behind my friends and family. Jonathon? He won't speak to me now. We've been best friends since eighth grade. We've done everything together, and now he won't talk to me..." he said like a lost puppy looking for a friend. "We moved here for you – and now I've lost Jonathon... " he said, looking distressed. "I think he was secretly in love with me and wanted to be my gay lover, so he won't forgive me for moving here with you," he confided.

Melody was taken aback. What a leap!

"What makes you think he's gay and wants to be your lover?"

He looked at her and shrugged with a smirk. "Trust me; I know he wants my ass."

Without another word, he left the house and got into his truck.

The house was silent again. The stillness was deafening. Melody looked down and realized that Joey had fallen asleep on her shoulder while she was standing there and watching her husband's work truck leave. She set the plate of breakfast food down, ventured out the front door onto the covered porch, and sat on one of the wicker chairs she'd carefully arranged there a few months ago. The cushions were still bright and clean; she had finished making them four weeks earlier. Melody stared at the fabric on the adjacent chair for longer than she realized. Lost in time and dazed, she was thinking about how there was nothing she was even sure of anymore. The sounds of robins in the surrounding oaks and the scampering of squirrels up the looming tree trunks caught her attention first. The tune of nature surrounding her soothed her. Across the street, her old neighbor, Clara, was busy tending her roses. Melody had planted flowers and hydrangeas across the front of this porch within the first weeks of moving in. In fact, she'd even dug into the earth and scrounged around for bricks to build an arched walkway to the front steps. Darkness crossed her eyes as she looked down upon the bricks and what used to be her flower bed.

Memories of an argument poisoned the moment. He'd made her redo the walk, accusing her of doing it wrong first. After he'd scorched them all with a blow torch, the flowers were gone because he complained she didn't weed well enough in the garden. In her best effort to change her mood, Melody got up quickly and moved with the agility and grace to not wake her sleeping baby and walked into her home.

The windows needed curtains.

Melody had fabric waiting to be cut and sewn for six large windows on the east and south walls of the large living room. Unwilling to feel consumed with loneliness or sadness, she walked to the nursery and put her sleeping son down in his bed. She hugged him just a moment longer than she needed to before laying him down and covering him with a small quilt she'd made of soft flannel.

Turning the Pachabel CD on for her sleeping son, she quietly tiptoed out of his room and set herself up in front of the sewing machine. Melody imagined how glad her husband would be to see the windows appropriately dressed as she laid panels, measured, cut, and sewed seams.

He'd mentioned several times that he didn't like how open and exposed they were in that room, so Melody created the sheer panels to hang behind the darker panels to allow light to come in and also maintain privacy for him in the room. It had taken weeks to decide on the fabric for the windows. There had been countless trips to the fabric store, getting swatches and bringing them back for her husband to approve this one finally. Melody had drawn the room repeatedly with various curtain patterns to show him before he finally agreed to a long valance tapering to a point in the center of the window. She'd purchased the fabric for the sheers and made them without drawing a picture or asking him what he'd thought. It was a gamble on her part that she'd hoped he'd like.

As Melody worked, she thought about the oldest woman in town and the stories she'd told about dancing in this very home when she and her husband were just married. Before the home had sat ruining for so long, it had been the mayor's home and had been grand. Rebekah had told of many happy times in the living room and parlor of the house.

Melody thought it was so wonderful to know the history of the home. Trying to bring it back to its splendor would take time and money, but she hoped to get it as cleaned and gleaming inside as her talents allowed.

She finished the last seam, snipped the last two threads, and went to hang the final curtain over the final window on the east wall. Satisfied with her work, she straightened one tassel that hung just at the center of the matching valance, which tapered to a point at the center of each window, all with matching tassels. Still imagining the dancers from eighty years ago swirling through the two front rooms, she heard Joey waking from his nap, so she rushed out of the room to clean up her sewing supplies before entering the nursery.

She found him lying on his tummy; he'd evidently rolled over in his crib during his nap. Melody was excited that he could roll both front-to-back and back-to-front now and ran to his baby book to jot it down. Lifting him carefully, she went to the changing table to change his diaper and then took him into her room, where she'd rock her infant and nurse him before he even cried out with hunger.

She hummed as he sucked. The sun came through the large bay window behind her, dancing in a brilliant light pattern over the suckling child as it cascaded through the lace curtain panel.

It looked as though his skin was alive with the breeze that caused the curtain to sway and display a special light show on the delicate skin of her little baby. His hair was brown and long for such a young baby. It curled up when it got wet, so Melody expected him to have curls as it grew longer.

Sitting with her nursing Joey in the silence of her home was a recipe for her mind to wander. It was often impossible for her to escape the thoughts and goings-on that tugged at her heart and attempted to force her to become sad. Melody knew how to channel these thoughts away. Without another moment of indulgence, she curbed her mind with prayer. Instead of thinking about how upset she was about the details, Melody quietly bowed her head and began singing her prayers softly. She spoke to God about her love for Him, her gratitude for this little baby, her house, and the time and fabric to make curtains. She kept the song going as long as she could come up with things to be grateful for.

She had exhausted herself listing her blessings and prayed for her husband to be happy, prosperous, kind, and honest. She prayed for him in every avenue that threatened to bring tears to her eyes –while holding back the details that sequestered such pain. She looked up to the height of the 12-foot ceiling and pleaded with God to take these thoughts from her mind and instead be pleased with a wife who was taking the time and choosing to pray for him instead.

Just as minds wander – even though she tried to stay focused by singing her prayers, she grew silent as thoughts filtered through her mind again. Abruptly, she was brought back to reality as she chided herself for "going there again" and decided to get up and busy herself to keep her mind from straying again.

Smiling and feeling quite at peace, she decided to make her

husband's favorite meal for dinner. Her young baby had nodded off as he nursed but hadn't finished yet, so she scooted her slim body forward on the rocker to get to a position where she could get up from the chair without disturbing him. She took him straight to the laundry room and opened the freezer to find frozen chicken legs and thighs. She should have thought to take the meat out sooner so it could defrost, but she hadn't. She brought it into the kitchen, balancing everything and her snoozing, still-nursing son as she moved gingerly to the sink. Running the tap to get it hot, she let the basin fill up and then placed the frozen meat into the hot water for defrosting.

Her son finished his afternoon meal and needed burping, so she delicately situated him on her left shoulder, where she could pat him and still use her right arm to get a few ingredients down from the cupboards. Happy with her son's long burp and his content, sweet, and smiling face, she set him on the kitchen counter in a tabletop swing and fastened his buckle.

She peeled potatoes and set them in the second sink basin for rinsing.

Moving quickly and easily, she filled a pot with water, set it on the stove, rinsed the potatoes, and gently set each potato into the water for boiling. Next, she fished around in the pantry for Corn Flakes cereal and various spices and set to work with her marble rolling pin to turn her cereal into bread crumbs. She swayed her hips to a rhythm only she could hear, cooed at her son, and set her creation to the side. One last dash of onion powder, and she was just about through in the kitchen for the time being.

She returned to the sink, removed the chicken package from the basin, opened the window, and pitched the water out so she could refill it with hot water again. The drain had stopped working in the sink six months earlier, but she didn't mind tossing the water out the window. It reminded her of the "olden day" times she loved reading about so much.

"We're going to take a walk, little manny," she smiled as she spoke to Joey. She moved to her son's room and changed his diaper before heading into her room and slipping on a pair of running sneakers. For practicality's sake, Melody kept her stroller in the trunk of her car and quickly pulled it out with one free arm, holding her child in the other.

It snapped together quickly.

Melody set her son in the seat, set him up enough to see the scenery, slipped his little booties onto his feet, adjusted the sun visor, and set off for an afternoon stroll into town. Only half a mile from the main square, she pushed him along the road on a sidewalk, heading first toward the library. Few storefronts were open anymore, so after dropping off her latest library book and choosing another to read, she walked to the other side of the road to see what new display was set up at the insurance company. A new Mexican restaurant had opened, and a Thai café was going in. The excitement of their small town getting more food venues was brilliant. Melody forgot the troubles of her heart as she walked forward, pushing the stroller and staring at the adorable tiny leather booties she'd made for her son to wear on his outings with her. One foot had a monkey head and the other a bunch of bananas, complete with a small blue sticker. She thought about how she'd worked out that pattern and collected various pieces of colored leather at the thrift store from pants and jackets others had discarded.

Walking, strolling really, she made her way around the square and was ready to head toward home. Hoping the chicken would be ready for breading, she couldn't help but smile, thinking of the satisfaction she would bring to her husband, having created his favorite meal. Her child needed nursing, so she stopped at the park and found a good spot to sit and feed him. Watching the other mothers and their children play mesmerized her until she saw another mom with a sleeping child under a nearby tree and felt instantly connected. She felt drawn to her and quickly got up to move near her and introduce herself.

CHAPTER 3

Three little boys met me in the kitchen, asking for breakfast. I was angry and had been defiled, but I tried to hide it with a false smile that even my kids could see wasn't real but didn't mention. Grabbing a frying pan from the cabinet and a carton of eggs with the other arm, I balanced butter in the crook of my elbow before setting up to make eggs for the boys clamoring for food. Within minutes, the eggs were scrambled and cooking in the cast iron frying pan I often daydreamed about whacking my husband with. As soon as I served the boys breakfast, I made coffee, carefully measuring the exact amount of grounds for a "perfect cup."

Peter walked into the kitchen, bending his six-foot frame to kiss me.

I held my breath as he pressed his lips to mine.

"Good morning, mine love." I'm not sure why he needed to say it that way, but he'd say it once a day, and then I was safe from his lips and poor grammar for another twenty-four hours.

I watched him as he completed the ritual and nonchalantly dumped the remaining eggs I'd made from the pan into the garbage. He put together an entire omelet in the same pan, complete with mushrooms, onions, and peppers, all remaining on the counter under the open cabinet doors of every cupboard he'd opened to make his creation. They were the vegetables I had intended to use to make the chicken a la' king for dinner, but I said nothing. I tidied behind him, watched him eat most of it, and then handed about an ounce of the meal onto our oldest son's plate. Jonah had already eaten and was full, so he passed the plate to Gregory, his younger brother.

Peter turned his nose up at the coffee, calling it "too sweet," and made another cup before heading into the den, where he sat in front of the computer with one hand down his pants and the Drudge Report on the screen.

I impatiently anticipated his leaving. I couldn't wait until he was gone so I could relax a little. Not wanting the criticism he was sure to dole out on my parenting and homeschooling methods, I moved the kids to the front room to begin their schoolwork for the day. Nine-year-old Jonah raged his disgust for having to do his math problems, and Peter was there in a second to defend our oldest son. I was chastised for forcing such work on him and reminded that homeschooling was supposed to be done in a way that made kids want to learn. Before leaving, he chided me for letting the breakfast he'd made for *me* get cold and wasted (this was the remaining omelet neither of the older two had eaten) and high-fived Jonah before disappearing. Six-year-old Gregory looked after him with the saddest look. He'd been ignored again. I say 'disappearing' because he was gone for three hours while his van remained in the driveway. Having no idea where he was unnerved me as the hours dragged on, and I worried his appearance would disrupt the flow of work the kids were doing and fretted each time I had to redirect or correct one of the boys. Feeling as though I had to look over my shoulder and anticipating a reprimand, we managed to make it to lunchtime. I didn't know how much longer I could stand him being around somewhere, eluding us yet being present in his evasive hiding spot that could be nearby or far away.

We were not through with our lessons, but I moved into the kitchen to make a picnic lunch to eat at the park. I packed up three bikes and our food into the minivan and got three young boys into their seats. Still a toddler, barely 3 years old, Andrew had a little three-wheel bike with a handle I could push and steer from the back. Before we left, I felt obligated to call out for my husband to say goodbye but was met with no answer. A nursery rhyme CD played softly in the background on this short drive before I switched the music to a math song with repetitive multiplication tables done in a rap.

We stayed at the park through Andrew's nap time, which I held him through as I sat under the giant oak tree at the local park. Sitting at such an angle, I could see the entire playground and the small entrance either of the older children would come through if they needed or wanted me. I noticed another woman sitting under a tree nearby, nursing a small baby. She was beautiful. Everything about her posture exuded grace and class. She was a woman who had it all together. I imagined her beautiful, happy life, feeling jealous, unkempt, and shamefully insignificant at the same time.

Every one of her brown hairs and beautifully sun-kissed blonde streaks were in place. She had her hair up in a French twist with a tortoise clip. Her baby was finished nursing, and she magically had him upright, being burped, and her top done back up appropriately. Somehow, her cover sat perfectly folded next to her, as if she hadn't just spent the last thirty-five minutes using it to cover her nursing son.

Even the baby's outfit was perfect looking. He had the most adorable, unique leather booties and a head full of curly, wispy hair, and he favored his mother.

She noticed me looking at her, and I was immediately embarrassed. From the corner of my eye, I watched this established younger woman stand to her feet with ease as if she were not holding an infant and just stood with more grace than I could have without a child even nearby.

"Oh, crap, she's coming over here," I thought to myself with a sudden feeling of panic hitting me.

Balancing her baby, she scooped her diaper bag up and pushed her little stroller over to my tree as if she were floating. She didn't get hung up on roots or even wobble as she gently sat beside me and said hello.

"Hi," the perfect woman said.

With my eyes diverted to the ground, I said hello as nicely as possible.

"What could she possibly want?" I wondered, trying to be polite but unwilling to make too much conversation and encourage her to stay.

She turned out to be perfectly beautiful and equally as lovely. She offered to be an extra pair of eyes on my other two children playing on the equipment, and our friendship flourished from there.

We talked as if we'd always known each other. She'd planned to homeschool when her baby was school-aged, so our conversation went that route for a little while until it was time for her to leave and make dinner for her husband in what I imagined was a perfect home with a loving husband.

CHAPTER 4

Melody looked at her watch and realized she had to get home to make dinner soon if she would finish it before her husband was home from work. Politely excusing herself, Melody got her things together and swiftly walked home.

In her haste, she didn't miss the stunning flowers along the way or the flock of grackles making their aerial debut.

Each fully synchronized swoop made her smile bigger; the way these birds twisted, turned, rose, and descended was an orchestrated masterpiece. The chirping from thousands of birds at once was a welcome serenade to Melody.

With a grin from ear to ear, Melody walked up her driveway, put her stroller back into the back of the car, and brought her little boy into the house and directly to the kitchen.

She put him in the swing, washed her hands, and set to work preparing the chicken and turning the water on to boil the potatoes. Half an hour later, she had dinner in the oven, potatoes whipped and covered to keep warm, carrots steaming, and a salad tossed. Smartly washing the dishes as she went along, she was ready to set the table.

Remembering to check on her latest class assignment for her school courses, she jogged to the front room and grabbed her laptop. Quickly logging in, she saw a short essay was due by the end of the week.

It was easy for Melody to type up an essay within half an hour, including all the required quotes and citations, because writing had become a passion for her. She was good at it, scored high, and enjoyed the ease of getting this degree through assignments, mainly writing papers and essays. She finished the essay at the counter next to her son, who still sat in his swing cooing. With a quick click on the submit button, she waited the moment it took for the assignment to send and closed her computer, sliding it to the other side of the counter and out of the way.

The familiar jingle of the keys meant her husband was home. Melody moved to the next room and waited for him to appear in the den, where she sat with their infant son.

The sound of water running through the pipes alerted her that he was taking a shower. Slightly disappointed he didn't even say hello first, Melody got up with her son and checked on the meal she was preparing.

Turning off the carrots, she suddenly realized she wasn't finished. Her husband's favorite vegetable was in the refrigerator. With one arm supporting her child, she washed and snapped the ends off the long asparagus stalks. She laid them carefully on the cutting board she kept near the sink, moved sideways in one graceful movement to reach a baking sheet from the cabinet, and, still one-handed, she set the baking sheet across the sink, straddling it over the basin and carefully arranging the asparagus. She leaned forward and on her toes to reach for some olive oil and gently sprinkled oil over the fresh vegetables. Melody put the oil away and reached over the stove to get the salt.

Carefully opening the oven, she gingerly shoved the tray under the rack the chicken sat on and checked the meat to see if it was finished yet. Melody moved across the room to set her now sleeping baby in his bouncing chair so she could lift the meat from the oven.

He appeared from nowhere in sweatpants and a clean tee shirt. His hair was wet but still looked unwashed.

"Smells good," he said, bringing a smile to Melody's face. She was so glad she'd taken the extra time to add asparagus to his favorite chicken dish. "Looks like you dirtied every dish in the house to make it, though."

The thrill of his compliment was immediately crushed as she looked to the sink and saw the dirty hot chicken dish and all the other dishes she'd used clean and sitting in the dish drainer by the sink.

Melody parted her lips to speak, to defend herself, and said, "Of course, I didn't use every dish." She stuttered a little, explaining the need for what she'd used, but was cut off.

"You could wash dishes as you go so there aren't dirty dishes all stacked up next to the sink, is all I'm saying," he said with a look of innocent sympathy. "I'm trying to help you make your life easier."

Melody felt frustrated that he wouldn't listen or see that she had done just that.

"Mel, you need to toughen up. I wasn't criticizing you, just helping you," he said again with the same look of concern.

Frustration melted into shame. "Alright," Melody said with her eyes darting past him, unable to look into his eyes. She stooped down and slumped a little, almost like a dog who had been caught eating from the garbage. "I just need to put the vegetables on the table, and we're ready to eat," she said, somewhat straightening with the pride of a woman who made dinner from scratch for her husband.

"I'm not hungry. I ate about an hour ago… but it sure smells yummy."

Melody felt anger and as though the wind had been beaten out of her.

"You could have called, you know?" Melody said softly. "You should let me know when you're not planning to eat."

"Why would I call? I work all day. I was hungry, so I ate," he retorted, looking at her with the menacing stare he knew would eventually quiet her.

"Because I cook supper every day. It's common courtesy to wait the extra hour and eat the meal you know I'm home preparing," she responded with growing agitation from this common occurrence but tried so hard not to let it be heard in her voice or seen on her face.

"Common courtesy would be you knowing your place, woman," he spit in her face and put his hand up quickly. She flinched, moved away from his reach, and saw a smug look across his face. He left the room and closed their door.

When he departed from the room a moment later, they met in the hall, crossing paths accidentally. She moved quickly to the other side of the 5-foot-wide hall and recoiled when she saw his hand move. It was her typical defensive move whenever she was in a confined space with him. She felt ridiculous every time she did this and couldn't quite understand why she wouldn't get past their previous rocky years together. He hadn't struck her in months, but fear still overtook her most often in their hallway. She excused him as she considered how stressed he'd been during that last year. They were starting a new life and job and getting used to the new surroundings. There was his friend Mark, who had also been such a poor influence on him. She knew that was why he had been as bad as he'd gotten, and it wasn't his fault – so she wished she could bring herself to walk naturally down the hall or into small spaces with her own husband.

Lost in her thoughts, she hadn't even realized he was gone until she heard the front door slam.

Frustrated, angry, defeated, and confused, Melody went to her child, still strapped in his seat. He was still sleeping, but instead of putting him in his crib, she took him to her bedroom and rocked him in her arms. She put him on her shoulder, breathed in the smells only young babies have, and cried softly as she gently rubbed his back.

She sat chiding herself for being so forthright and yet replayed the events of all the nights previously when she'd been too timid to say anything and chided herself for that. She didn't know if staying quiet was right, but confronting her husband never accomplished anything, either.

"When will I learn to just be quiet?" she thought to herself, resigning herself to defeat.

Several hours later, the lights of his work truck lit their bedroom and drove a light around the room high above her head. He came in loudly, as though he expected her to be awake. She was. She had been lying in bed praying that he would return, preparing her apology, and going over it in detail because she could think of nothing else anyway.

Wide awake and eager to tell him she was sorry because she knew it was the only way to fix this, she waited patiently for him to come to their room. He didn't come.

She pulled the covers back and swung her smooth legs over the side of the bed, grabbed her bathrobe from the bed knob, padded through her room to the hall, and looked for a light to give her a clue as to which way he might have gone.

He was in his office, the door closed and a pale stream of light pouring through. Of all the projects this old house needed, turning the enclosed back porch into an office with a door he could close and lock had been his priority.

She knocked softly. There was no answer. She knocked again. Finally, she heard his chair creak, and the door opened. He took his seat and returned to peering at the computer screen at an angle that made it impossible for her to see. She could easily see the lump in his pants and hoped her going to him had created the reaction.

Melody sat on the floor. She felt as though she had to be lower than him before apologizing. It was a move she couldn't explain or actually resist.

He wouldn't look at her, but she apologized anyway. Ignoring her, he kept staring at the monitor's glow before him.

Since he didn't respond, she thought he either hadn't heard

her or needed a further, more detailed apology, which she freely offered.

Still, he said nothing.

Melody was feeling desperate for him to accept her apology. The anguish grew and twisted like a gnarly tree rooted deeply within her gut and crowding in her lungs and heart. She could feel a sharp pain as though the tree of anguish poked into her heart and pressed the breath out of her lungs.

Reluctantly, Melody got up and retreated to her room. She heard the baby stir in the adjoining nursery, so she went to him, brought him to her bed, and nursed him there.

She couldn't sleep, but lying there with her infant salved her broken heart just a little bit.

It was 4:03 when he finally came to bed. Their baby was sound asleep in his own bed when he finally came to bed.

Melody reached out to him; she put her arm around him, trying to pull a rigid body to her, moving her hands to massage his back and rub tension from the left side of his spine where she could reach. She told him that she loved him and was sorry once more. He did not respond. She reached her hand toward his front to stroke him, but he moved her hand away abruptly.

Melody wept softly beside him, wishing she could control this emotional outburst and scolding herself for every tear, sniffle, and involuntary sob that shook her body and made it evident that she was crying.

CHAPTER 5

I called for Gregory and Jonah to come to me at the park. Andrew was awake from his nap by then. The older boys came over soon after I'd called them and asked to ride bikes. I was actually happy to oblige, having no desire to go home, so we stayed at the park for another hour. They rode bikes down the hill, and I diligently tugged them back up so they could ride down again. Single-handedly, Gregory was the son who had taught me to smile again. He forced me to pay attention to my own face.

He was cranky as an infant if I couldn't muster a smile. I could fake a "happy face" just for him. I had gotten quite used to doing so. I walked through my days with what I imagined was a pleasant smile plastered across my face. If anyone cared to look closely, it would be easy to see dull, hazel eyes with no smile lines around them.

Gregory needed me to get his bike and bring it up the hill. I could see him studying my face and realized I needed to replace the scowl across my brow, which contradicted the smile I had planted there just for him. I relaxed my eyebrows and immediately saw him relax too. Jonah was trying to bring his bike back up, and Andrew eagerly waited for me to let him go down the hill with my assistance.

The boys tried to wear me out with their bike-riding antics. They kept giggling until I noticed their hunger for dinner outweighed their fun.

Before they could become grumbly, I rounded them up, packed their bikes, and buckled them into their seats.

The CD player in our old minivan was put on again as we drove the short distance home, and we sang "number raps" together.

His van was in the driveway. I could see it as I turned onto our road. I wondered if he was actually home or not.

Apprehensive and unwilling to face him, I hoped and prayed that he was still gone, but he was inside, sitting in front of his computer.

"What's for eats?" he wanted to know.

I rushed into the kitchen to fill a pot of water for spaghetti and quickly warm up some premade meatballs and a jar of sauce. I turned the heat on low, set the lid off the side, then dug through the freezer, looking for bread to make into garlic bread.

Within 20 minutes, I called everyone to dinner and sent the boys back to wash their hands as they rounded the corner one by one. Peter remained in front of the computer, engrossed in nothing I cared to know about. I'd grown so used to him not eating with us that it actually only bothered me when he did now.

The boys and I ate together at the kitchen counter on stools that swiveled.

They pretended their food was a bowl of worms and the meatballs were supersized beetles. They were boys and boys who could entertain even a tired mother.

When they were through, I cleaned up after them, loaded the dishwasher, and took Andrew to the bathroom for a bath. The bare floorboards creaked under my feet. I leaned forward to test the water with my wrist. I couldn't tell if the water was too hot by my own hands and didn't trust myself, so I grabbed a thermometer and tested the water to be sure this would be a good bath for my youngest son. Andrew stood staring into the water. He reached for the toys he wanted in the tub with him. I poured in bubble bath, which was actually an organic shampoo that I loved to smell, under the running water as I hugged my boys close to me. I sat cross-legged on the floor next to the tub, dodging water splashes from my excited little son.

Jonah and Gregory brought books for me to read to them and sat just outside the bathroom door. I read until Andrew's bathwater grew cool. Reaching in to drain the water and put his toys away, I moved to help the slippery toddler out and wrapped him in a towel.

After dressing Andrew into his pajamas, drying his hair, and tucking him into bed, I left him in the bed with a night light and went out to the den where the older two boys had moved to and were playing with their trucks.

I smiled at the two playing boys. Gregory was chanting,"*pew pew pew pew*" as he aimed his tank toward his brother's truck. Jonah played along and tumbled his vehicle to the right. He sputtered and shuttered the sounds of a truck explosion and played dead. Gregory moved over to his brother's aid and tuned his tank into an ambulance and wrecker to save his brother, but Jonah wasn't having it. Gregory shrieked at his brother for not playing right and lifted his arm to smash his truck across Jonah's face. I caught Gregory's arm in time to prevent a brawl.

"It's bath time for you two," I told them. They both looked up with pleading eyes asking to bring their trucks into the bathwater.

"These don't make very good water trucks, but you can use your foam cars your aunt sent for your brother's birthday last month," I told him with a gentle look.

They both jumped up and into the bathroom, stripping their clothes before turning the water on. I helped them fill the tub, gave them some of Andrew's bubbles, and left the room to get a book.

It was my turn to sit outside the bathroom, near enough to supervise and far enough to give them both privacy.

Engrossing myself in a book was my favorite way to escape the thoughts that plagued my mind, constantly warring for a place to thrive.

The boys splashing and playing reminded me to tell them to wash their hair and help each other rinse it, which they did quickly.

I returned to finish the last chapter of the latest Jody Piccoult novel I was reading. When I read her books, I could use my own mind, form my own opinion, and agree or disagree with safety and peace. The controversial topics played out in these books, feeding a need I had from the depth of my soul. Before closing the book, I told the boys to drain the tub and ensure they were rinsed.

More water splashed around, and the loud noises from skin slipping in the water against the porcelain tub cut through the quiet of the home.

"I'm okay!" Gregory's little voice said. My clumsy little boy was famous for that saying. I giggled, glad he was okay, and laughing because of how many times I heard that each week. I passed towels through the open door and reminded them not to drip dry like they were prone to do as they continued to play.

"We need pajamas!" the two chorused in unison.

I passed two sets of pajamas and clean underwear to each. They dressed quickly and prepared for me to dry their hair.

Jonah sat on the closed toilet as I dried Gregory's hair first. They switched places when I finished, and I sent them to tell their dad good night. We all tiptoed into what used to be the nursery and now housed all three boys, complete with bunk beds and a toddler bed. I tucked them in, kissed their foreheads, and crept into the hall again.

Now, I was stuck. I contemplated my next move carefully. If I went through the bathroom and out the second door, I could get to the laundry room, finish the load I'd started earlier, and maybe not be seen. Still, if he was near the door to the den or happened to look up when I passed the doorway on my way to the laundry room – I'd be seen… or I could leave the laundry for tomorrow and just rewash it.

I decided the grown-up thing to do would be to go ahead and

finish the laundry now. I turned the door knobs very carefully. Opening the door fast kept it from creaking, so I did so and held my breath, pausing in the bathroom doorway for a moment to make sure I was still in the clear. I moved quietly and with agility into the laundry room, where I worked by moonlight so the light wouldn't draw attention.

Feeling relieved and quite confident in myself for eluding him, I tiptoed back from whence I came, down the hall to my bedroom, where I'd fold the laundry and stack it on my dresser to put away in the morning. Before I managed to reach the light switch, the looming voice of my husband shocked and scared me. I jumped backward, slightly ready to flee, and quietly calmed myself.

I spun around to leave quickly, apologizing for bothering him as I left.

He followed me to the den and began finding a movie to put on for us to watch together. I used the laundry basket as a barrier and built a wall of clothes surrounding me on both sides so I was not easily accessible.

"Babe," he said with a forced softness I wasn't used to, "let me rub your feet for you."

I swallowed hard. Any other woman would jump at the opportunity and offer from their husband– not me; it tugged on the knot I had in my stomach. The clothing I'd just folded was pushed aside and crumbled as he lifted my foot and massaged one at a time.

I would have melted seven years earlier and succumbed to his "affection."

I would have felt he finally loved me and been grateful for the love and attention. That woman wasn't around anymore. A bitter, guarded, hateful woman remained in her place, and she didn't want her husband touching her, even for an otherwise much-needed massage.

He massaged and gently reminded me of what a great husband he was. He listed the half-drank cups of coke he brought home to me frequently and this massage. He confided his "stress" about money, as he stayed home every morning to make breakfast for the boys so I could supposedly shower in peace and have some alone time. I refrained from rolling my eyes so he wouldn't accidentally see me.

Aggravation flooded my body as I listened to this obviously well-rehearsed spiel, a rewrite of history as if he did stay home to cook breakfast, and I got to shower alone. I wondered how many people he had already told that to, cooking up excuses for his regular tardiness for work while painting a picture of himself as a hands-on father.

"Come to me, mine wife," he said with the same practiced effort. "I shall bed thee."

In my mind, I stayed right there in the den. I watched the rest of the silly movie that had been playing and then fell asleep feeling empty. My body, however, left the room and reluctantly followed him to the bedroom, where tears streamed from my eyes, and I mouthed the words that I hated him several times in a row under the cover of night.

CHAPTER 6

The sound of birds chirping in the tree outside her window woke her early. She rolled over toward her husband and laced her arm through his. He was still sleeping as she cuddled up and maneuvered to get his arm around her. She whispered to him that she loved him. He was woken by her movement and pulled his arm away from her to roll the other way.

She stroked his arm in an attempt to get him interested in her.

"I haven't showered yet!" he growled at her as he shifted to stay away from her.

Melody rolled the other way too. She was busy telling herself not to talk. She didn't want to be ignored again but still couldn't stay quiet.

As long as she'd known this man, she'd had always been told stories of the Casanova he thought he was.

His sister, mother, and he shared names and descriptions of his prowess with women. She knew she was number twenty-something in his line-up of women he'd slept with. Knowing of his previous promiscuity and his literally pushing her over her dining room table and forcing himself inside of her to get the sex she'd withheld from him before their wedding day flooded her with shame, and her face flushed with anger. She couldn't stop thinking about how dirty he'd made her feel and how ashamed she was for not doing something to have stopped him then – but now she was his wife of three years, and she couldn't get him to have sex with her.

A mix of anger and confusion swelled up inside Melody. In the quiet of the morning, she heard her own voice but didn't feel her mouth move as she spoke.

"This morning, you don't want sex because you haven't showered yet; it's usually because you had just showered… " Melody paused and thought she heard him chuckle.

She peered around the cover and saw the side of his mouth turned up in a smile.

He caught her eye with his and answered.

"I guess that's true, isn't it?" he said still grinning. "Maybe I'd be more interested if you'd be willing to take it in the pooper."

Melody sat frozen and heartbroken. He wasn't ignoring her but laughing at her and wanting anal sex, which repulsed her.

"Mel, I don't want to hurt your feelings, but I'm a man with needs – needs you just can't meet. I don't find you attractive. In fact, you couldn't be sexy if it fell out of the sky and landed on you. I can't even cum unless I imagine you're another person."

He paused for what seemed like an eternity as she sat, feeling the sting of his words.

"I've always told you that your sister has a nicer body than you; it's not your fault that your butt is flat, your chest is small, and you just don't have that 'package' a man is looking for – if you knew how to overcome not being sexy, a guy could overlook your body – but seriously, Mel, you don't have a single sexy thing about you, and you know that. I've been with people who know what they're doing. It's hard to know I'm stuck with a woman who won't give me the hole I need… "

If he said anything else, Melody did not know. She turned him off in her mind. She felt hopeless. She didn't want him to see her cry, so she harnessed the emotion from emerging. The pain of holding back the crying ambushed her, beckoning her to just let loose, but she felt a sudden sense of strength and even an empowering surge shoot through her in overcoming the pain instead and not allowing him to make her cry. Tears were streaming down her face, but he couldn't see them with her back turned to him, and she didn't cry.

She didn't know how long she had lay there in bed; time seemed to stay still and drag on forever at the same time. She finally pulled the blankets back and got up to go shower. She went straight to the bathroom and undressed.

A full-length mirror taunted her from the corner of the room. It pleaded with her to look herself over and to see what her husband had just described.

She glanced at her nude body reflecting back at her and saw herself as he had described. She tried changing her posture but to no avail. She was unattractive, unwanted, and married to an 'experienced' man who needed more than she could give.

She quickly showered, dried herself off, and dressed in the bathroom solitude where she couldn't be seen by her husband. She was careful not to look herself over in the mirror again. She already knew what would be reflected back at her.

Her son was waking up, so she moved quickly, brushed her teeth, and went to the nursery. This morning, she changed his diaper, put him in an outfit she'd just gotten from the Goodwill a week earlier, and sat in his room nursing him. Depression was creeping in and trying to consume her thoughts and her heart. Not willing to be consumed with sadness, she changed her thoughts to the child in her arms and started singing softly. It wasn't a song but rather a prayer. She sang from the depths of her soul as she gratefully held her child close to her.

Melody got up with her child and went to the kitchen for breakfast. She debated whether she would prepare coffee or breakfast for the man who skipped day after day, but fear of being petty led her to the oatmeal canister from the cupboard, and she set to work making two bowls of oatmeal. With one arm holding her baby, she reached for an apple with another and realized she would have to put him down to finish preparing this small meal.

Setting him in the swing, she clasped his straps and turned it on. She went straight to work cutting and slicing apples and collecting and sprinkling in cinnamon, a pinch of nutmeg, a dash of salt, and the smallest amount of sugar lest her husband tell her she made it too sweet. She cut a pat of butter from the dish, added it to the pot of bubbling oatmeal, and stirred it all together while talking to her little boy and telling him about her recipe as if he could understand.

"What are your plans for the day?" he asked her as he walked into the kitchen in jeans and a clean tee shirt, speaking to her as though he hadn't just cut her down and torn any shred of femininity she had for herself away.

He was being pleasant and interested in her; he was talking to her. An unexpected joy ran through her veins as she quickly thought of what she would do for the day so that she could answer.

So quick to forgive and forget, desperate to be loved by the man she married, she answered him with a genuine smile.

"I'm going to make matching throw pillows in the living room to coordinate with the curtains I made the other day," Melody said with anticipation of a conversation like she'd dreamed of having with him.

She watched as he made coffee and took the spoon he'd stirred his sugar and cream with to sample the oatmeal she'd been making.

She was proud she'd resisted the urge to make only enough breakfast for herself and embarrassed that she hadn't yet made the coffee, leaving that for him to do. She stood there smiling, waiting for his answer.

Without so much as a grunt or a wave, he left the room with his mug and went to his office, where he sat in front of his computer, presumably with his hand down his pants and several tabs being opened behind The Drudge Report.

The letdown was a feeling of monumental rebuff.

"Why did he even asked what I was planning to do today?" she wondered to herself.

Melody picked up her infant son from his swing, turned off the stove to let the oatmeal cool, and walked, shaking, to her husband's office. She was angry but tried to remember to keep her feelings in check. Melody was going to get this marriage right. She was going to go into his office and explain to him how hurtful his ignoring her was, and he was going to be enlightened, apologize, and they would go on in marital bliss. Melody would remember to use the word "I" and not use the word "you." She would be sure to watch her tone and keep it completely level and low. Breathing in through her nose and out through her mouth, she made her way to the back of the house and around the corner to her husband's office.

She walked in after knocking and waiting a moment for him to respond, took her usual seat on the floor, this time with her baby in her arms, and began in a quiet voice with the words she'd practically rehearsed on the way in.

He didn't look at her as she spoke. He didn't smirk, grin, or respond in any way. Melody's frustration grew; her voice naturally tried to rise higher, but she fought it, putting as much base into her speech and speaking even lower as if that would affect the tone. She pleaded with her words to get a response that would fix this.

"I just wanted to talk about how I feel when I am not listened to...."

When he did finally respond, it was to tell her to "shut her hole" and inform her that her voice irritated him. He scolded her for raising her voice at him and actually got up from his seat to confront her.

Melody's back bristled up; she moved to her feet, and feelings of fear vibrated from her soul to the outer parts of her whole body.

His words pierced her broken heart as he told her that her tone of voice was wrong and he'd never hold any sort of conversation with her if she was going to address him with that sort of "demeaning candor and disrespect."

"You badger me by saying the same thing over and over, again and again and again in a tone that I will never respond to. You're crazy," he told her in almost a whisper as the veins in his forehead throbbed, his eyes grew red with anger, and spittle showered her in the face.

Not willing to back down, she stood up to him and thought if she could look like she had no fear of him, he'd back down. She softened the look in her eyes and paid attention to counting the length of her breath. "Stop shaking," she chided herself silently.

"I just wanted to share my plans for the day with you… "

First, he grabbed her by the throat, jabbing his thumb under her jaw and lifting her to her tippy toes. Then, before she even registered what was happening, his arm was in the air and making contact with her face. Melody covered their child and shielded him with her arm.

She cried out in rage that he was a monster – and was met with the retaliating rebuttal that he would not leave the house that day.

"I'm going to have to call my customer to cancel work today because I can't leave the baby home alone today – you're crazy. You're the monster," he fired at her as he reached for their child to take him from her.

Melody followed him to their son's nursery with empty arms, and unsure of what to do. She listened to him tell their infant son that he would protect him from his crazy mother and set him in his crib.

He heard Melody behind him, turned, and screamed at her to leave the nursery; he was going to put his baby down for a nap. Melody didn't know whether to oblige him or fight over their infant. Before she had time to decide what to do, he pushed into her, sending her crashing into the closet door across from the nursery.

He grabbed her face into his hands and pulled his face very close to hers.

"I will not be disrespected in my own home by a woman," he lifted her to her feet by her face and shook her hard enough to knock her glasses off and down the hall.

"I didn't hit you or leave a mark, so don't whine that you're abused," he told her as spit flung from his mouth and veins throbbed like a 'v' on his forehead.

She backed away quietly and went to the bedroom and cried. She tried figuring out what to do next. She sat on the edge of her bed, facing the window, remembering the "Lifetime" movies she'd seen of women being beaten by their husbands.

She felt dramatic, considering whether she was abused or not. Indeed, this wasn't like the abuse she'd ever seen on television. She still sat there in a quandary. Something unfamiliar filled her soul as she concluded that she would leave…

Packing a few of her own clothes and stuffing extra diapers and outfits into the already-packed diaper bag, she slipped out to the car and set everything in the trunk beside the stroller. She walked back inside as casually as possible, trying to sneak in to assess whether he was back in the office. He was. She swiftly picked up the little boy, who was not sleeping, quietly strapped him into his infant seat, grabbed her purse, phone, and charger, and silently sneaked out the front door. She didn't know where she was going or what to even do. Her hands shook as she got into her car and put it into gear. She picked up her phone to call someone. She didn't even know who to call. She was alone, with a small overnight bag packed for the two of them, and had no idea where to even go or who to talk to. She drove for a while, fretting at the waste of gas and the indecisiveness of what to do. Eventually, she called her pastor and began to tell him what had happened. As tears formed in her eyes and the anguish of her crying couldn't be contained, her pastor cut her off mid-sentence and put his wife on the phone.

Melody heard the soft southern drawl of the pastor's wife say hello to her.

"Honey, you need to put your big-girl pants on, drive yourself back to your husband, and apologize."

Melody slumped in the driver's seat. She looked in the rear-view mirror and saw little Joey sleeping in the rear-facing safety seat. Melody began to protest. The pastor's wife, Glenda, told her to go home, put the baby down for a nap, and seduce her husband.

"Men have needs that women have to meet for them, or they will look elsewhere," the older woman sang into the phone.

"You don't understand – he doesn't want to have sex with me. I keep trying, but he won't. I just need to talk to someone for a minute and sort out what happened this morning," Melody cried. Melody didn't wait for Glenda to respond. "There is something wrong. He won't have sex with me; he acts like I'm not talking – and this morning, I used my 'I statements' to tell him how that hurts my feelings, and he ended up dragging me by my jaw to my feet, pushing me into the closet door, and calling me crazy. I don't know what to..."

Glenda cut her off. "I'm only hearing your side of the story. Every story has two sides, and I'm sure his side would sound very different. Nobody is perfect, not you or him, and I really like your husband and don't want to hear any more of this. Get yourself together, child. Wipe your tears and stop giving him cause to be angry with you. Men require respect. You are clearly not respecting him and ambushing yourself with this childish emotional drama. Go home, and beg for his forgiveness before you send him out looking for another woman."

Melody felt her heart beating hard inside her chest. This was her answer. She was making something out of nothing, and now, she'd left the house and would have to figure a way back home to fix things.

He met her at the door. Melody shivered and considered for a moment that she should just leave again, but she remembered that she was the one being childish. He looked at Joey in her arms, still sleeping, and told her to put him to bed where his proper nap

49

should have been.

Following her down the hall, he berated her about his fear for their child.

"You worry me so much I can't leave you and the baby alone – I've got to take care of him for you, take care of you, and explain to everyone else that you're just not cut out for being a mother, so I have to help you. My work is suffering because of all the time I have to take off work to be here with the baby – and then I find out you're airing all of our dirty laundry to the pastor of my church. You do everything you can to make me look like a fool. You provoke me...." he said, seething with anger that caused the veins in his forehead to stick out again as he poked her with his finger in the chest, harder and harder with each poke. "You're a laughing stock around here. Everyone knows you're crazy. The neighbors know, the pastor, your friends. After all I do to keep this family together, you provoke me. It's like you want to be hit. You know you deserve it, and I'm trying to be patient with you, but I'm insulted, disrespected in my own home, and provoked. You won't leave me alone. You've got to say it, and say it, and say it again. Constantly pushing for a fight, trying to get hit and put in your place," he grabbed her by the arm and swung her to the ground. "Get up! Get off the ground and stop being dramatic," he growled as he grabbed her by the hair and pulled her to her feet. "You're going to learn some respect."

He grabbed her thigh as if trying to pick her up. "You're so fat, I can't even lift you." He dug his fingers into the back of her leg, trying to get under her, and slammed her into the bookcase at the end of the hall. Scurrying around him, she tried to get away and made it back into the living room. He caught her and pushed her into the edge of the couch. Her back crashed against the edge of the seat, just below the cushion, and she winced in pain. She didn't try to get up.

"You're irrational. How dare you treat me like this. Did you tell Glenda how angry you get and the tone of voice you use to talk down at me? Did you tell her how crazy and terrifying you are and that I'm only subduing you and protecting our child from you?"

She coiled up against the front of the couch, willing herself to look him in the eyes as she apologized.

He spit on her before he got up and walked away. She could hear his keys as he slammed the door behind him and heard the roar of his work truck start, then peel out of the driveway.

Melody stayed there in the same spot for some time, crying, thinking, praying, and pleading with God to help her. This was the last time! This was the last time he would touch her, even if the pastor and his wife both thought she was wrong. She should have never come back home.

Before lunch, Melody had arrived at an undisclosed location where she would stay with her son. Large wooden gates were opened for her to drive through. It was a home she'd passed before, and she'd wondered why it had looked different. She was supposed to be safe now. They showed her to her room and explained the paperwork she would fill out. Guilt consumed her as she felt like a traitor for going there.

Melody's mind was in a whirl. She didn't want to admit that he'd ever hit her before; she knew they would automatically assume that made him abusive. Memories thrashed through her mind of being picked up and thrown into various pieces of furniture or walls after making him frustrated. She recalled several times that he'd 'accidentally' pushed her into their hallway wall when he was his maddest and Melody hadn't been smart enough or swift enough to avoid him. She had gotten better about keeping quiet then, and if she'd maintained that habit now, she wouldn't have even been grabbed or hit.

She was ashamed and couldn't take her mind off that.

Fear was taking over. The more Melody allowed herself to say, the more these abuse rescuers told her she was a victim of abuse, and the more she could hear his words echo in her mind that she was not to "air their dirty laundry." Melody feared she'd somehow misrepresented her marriage and was getting quite the wrong diagnosis.

Backpedaling and retelling the same stories to make them realize she wasn't an "abused" wife turned into a quick appointment with the therapist and a handful of pamphlets about abuse to look at.

They let her go to the room she'd be staying in and offered her a variety of clothes to try on for her temporary stay. As her mind slowed, she noticed it was a normal house with many additions and renovations. The room she had was formerly two rooms with a carpet over the floor to hide the poor seams there. After trying on her "new" clothes, Melody made her way out to the rest of the house again. The common room was the original living room of the house. She was given a tour by another employee and shown the kitchen and bathrooms, which seemed untouched by any renovations. Tiled in 1950's blue, the bathroom had a tub and toilet to match. The kitchen was just a galley kitchen, but she paid little attention to details as she wondered what would happen…

CHAPTER 7

I sat at the park for the fourth day in a row, hoping to catch my new friend there again, but she hadn't returned so far. Day after day, I packed a picnic lunch and homeschooling supplies in the hopes of being at the park to see her again. I began to wonder if I had merely imagined her. The boys enjoyed their new school surroundings and played for hours after finishing work. Andrew had skipped a couple of naps, as he didn't want to stop playing, but he didn't seem too grumpy, so I allowed it. I was really enjoying these daily excursions from home and the looming eyes of Peter far too much.

We managed to be gone most of the day; the boys were doing well on their schoolwork and loving the time at the playground. Gregory had even begun riding his bike without training wheels. He was just as proud as he was excited about his newfound skill. I promised them ice cream to celebrate Gregory's achievement.

With one final look around and down the street to see if she was coming, I succumbed to the fact that she wasn't coming again. I gathered our belongings to bring to the minivan and headed for ice cream. Jonah was wondering why we'd been to the park all week, but I sufficed with an answer about nice weather and loving to watch them have fun playing.

This wasn't untrue; it just wasn't the motive for my frequent visits. I wondered if I'd ever see her again and chided myself for not getting her phone number.

We drove with the familiar music of math rapping going on in the background.

There were few ice cream shops in this area. Our choices consisted of an overpriced popular dive several towns north or McDonald's.

Fortunately, these boys were young enough to think McDonald's ice cream was the best. I just hoped their machine was working today.

As luck would have it, McDonald's ice cream machine was down.

This meant a drive to the overpriced ice cream shop. I was already dreaming up the sundae I planned to eat and reminding myself to get the kiddy size for everyone, or no one would be able to finish theirs. We went through the drive-through, where I ordered and practically choked as the voice from the speaker gave me my total for 4 ice creams, totaling over $26. I smiled and drove forward to pay for it. The indulgence of soft, velvety ice cream with strawberries, whipped cream, and chocolate syrup made it worth the extra drive and cost. The boys ate happily in the back of the minivan.

I drove to the town square and parked to enjoy my ice cream before it melted and stared off into nowhere as I got lost in thought again.

After finishing my ice cream and wiping six little sticky hands, I reluctantly turned the car toward home. I knew the boys and I wouldn't be hungry for a while, so I had no reason to run home and cook dinner, but we had been gone all day, and the dog needed to be let out and fed his own food.

There was a massive flood of relief when I pulled up to our home and saw Peter's van missing. He was still gone which meant peace for the rest of us.

The van pulled up not a moment after getting the boys into their house, though.

Peter was on his phone and sat in the driveway for the next forty-five minutes, which was both a reprieve and nerve-racking because I felt as though, at any moment, he could manage to sneak up on me.

None of them were hungry after I let them have ice cream so late in the afternoon. I figured Peter had already eaten too, but I went to work anyway, pulling the roast and potatoes I had been cooking all day in the crock pot out and serving them onto plates in small portions so, should he come in, he wouldn't know they had filled up on ice cream instead. I hoped it would look like they had sat down long ago and eaten more of their dinner than they actually had. Fortunately, the meal was tasty, so my little boys ate what was set before them and were handing dishes to me at the sink when their father came in holding a cup of Coke from the gas station.

"Here, this is for you, mine lovely bride," he said as he tried to kiss my lips and got the cheek I turned to him instead. "I saved half this soda for you, but I could take it back if you are going to be so ungrateful," he warned.

I turned to the sink to wash dishes, pretending I didn't understand what he meant.

Peter acknowledged our oldest, Jonah, his "number one son," but moved into the den and sat in front of his computer without noticing the other two boys.

I hadn't even offered dinner to him.

I figured he knew where it was and certainly wasn't shy in helping himself to whatever he wanted from the fridge or anywhere in the home or yard, but this was one place I could control the avoidance of rejection.

I moved from the clean kitchen to the bathroom with the two youngest boys. They all needed their baths, and so began the nightly ritual of bedtime stories and routines. I stayed in their room a little longer than usual tonight. I stood over their beds, silently praying for them, hugging them longer, kissing them a few extra kisses, and letting myself feel love. These were my babies, the reason I was still living and going through the motions. It had been a long ten years as Peter's wife. Many ups and downs befell us. I'd worked hard to turn it into something it would never be. It seemed like I had no friends left, no one to talk to or scoot out to and visit. It was them and me… and Peter.

I briefly thought of the woman I'd met in the park earlier this week and wondered if I'd ever see her again. Even if we only sat at the park together, I had hoped we would become friends.

The verse about "dying to self" fleeted through my mind.

"I think I've succeeded in that… " I thought woefully. "I've died."

At thirty-five years old, I felt old and little else. I pondered. My interactions with Peter seemed to lessen, yet I still felt the plague of darkness all around me, the hatred of life, and the lament of my existence. I felt kept. I'd long since forgotten I could sing, that I was a talented artist, that I could ride horses, and that I could train students and horses alike. I had even forgotten that I was smart and had a Bachelor's and Master's degree in Education and excelled in teaching and tutoring. I could more adequately say that I forgot I used to be smart. Life itself was a routine. I went through the motions to get through another day and was almost disappointed each morning as I woke to another one to get through. Standing in the darkness of this room, hidden by the shadows that had taken over, I slid my back down along the wall, listening to the steady, even breathing of all three boys sleeping, and wept. I sat consumed by darkness for longer than I could say.

Tears rolled down my cheeks as the familiar silence of my crying engulfed me. It didn't hurt anymore to keep from crying like it had when I was younger. I didn't want to get up and go out to the den or go to my own room to sleep.

"So, this is it. This is how adulthood plays out," I thought dully. I couldn't wait to get married, have kids, and be a homemaker, and now that I'd gotten it, I was in pain and sad and had become nothing. I guess I was depressed, but since I wasn't allowed to leave the children with a babysitter, I really couldn't get to a doctor or therapist to deal with it. It was an infuriating and defeating feeling all at the same time.

Chapter 8

Melody sat in the room she was borrowing as a bedroom in this battered woman's shelter. She stared at the walls, wondering what was next. She waited for the therapist to come in for the day. She would have to answer the same questions again, but she had hoped she'd get answers for herself this time. Her stomach was twisted in knots that kept her from thinking straight. She felt like when she was a child and knew she was about to get into trouble for something. Being in this place – away from her husband – she could almost hear the accusations of her stealing their child and his frothing anger over airing their private dirty laundry. Agitated and anxious, she picked up her sleeping son and moved into the living room quarters to sit on the couch, waiting for the therapist.

Once she arrived, the knot in Melody's stomach only twisted to the point where she feared she'd throw up any minute. Breathing slowly, deeply, and willing herself to relax, she looked at the therapist.

She was an older woman with chiseled features. She had a tight bun pulling the skin back on her face, although her expression was soft and empathetic. Still, Melody sat looking into her eyes as she spoke, trying to understand how a woman who had just met her could tell her that the few anecdotal stories could confirm she was abused in every single form of abuse there was and yet offer no assistance but talk.

She'd just had a harrowing discussion with the housemother, a heavy-set woman with the exact housedress she imagined every housemother would wear.

Melody was shocked to find out that her stay was limited to 14 days. After that, there was nothing. Somehow, Melody felt like the extraordinary courage to escape from her husband had been lunacy instead. A two-week maximum stay, and then there was nowhere else to go. They wanted her to move back home to her parents' for help but abruptly stopped discussing that option when they learned they lived two thousand miles away in Vermont.

"No, you can't move out of state that far, or your husband could claim abandonment and abduction of your child and gain sole custody."

"I'm a stay-at-home mom; I have no family here, no one to help me while I figure out a job and home for us… there have to be other women like me who come here?"

Melody busily played the previous conversation through her head as she studied the lack of symmetry in the bedroom paneling. The therapist looked at her sympathetically and nodded.

"I understand your frustration," she said in a kind voice that couldn't match the severity of the situation.

"How can there be nothing to help me and Joey?" she wondered aloud.

The therapist nodded again. Her eyes exuded empathy, but her words were empty as she told Melody that she knew this was hard. Still, she had to devise a plan to escape her abuser.

Melody looked at the woman incredulously but said nothing.

"Why is this place even here? What do they think they are doing to help? I wasn't looking for a vacation. I came here because I had nowhere else to go. I'm sure lots of women come here with no other options… there should be something. We get food, clothes, and a roof over our heads for a couple of weeks and then get turned out. I didn't want a vacation from my husband. This is going to make it worse. I have to go back to him sooner or later," Melody thought hysterically. The thoughts wouldn't stop coming as she pieced this news together, trying to make sense of it, but she knew better than to say any of it. "Why don't they realize if I don't have a safe place to live set up, then he will take my Joey?" Melody chided quietly. "I thought they would have services, help, other people, and steps to get out of supposed "abusive marriages.""

She wasn't a nail-biter but wanted some sort of vice to release the pressure and tension rising within her. To make matters worse, Melody was slotted for a later therapy session that she wanted to skip. She wondered what sense there was in knowing she was "abused" if there was nothing she could do about it to fix it or get out of it. She needed a job fair and someone willing to let her stay somewhere for a couple months while she saved enough for a deposit and the first month's rent.

She'd need to find a babysitter or daycare for Joey and had no experience nor had she ever thought of such an arrangement. She struggled to put the pieces in place to escape her husband safely.

The thoughts, fears, and details of what she needed but didn't have any help with swirled around her mind like an angry twister with a wake of depression growing with every twist of the evil monster driving through her mind.

Melody heard her name being called through the noise of her cyclone tearing up her thoughts and first checked that Joey was still sleeping.

Her housemother and the therapist were sitting at the computer. She was motioning her over to come to join them.

Slowly, she made her way over to a situation she knew would only grow her frustrations. She eased herself into the seat across from them.

"We will ask a few questions together so you won't have to repeat yourself later when we sit together to chat. Full name. Current address. Age…"

The banter went back and forth for several minutes before they asked about education. Suddenly, she felt panic wash through her system. In all of this, Melody had forgotten about her college classes.

Seeing the panicked look in Melody's eyes and her explanation for them left both women offering the computer for her to look up her school assignments. She could see only her husband's name as her email pulled up. He'd emailed her scores of messages. She had to scroll down quite a bit to get past them. This was more cause for alarm that also did not go unnoticed by the pair sitting in front of her. The awkward pause had created interest.

"Has he emailed you?" they asked her.

Melody answered quietly, "Yes. There are emails from him... I didn't read them, though."

"We don't allow you to have contact with him. You can't answer him back. Remember you've signed a form that there is to be no contact while you are here, and you are never to let anyone know where this place is."

Melody knew this therapist could sense the looming dread mixed with a warped curiosity for what was inside those emails.

"Would you like to read them now?" she asked.

Melody was dizzy with trepidation. She wanted to read them so badly she could think of little else.

Fear gripped her heart as she cleared her throat and licked her lips to answer.

She did want to read them.

The therapist turned her computer monitor toward Melody and offered her the keyboard.

She pulled up his first email and felt fear stab her and twist in her guts as she read. Her therapist noting this response added more upheaval to Melody's mental state.

She turned the computer back toward the therapist to let her read.

"You can read them all... " Melody said as she sat back in her own seat with tears streaming from her eyes.

Melody,

Allow me to ramble a few noncohesive thoughts at 2:00 a.m., not incoherent, just noncohesive.

I don't understand the silence and the keeping Joey away from me. For the record, neither does our pastor understand the Joey part. Is it just part of the template of this Rescue House place, if that is where you are? Does it make sense to foster further mistrust and resentment by keeping a man's child away from him? Surely, you are smart enough to discern between good, sensible practice and that which is nonsensical. In my very humble opinion, what you are now doing is nonsensical, particularly in light of how this came about Saturday.

I am not in denial about what happened Saturday. I am being highlighted here as the typical domestic abuser, I assume. Perhaps as the theory goes, it's a good idea to let the violent man cool off for a few days before any contact is made or allowed? The irony in that to me is who, I believe, is the one that needed the cooling down on Saturday. Melody, you know that I think you are a good mother, but with that said, you know that I sometimes feel you take your anger with me out on Joey. I have not gone to work on at least one occasion and maybe twice for this very reason. Now, for argument's sake, let's say I go along with the premise that a man should never lay his hands on a woman... even if she is attacking him! If I go along with that premise, then I was wrong, and I know I made that mistake, but for you to lie about it or at least its severity serves what purpose exactly? And let me ask you this question, which I feel is very reasonable… if a plumber leaves gas running in your home and tells you it is unsafe to enter the house, and you do so anyway and then light a match, whose fault is the explosion? If you do not see the obvious parallel, I more bluntly ask why you try so hard to push my buttons during these heated arguments? Suppose a man leaves the room when his temper flares, and she follows, which repeatedly happens in different rooms. Is he not justified in pushing her aside when she attempts to trap him? Are you not trapping me when you stand in the doorway when I try to do the right and most practical thing in leaving to cool off? For a moment, let's forget how the law looks at it, and let's look at how God is the ultimate judge in this, isn't he? I believe God is disappointed in me that I do the things that cause you to get so angry and frustrated with me. I think He is disappointed that I said some of the things I said to you during our argument. I believe that He is disappointed that I swiped your eyeglasses across the room!

I believe He is disappointed in my anger toward you the rest of the evening and the next day. What would God say that you could have done better that night, though?

I don't want you to answer that question to me but to yourself. Again, don't answer this question to me but just yourself. Am I wrong to feel that you set me up for this? You have in the past dared and enticed me to hit you, you have in the past, and even Saturday night, followed me around the house, verbally attacking me, trying to trap me as I tried to get away to cool off. Am I so wrong to feel like you said, "Yes, now I got him, now I can get away?" And again, I am not talking legalistically here; I am speaking in the eyes of God.

I could undoubtedly handle our arguments better, but damn sure Melody, you could, too! The evidence of that is last week's talk that we had. That talk was civil, and you did get your points across. That argument did not get ugly, and I was not attacked! You did not berate me or put me down in a nasty way. You did not raise your voice and say hurtful things to me. You don't think you say nasty things to me? Melody, it is so obvious that you have zero respect for me... I'm not blind to that!

You were very bothered by a comment that I lightly threw out at you recently, and that was obvious because you did not let it rest for a good day. I wanted to help you figure out how to make your work at home easier, and you tried to make it into something.

I could go on and on with these examples. Now, I could make more comments to you like the ones about your weight.

Your ass, Melody, has more dimples than a Shirley Temple fan club. When I see you getting out of the shower, I shudder.

Do I dislike you and even have hateful feelings toward you at times? YES, of course, I do, and I would be a liar if I said otherwise. For the record, I have been praying hard for months about what to do about my life.

I've always done what I wanted to do and never considered what God wanted me to do. I have been asking Him what He wants me to do.

But you know Melody, part of why you don't know these things about me is because talking to you is very frustrating for me! I know that's a switch for you because I am the one that is so obviously impossible to talk to! And I know I am difficult to talk to, but do you want to know how I feel about talking to you? Melody, you have no right to do what you are doing with our son right now. You are keeping him from me and me from him. I am not telling you but asking you this time. Please call me, and let me know what the deal is and where my son is.

This silence is not just punishing me but is creating a great deal of resentment and distrust. It is truly letting Satan in the door, allowing him to further damage our life! Melody, if you don't think Satan has a great deal to do with what is going on with us right now... ??? I think you know I am truly a Christian now. I pray for me, I pray for you, I pray for us, and I have been encouraged by the pastor's sermons to pray that God saves our son and gives me and us the wisdom to bring our son up to be a better man than I was and am. I feel Satan's influence in my life is stronger than I feel God's often. I am not saying he is more powerful than God, but he is more direct! Would you not agree that it is highly likely that Satan has a very intense focus on us right now? Would you not agree that he scored an amazing victory this week? I'm tired. I've been writing for 3 hours. Just call me.

Your loving husband.

The therapist looked up at Melody with pleading in her eyes. "What do you think about these emails?" Melody knew she was trying not to tell her what to think and dying to see if she already knew what these emails meant.

With all her heart, Melody had wanted to find that her husband was apologizing and begging her to come back; she wanted to see his confessions of love and sappy promises that he'd change. That was not what the emails said, though. They were allegations that Melody had intentionally made him hit her so she could run off. Melody had stopped reading only partially through the first one and opened each of the others, looking for the apologies and the professions of love but found none, only threats and accusations that filled her with such a fear she'd never known.

There was an eerie silence in Melody's mind. Pain, disappointment, frustration, fear, and questions. The mix of emotions paralyzed her and dumbed her speech.

She could hear the therapist prying. She wanted Melody to tell her what she wasn't going to say. Wasn't being at a battered woman's shelter enough admittance that she thought he might be abusive?

Melody wasn't ready to say it out loud. She wasn't ready to tell herself.

"Do you see the manipulation he's using?" the therapist asked, forgetting to let Melody see it herself first.

The pause and silence that followed was a statement of denial. It was the loudest way that Melody could refuse to accept that she'd married a man who intentionally hurt her.

"He's one of the most manipulative people I've ever encountered," the therapist boldly stated.

Melody wondered how she could possibly make such a statement after reading a few emails and dismissed her as one of those therapists who found everyone abusive. She was mentally disengaged from the conversation as she thought about plans to fix this.

"He's so mad. He's going to take Joey if I don't go home," Melody chanted over and over in her mind.

The pressure was so strong for her to leave him. She didn't want to be that abused wife who returned to him for more abuse, so was it easier to deny there was abuse? Could she go home and just avoid him? Could she stop antagonizing him? Maybe he only "abused" her because she provoked him. Could she perhaps subdue her crazy and be a better wife? Melody seriously pondered.

At an impasse with the therapist, their time slot ended.

The night was sleepless as she tossed and turned, trying to find a way to leave the facility and not upset anyone there.

CHAPTER 9

A new day was dawning bright and early. I could hear the birds outside and lamented that they no longer gave me joy. I lay in bed with my eyes closed for a moment longer, trying to feel something other than dread, but nothing happened. Peter would "want" me that morning if I didn't get up soon, so I hurried out of bed, careful not to wake him. Grabbing my laptop and Bible, I began topically looking for verses on 'joy.'

Several scriptures flashed up on my screen, which I read there instead of flipping to my Bible. Nothing stirred in my heart. Nothing happened as I read them and reminded myself of the joy I was supposed to have as a believer with a home, three beautiful children, and food to eat.

Disappointed, I flipped over to Proverbs and dutifully read the Proverb matching the day's date, wondering if there would ever be any breakthrough in my heart. I tried to pray again, but nothing came out. I tried singing a praise song but couldn't get past the first verse. I felt God had abandoned me, and I was hanging onto Him by a thread. I wondered why he felt so far away.

A pitter-patter through the hall got me up onto my feet. The boys were waking up and would need breakfast.

The day was beginning, and I was the only one who was going to attend to it.

Peter was quicker to join them that morning than usual. I felt disgust wash over me as I moved about the kitchen, cleaning up the dishes and finishing the last of my coffee.

"Good morning, mine beautiful wife," he said to me as I turned my back to him, looking busy with the spice cabinet.

"What have you got planned for this fine day?" Peter asked with a smile that looked more like a smirk.

"I haven't got any plans for today," I said with deep sadness, thinking of how I'd wished Melody would have returned to the park by then.

"If you're going to be around today, I need you to go to the plumbing supply store and pay my overdue bill," he asked in a way that sounded more like a statement.

"Do you have a check or cash ready to go?" I asked, afraid to hear the answer.

"You have to use the money I gave you last week," he answered as if he'd given me some exorbitant amount that could pay the mortgage, electric bill, and his plumbing supply invoice.

"How much is it?" I asked, trying to figure out how he expected this to get paid.

"It's about a buck and a quarter."

"A hundred and twenty-five dollars?" I asked for clarification.

"About that, maybe higher," he answered.

"You only gave me seven hundred fifty dollars last week. I put it with the two hundred you gave me three weeks ago and paid the mortgage and electric bill the day you gave it to me."

"This is exactly why I can't give you all the money I make! What did you spend the last nine hundred I gave you on?" He charged toward me, asking angrily. "This is exactly why you shouldn't have stopped tutoring and making your own money. You need to contribute to our finances, too," he said angrily as I grabbed my bill book and flipped quickly to the page where I listed the money he gave me and showed him that he'd given that to me seven and a half weeks earlier, and it had paid the previous month's mortgage note, gas, electric, and water bill, and I made a payment on his account with Visco Lumber.

Screaming and cursing, he grabbed my book, looked at it, and called me a liar.

"You don't know how to do the math, and I gave that to you last week. It wasn't over a month ago."

"I keep track of everything you give me and what I pay for in here. It's all there and all mathematically correct," I said dully and under my breath because he wouldn't listen anyway.

"What did you say? ...How dare you talk to me that way?!" Peter sputtered furiously. "I'll pay this bill, but you aren't getting another cent from me until I finish this job next month so I can make sure I have money in my pocket and you're not spending it all on bills. Don't expect me to be around much. I won't be here to make breakfast for the boys or babysit the boys to give you time to yourself in the morning if you're spending all the money I make around here... " he retorted with confidence as if he actually made breakfast for anyone or watched the boys for any amount of time.

I was just as angry as he was, but I knew better than to say anything. With lips pursed and eyes staring straight ahead, I breathed deeply and told myself to stay quiet.

I didn't have to wait long for him to leave. The front door slammed, and he was peeling out of the driveway in his van.

After a deep sigh with my eyes closed, I went to the den with the boys to get their homeschooling started. Jonah was particularly quiet this morning. I looked over at him and smiled.

"Why do you always have to get my Daddy mad?" Jonah accused before slapping his math workbook shut and telling me he refused to do his work for a mother like me.

I passed my oldest son a baggie with nouns and adjectives I'd written on card stock and told him to sort the words into a stack of nouns and adjectives.

Even though I'd thought Peter was gone and I'd be able to school in peace, he was suddenly there. Jonah squawked his disapproval, and Peter was immediately beside "his number one son," telling him to put the cards down and that he didn't need to do such a "ridiculous task."

Jonah looked at me with a smug look of satisfaction and back to his father as if he were a savior as Peter high-fived him.

"I'm taking Jonah with me today so he doesn't have to be subjected to your ridiculous and abusive school lessons," Peter called over his shoulder as he patted our son on the back and told him there were "goodies" for him to eat in the front seat of his van. They both left abruptly as I sat fuming. Jonah would fall behind if this happened as frequently as it did, but I knew if I'd waited until I knew that Peter had left, I could have avoided the whole scenario. I needed to do better.

CHAPTER 10

Melody had her bags packed, and Joey was ready for early departure. She hadn't come up with a solution but was going to go on a hope and a prayer that she could explain to them that it had been a big mistake for her to have come there.

The housemother wouldn't let her go without seeing the therapist again, so Melody was forced to wait hours for her to arrive. The time seemed to slow to an unbearable pace as she sat around trying to keep herself occupied as she waited. She kept running scenarios through her mind, thinking of what she would say.

When the therapist finally arrived, she went into her office with the housemother for what seemed like an ungodly amount of time. The time slowed even further…

Once they emerged, Melody sat at the edge of her seat waiting for her turn to talk to the doctor.

The therapist approached her and sat down near her on the couch.

"You and Joey are ready to leave?" she asked with a look of disapproval so strong Melody shrank back.

She looked at the woman before her wondering what she could say. Her chiseled facial features seemed more pronounced as her disapproval showed on her face.

"I think I shouldn't have come here. I don't think I'm really "abused" like the others are... but even if I were – I have no way to get away from him right now. There are no services beyond these two weeks... We've been through the options, and I realize I have none."

The therapist sighed but said nothing.

Melody went on. "I need a place to live, a job, and a babysitter. I need a plan to make sure that all of this is in place so he can't take Joey from me. I don't have family around me or willing to help me. I don't have any money. I have no way to get a place and nowhere to be within a few days except for my own home."

"We can get an extension for you to stay here," the housemother answered quickly.

"How long?"

"Another two weeks, perhaps?" she replied with uncertainty.

"Then what? I haven't worked since I've been here in Mississippi. I can't get a rental with no real job to list for income. What would you do if you were me?»

"Not go back to him," both women said and sighed.

"Then tell me how to not have to go back to him!" Melody said with determination she hadn›t heard in her own voice for years. "If I'm homeless, he takes Joey. If I leave here, in a couple of weeks – I'll still have no home to go to and have an even angrier husband who will retaliate against me worse than if I go back now," Melody said with a desperate resolve that broke both of their hearts.

"You need a plan of action, then. Let me walk you through the instructions for living with an abuser so you can have a safety plan in place for when he gets violent again."

They spent an hour reviewing the plan, forcing Melody to answer each question and sign a promise that she would follow through when the time came.

"I know this is a lot to take in. Many women believe they have to be bruised and bleeding regularly to be considered abused. He isn't going to change. I'm sure you've tried that with him before ever coming here. Trying to get him to see what he's doing to hurt you physically, emotionally, spiritually, and financially… only 1 percent of them ever make lasting change… let's look at the stages and cycles of abuse…." the therapist tried to talk to Melody, but after that, everything turned to the same tune as Charlie Brown's teacher.

The last-ditch effort to keep Melody was foiled before it started simply because no services were available to help a woman like Melody get on her feet. She needed a benefactor to support her for a month or two as she got her life together, and that just wasn't going to happen. There were no low-cost apartments or services they knew of that could put a roof over her head as she figured out how to support herself and a baby.

They were at an impasse. Without any further words, Melody and Joey left the facility. The housemother and therapist waved goodbye with their heads low.

Melody felt she'd let them down but didn't know what else she could do.

In her mind, she devised her plan to make life at home as pleasant as possible while working toward her escape.

She slowly drove home, avoiding the inevitable. With her baby sleeping soundly in the back seat, she zig-zagged across the northwest corner of Mississippi, meandering toward home. She felt defeated yet inspired to fix things at home, to make that marriage work until she could get on her feet. She had her schooling to think about. If she finished her degree, she could get a job teaching, and surely she could support herself and Joey that way.

A plan was forming in her mind.

She remembered a book she'd ordered a year earlier and hadn't liked at first.

"What was the name of it?" she thought, tapping the steering wheel as if that would help her recall it.

She could picture the cover; it was something about being a "Help Meet."

Suddenly, she remembered where she'd shoved it the last time she'd tried to read it and couldn't.

It was in the window bench in the dining room. Melody knew it would be a hard read; she'd already tried to.

The author swore that the woman could change her husband to be nice, provide, and be a good man if she did everything meekly and in service to him.

She made it to her home much too soon and found no one was there. She carried Joey inside, unpacked their things, set a pot of water to boil for baked ziti, and plopped herself on the floor of the living room with Joey on a blanket beside her with a few baby toys and herself with this book.

Melody felt ill. Her husband didn›t come home with people over to eat. He didn't even eat what she made… and sex? She'd hang from a chandelier if she could get him interested in her.

"What about me? Where is my chapter? How do I get him to eat what I make, want to have sex with me, or even just hold my hand or talk to me?"

Melody got up and threw the book in the garbage. She couldn't keep reading it; her frustration only grew stronger with each word she read. She scooped her child up from the blanket on the floor and took him to her favorite rocker in her room to feed him. She prayed for God to give her wisdom, to make it so she could win him over to her and be a good enough "help meet" that he'd want to be around her, talk to her, and want her.

The familiar creak of the front door startled her. He was home now. Feeling almost panicked, she moved to put Joey in his crib. She dashed across the hall to the kitchen, where she'd nearly forgotten about finishing dinner, and got right to work. She heard the water running through the pipes and knew he was taking a shower. Obviously, she was home now; her car was in the driveway, but he managed to avoid her as he moved through the house and past her without looking for her.

She wasn't sure if it was a good or bad thing that he hadn't gone straight in to see her.

She quickly mixed sauce, cooked penne, and mozzarella cheese and shoved it in the oven to bake. Within 10 minutes, he walked into the kitchen. She lost her voice for a moment. She hadn›t even thought about what to say when she saw him.

"So, you're back?" he asked her without emotion.

"We are," she answered.

Pretending she'd never seen the emails about his threats, she apologized for leaving and asked him if he wanted to talk about it after dinner.

They ate in silence. He ate her baked ziti. They moved to the living room and sat together on the couch. It was the first time in months that she could remember him being that near to her. He leaned in and told her he "was sorry *if* he'd done anything wrong."

She immediately began crying.

He looked at her with what appeared to be compassion. His lips turned up on the right side to a half smile, and he brushed tears from his wife›s eyes as he spoke tenderly, telling her that he forgave her for pushing him to react to her.

His words didn›t match his tone or seemingly caring touch as he accused her of intentionally «pushing his buttons» to hit her so she could leave.

"You get so angry and force me to fight with you. I don›t want to fight with you, but you follow me and hammer me with everything you hate about me repeatedly until I can't stand it," he explained, looking deeply into her eyes.

She wasn't sure which part to respond to, but her heart decided for her instantly.

She melted at his touch, the softness of his eyes, and his closeness. His accusations and falsity evaporated as he told her he loved her. When had he said that last?

He fondled her and told her he would never be pushed to hurt her again and wanted them to have a happier marriage.

His fingers made her tingle. She cried on his shoulder and told him she wanted to be loved. There was nothing logical or rational going on.

Nothing Melody had thought of had prepared her for this emotional outpouring. He cried too. He held her face and kissed her tenderly. She remembered who she'd fallen in love with, and suddenly, her schemes to get through this as nicely as possible until she could graduate and support herself dissolved. He carried her to their bed and told her everything she'd longed to hear from her husband. His touch was delicate. He didn't force himself on her, but he wanted her. He assured her that he wanted her and that their marriage would be different from now on. He held her and wrapped his arm around her, giving her the feeling of safety and comfort. In the darkness of the night, she felt loved, safe, and like a foolish woman for ever having left or fearing him. She knew she was right to return and that all the talk from the therapist was rubbish; this man was not an abuser. He was forgiving, loving, and just stressed by her neediness. He was going to help her be less needy and love her through it.

He would be that one percent who changed or never was a real abuser. Whatever it was. She knew she was glad to be home. She slept soundly for the first time she could even remember.

When Joey woke up in the room next door, he put his arm over Melody and lovingly told her to wait there; he'd get him for her. She waited with feelings of love and admiration in her heart. That book she›d tried to read wasn›t for her because her husband wasn›t an abuser. She would work on herself and be careful not to push his buttons and antagonize or patronize him.

CHAPTER 11

I rolled over to the sun shining in my eyes. I hadn't slept that late in a while. For a moment, I wasn't even sure what day of the week it was. I had to think hard for a moment to figure it out and finally realized it was Sunday.

"What time is it?" Panic filled me as I realized all that had to be done before leaving for church. Peter slept next to me, oblivious to the time and my rush to get up and get the boys ready for church. I jumped into the shower first, got out, did my makeup quickly, grabbed a dress from the closet, and threw it over my head as fast as possible. I grabbed the hair dryer to dry my bangs and threw the rest into a clip. I went into the boys' room next to get them up and their clothes laid out for church.

They got up quickly, dressed in the clothes I put on their beds, and followed me into the kitchen. Jonah poured cereal for everyone while I threw together several ingredients into a crock pot to take with us for a potluck.

Peter sauntered into the kitchen to make coffee and then proceeded to his usual spot in front of the computer.

Sending the boys to the bathroom to brush their teeth, I went to my room to get the hairbrush and combed the boys' hair as they did their teeth. We were ready to go and went to the den to sit in front of the TV until Peter got ready.

He looked up long enough to tell us he didn't like the cartoon we had on because it was "of the devil" and made tus change the channel. I knew better than to remind him of the time, but we had to leave within ten minutes to get to church on time, and he was still in his holey sweatpants. Tension coursed through my body as I mindfully breathed deeply to settle down.

"What?" he asked. "You sighed."

"Nothing, just watching this with the boys," I lied as we watched a PBS special about making baseball bats because it was a safe show to watch while he was around.

He got up and went to the bedroom.

A feeling of relief washed over me. I got the boys up to get them ready for the car.

"Let's carry out our Bibles and the crock pot so we're ready to go when Daddy finishes getting dressed."

We sat in the car for several minutes, waiting. What was taking him so long? Fifteen minutes had passed, and the boys wanted to know what we were waiting for.

"We're waiting for Daddy."

"Are you sure he's coming?" Jonah asked with sincerity. "Did you fight with him and make him mad?"

I didn't have to answer or deal with the sting of my child's words as we watched their father stroll out of the house. He had that half-cocked smile he wore when he thought he was something special and got into the driver's seat of the minivan to take "the family" to church.

We drove in silence to church. I knew better than to mention the time or that we'd be late. As usual, I was lost in thought as we drove the twenty-minute drive to the Reformed Baptist Church we'd been attending for a few years.

Late as usual, I reminded the kids to be quiet as we walked into the service. I asked Jonah to take my Bible as I juggled the crock-pot with one arm and my waist and had Andrew by the hand on the other side, with Gregory at my hip to keep them from running inside and making too much noise. We went straight to the kitchen, where I set up our pot and went to fill the water pitcher with water and ice for after the service.

Peter had gone into the sanctuary with Jonah and taken our regular seats. I tiptoed in with the other two boys and sat next to him. The Elders took turns preaching at this church; it was Brother Willis' turn today. He was a year younger than Peter at 48 years old. He was fully grey-haired, slightly shorter than Peter, and clearly not practiced in preaching. His wife sat in the pew beside us, making faces and hand gestures to control her husband at the pulpit. His eyes remained locked on her even when you could see him trying to look away. She kept flailing her arms as if she were part of the landing team for a Boeing 747, nodding or frowning her approval or disapproval.

Brother Willis gave the most basic message from every text he was given to preach on. I sat bored and wondered if he would ever make a point. Brother Willis and his wife had the opposite of the family dynamic this church preached about. They chanted about respect and male headship whenever they could. They commanded female submission, but Sarah Willis sat in the pew directing her husband as clear as day. Once he was off the pulpit, she dictated how he had to handle the children and anything else that came up between the two. It was frustrating and confusing. The more they preached about this submission and the fruits of a good, submissive wife, the more these women bantered on about it being the glue that held marriages together. Then, there were Sarah and Elder Carl Willis with this display as supposed role models for the rest of us. I couldn't figure out how that counted as respect and submission, and my behavior toward Peter did not.

Looking around the sanctuary, I noticed families all sitting together. Couples arm in arm, mothers with babies on their laps, and siblings helping their younger brothers and sisters. They were perfectly happy families that all homeschooled and lived in some sort of marital bliss. The lesser-off families had husbands who made three times the money mine did, and all managed to be home lovingly supporting their wives.

Everyone looked happy, but so did we. At least, it seemed as though no one knew we weren't happy. It made me wonder if they were actually happy. I wondered again if I was the single problem in our marriage. These couples were so happy. They seemed blissful and content with their lives. Perhaps it was true. Peter often told me that I thought too much.

"Maybe I can't be happy because I'm always thinking and analyzing?" I thought.

Eleanor sat down the row from us. She and her teen daughters wore "church hats" and had the latest in homeschool fashion, which was apparently a thing. Months ago, the church had a women's meeting with a webinar for choosing the proper attire to keep our men happy and be modest at the same time. The final session was of a color swatch sampling to figure out which colors looked best with our skin and eye tones so that we could "get it perfect for our individual, God-given looks," and this mother and her two daughters had been studious participants. There was another family in front of us with eleven children and another on the way. Each female had long curly locks, makeup done as if professional, and the same skirts and blouses with scarves and accent jewelry. Further across the church was another family with yet the same attire. The youngest wore a precarious bun on the top of her head with perfect ringlets falling down and cascading around the whole ensemble for the final touch.

I looked down at my own attire. I wore a skirt, too, one I'd gotten at the Goodwill for three dollars, and a blouse that seemed to coordinate, yet somehow, I couldn't get the same look. My hair was neither long nor luxurious, curly nor straight. No matter how I tried to dress, I looked sloppy. Peter didn't like for me to wear makeup and often told me I looked like a clown when I attempted it. I wasn't sure if I looked like a frumpy clown today, but I most certainly didn't feel I fit in with this Reformed Baptist Church.

The sermon finally ended, and all the women headed to the

kitchen to finish the final touches of our weekly meal. Women and children filled their plates first, and then the men lined up if their wives hadn't already made their plates while in line. It felt like I was in school again, looking for an empty seat at the popular table only to be ignored by everyone, so I looked for an open table instead. I hoped Myra would come to sit with me; she and I were both the fashionable outcasts.

She had a larger family than I had, but her crock pot was usually left with food still in it, and her skirts and scarves didn't look like the rest of the other women's either, so we had that in common.

Fortunately, she came and sat with me.

She and I ate and ensured our kids ate while we chatted about vitamins and supplements.

It was the highlight of my week, sitting with her and chatting. I didn't dare tell her about my marriage issues; the kids were all always so close, I wouldn't have had a chance to say anything out of their earshot anyway, but I feared she'd tell me to pray and be more submissive if I had an opportunity anyway, so I kept quiet.

"Oh, I forgot to tell you, I ordered the Magnesium you told me about last week. Chris said he'd want to try it out to see if it helped him too," Myra said in her usual chipper voice.

"I hope it works for both of you. I really think it's made a difference for me… "

Out of nowhere, Peter joined us. "What sort of difference?" he asked, looking at Myra for an answer.

"We were talking about Magnesium supplements," Myra cheerfully offered, oblivious that he was trying to catch me talking about him.

Peter looked intently at Myra, who seemed ignorant that he was studying her to decide whether this was true or a cover.

"Your wife is so helpful," Myra said again in her never-ceasing joyful voice.

Peter's eyes shifted to me. The gaze was steady. No blinking. It was heavy. I could feel his eyes burning a hole into my soul and my insecurity rising with my pulse. I didn't meet his gaze and pretended I didn't realize he was looking at me.

Myra broke the silence and asked Peter if he was taking any supplements.

She was so innocent; she didn't know he was in the middle of intimidating me and offered to move over for him to join us. I kept my eyes diverted to the ground or toward Myra with a fake smile to look as though I was completely relaxed, but inside, my heart was beating out of my chest, and my mind was racing. I wasn't sure why he was hovering this time, but I couldn't stand it any better than any other time he did this.

I used the kids as a good diversion to get away from the table and brought them with me to throw their garbage away. I lingered at the garbage pail, watching Peter turn his half-cocked smile and squint his eyes just enough to think he looked charming for Myra.

"Ok, as soon as he finishes flirting with Myra, we'll be getting out of here," I thought, looking at the three boys who were wondering why their mother had been loitering at the garbage pail for so long. Myra was a beautiful Asian woman with nine children, and unfortunately, I knew his preference was Asian women – not me. We moved into the kitchen to collect our crock pot, and the four of us walked out to the car to put my Bible and our crock pot in the car to be ready. As I stepped through the front door, I couldn't help but take a deep breath.

I must have been holding my breath without even realizing it. The sky was bright blue with a few puffy cumulous clouds high above, and the sun felt amazingly warm against my skin. I didn't hurry back into the building. Trying to keep three young boys wrangled in the church parking lot pushed me toward the building much sooner than I would have liked. I went back inside and tried to look busy at the bookshelf looking for a new book or DVD to bring home. From my place, I could see the O'Dell family laughing with the elder who had given the message today. Politely, they motioned for me to sit with them for a while. It was a welcoming gesture that I took them up on to avoid being rude. Jenna patted the seat beside her to say I should sit beside her. I sat, as was expected, and tried to follow along in their conversations. Moving into a topic I felt well-versed in gave me a much-needed outlet to join in.

All the eyes on me were overwhelming, but I only stuttered a little as I provided some verses I'd been looking at to help me interpret the meaning of this other. Smiling faces turned tense, and eyes went over my head as they watched my husband approach. I felt suddenly awkward and didn't realize what had changed the atmosphere of the small group of people sitting there. Peter slid into the chair beside me and took command of the conversation.

The same half-cocked smile and squinted eyes with a mild lisp (which only appeared when he was trying to sound smart) had followed me to this table. I sat with my eyes directed to my lap. The boys had gone off to play with the other children, and I felt suddenly alone and helpless. The entire demeanor of the table had changed within a moment. Polite smiles were aimed toward Peter. I thought I'd noticed Jenna look toward me with sympathy, but I wouldn't look at her directly lest I make eye contact, so I couldn't be sure. I was probably wrong.

Silently, I wondered what all these families' lives were like. I wondered if their husbands lied about their whereabouts or disappeared for hours on end without notice. I wondered if these wives were ruled at home with that "under a thumb" feeling I'd grown used to after so many years as Peter's wife. I wondered if this was just the way Christian marriages were. If Jenna had looked at me with sympathy, then did it mean she knew something was terribly wrong within my household? Did others know?

The group disbanded one by one while Peter went on and on until it was just him, me, and the elder who had preached that morning. I looked up and saw what looked like a glazed-over look on Brother Willis' face. But maybe it was just my imagination and hope that others also couldn't stand getting stuck having to listen to him.

Realistically, I didn't want to leave yet. I didn't want to be in a car alone with him for the drive home or to be home with him. I wanted to avoid listening to his recap of how much everyone loved him or how smart he was.

I needn't have worried about all that after all; he was angry with me for some reason. Our drive home consisted of a heavier foot on the gas pedal, shorter turns, and screeching halts. I knew I was supposed to ask him what the problem was so he could ignore me and get angrier, but I didn't have the energy to play today. I stared out the window involuntarily, wondering what I had done this time. Scanning my memory of the morning and lunch hour with our church family brought nothing to mind, so I scanned again. I worked through each conversation I'd had and emphasized the parts where he'd come by to join, wondering if I had said or done something to make him legitimately upset with me. I could come up with nothing, and while I was too tired to do this today, I couldn't stop the anxiety from swelling within my core. I could feel my back tighten, my shoulders droop, my face pinch, and my pelvis tilt inward. I looked like a dog with her tail tucked between her legs. I tried breathing deeply to wash this physical and emotional feeling away, but it was useless. The boys were in the back giggling about something; in my head, I wanted to tell them to be quiet. Didn't they see that their father was mad about something already? I sensed his agitation next to me and braced myself.

I turned myself toward the children and into his direct line of fire as I pleaded with them to be quiet and passed out a package of fish crackers to each so they'd chew and stop giggling.

I didn't know how we got home. It was a long blur, but we were suddenly in the driveway. I helped Andrew undo his buckle and carried everything into the house. Peter was out of sight when we got inside. I put Andrew down for his nap and set up a game with the other two in the living room to keep them entertained and away from their father. When he came through the living room, he glared and commanded the television be turned off. He sat spewing all the reasons he didn't like the Canadian-based horse ranch saga we had on again. I wasn't sure if I should be happy he was talking to me or annoyed at his nitpicking about the show we loved to watch. I decided on the former and then braced myself as he began berating us on how much he didn't think our game was appropriate.

"Why are you having the boys play with toy horses? Weeding needs to be done in the garden, and all of you need to go out there to weed."

It was my garden, which I'd been building for the last several years. The one he wouldn't make garden boxes for because he didn't think I needed them, and the garden that he couldn't even water for me if I asked him to. But suddenly, it was his garden, and the weeding was never done right or well enough. He was forever adding new sections to the garden all over the yard and planting vegetables in preparation for the great "Zombie Apocalypse." It was no longer my garden or my place of solitude. It was his garden now and my work, a burden to weed, which I never did right. It was a project for me to keep putting dirt into boxes and find more seeds to be planted, cultivated, nurtured, and weeded.

I loathed the garden. I didn't even want to eat vegetables anymore if I could have gotten rid of the garden.

Nobody moved fast enough for him, so the veins on his forehead began appearing. I rushed them to finish cleaning up our game and had the television turned off, trying to stop the frothing rage. I kept one eye on him, the other on the boys, and somehow got us outside and weeding.

He stood over us, watching our work, pointing out weeds that were missed, and tapping a long stick against the garden box Jonah worked in. The constant drone of the tapping grated on my nerves, but I would not say anything.

The kids were whining as we worked.

They didn't want to be out there as much as I didn't want to be, but their youth overcame any sense to remain silent.

Miraculously, he walked off and left us to weed by ourselves. We finished working; I picked weeds after the boys to be sure it was good enough, then let them get ice pops afterward and brought Andrew outside since he'd woken up from his nap. By dinner, I decided to load them up to get a five-dollar pizza for dinner and left a note for Peter that we'd be back with dinner.

He was in the kitchen when we came in with two pizzas. The look on his face was grim. I considered several possibilities that could cause his anger this time but came up with nothing.

The boys were busy chatting and declaring which type of pizza they wanted. Peter was sitting, stewing, at the head of the table, staring at me as I moved about the kitchen, giving each of the boys pizza. Finally, he spoke.

"Why don't you come outside so I can show you something?" he said between clenched teeth.

I looked at him, sighed, turned to the boys, and told them to stay there as I followed their father out of the kitchen and into the backyard. He took me to the garden and began pointing toward the earth.

"You call this weeding? Look at all the weeds that you've missed! It will take me an hour to get this looking right while you had help to get it done and spent – what, two minutes? You didn't weed. What kind of example do you think you're setting for these kids?"

I turned toward the house, then back to him. "I'll come out after dinner and work on this again."

"NO – YOU will stay out here NOW! This should have been done before you left the house; you don't need any dinner tonight. I'm going inside to be with the boys and make sure that no one chokes on pizza because someone has to care about their upbring-ing. I'll come out later to check on you." Peter grabbed me by the arm and sneered in my face; the scent of rotting teeth wafted in my face as I stared him back in the face trying not to look scared. "Don't ever speak to me that way again. Do you think you can spend your whole lunchtime telling everyone at church how hard it is to be married to me? I'm the one who's suffering. You're a lying, filthy bitch. They know you're a liar. I can see it in their faces as they try to get away from you so you won't start whining about your poor life. No one wants to hear about our dirty laundry," he hissed. "Nobody even believes you! They all know how much you disrespect, belittle, criticize, and are just nasty toward me!"

I stumbled toward the house understanding now that he'd been ignoring me all afternoon because he mistakenly thought I'd been speaking poorly of him.

"I don't talk about you or us at church," I said over my shoulder, annoyed and confused. It was like he could read my mind. I wanted a friend to talk about our marriage to. I wanted a therapist to cry to. I wished I had someone in my life who would or could listen to me and help me feel less defeated and depressed, but there was no one – and now he was angry with me before I'd even said anything. I deserved his anger and wrath simply because I would have talked poorly about him if I'd had the chance to.

Chapter 12

The birds chirping outside her window seemed especially chipper this morning. Melody stretched and untangled herself from her husband's arms and legs. She was so happy to be in a good marriage now.   She thought she saw him smile at her. Grabbing her robe, she gently swung the light fabric around her shoulders and found her sleeves as she walked toward the bathroom for a shower. She smiled and hummed softly to herself as she prepared to shower. Still unable to look at herself in the full-length mirror, she quickly glided into the shower to prepare for the new day. She continued her song, singing softly as she washed and made plans for her day.

Joey was waking up as she dried off and dressed, so she hurried to finish and get to his bedroom. It didn't bother her that her husband remained in bed. Melody sang to her little one as she changed his diaper, fed him, and made her way to the kitchen. With complete faith that her husband would want coffee and breakfast, Melody quickly assembled the ingredients she knew he always liked in his omelets. Everything was prepared, hot, and ready when he entered the kitchen. With a gleaming, happy smile, she offered breakfast to her husband and suggested they all sit together at the breakfast nook. She watched her husband sip the coffee she'd taken great care to make right for him. He immediately moved to the sink and dumped it. He looked at the eggs and asked if she'd put peppers in them, pushed them forward on the counter, and told her he didn't have time to eat. He sauntered out of the room and toward his office where he locked himself in for the next three hours.

Melody was heartbroken. Instead of dwelling on it or rushing off to tell him how she felt, though, she went straight to the garbage can and began digging for that book she'd thrown away the day before, forgetting she'd already taken the garbage out. As she got to the bottom of the bag, she realized the book had to be in the outside garbage can. Making sure Joey was secure in his swing, she dashed outside to find the book covered in what looked like chicken soup. She retrieved the book and brought it inside to clean it off as well as she could and then took her son into the living room where she could nurse him and pick up reading where she left off.

Story upon story was written in this book depicting women who died to themselves against the cruelest and even most abusive men. Each story illustrated a woman who didn't let her husband's human tendencies move them. The women worked harder and provided "more." Every story ended with a blissful marriage.

Melody sat for hours with her sleeping infant on her lap, reading every last page. There were success stories in the back that others had written in describing their happy marriages after the women submitted to their husbands. She was determined to become a success story. She would not react to anything. She was to serve her husband. If she'd serve him well and remember that he was only human, with so many stresses on his shoulders, then she could win him over to being a godly, loving husband like these other women!

At about the same time she finished reading this book, she heard her husband coming from his office. Ready to be the most dedicated wife possible, she smiled warmly and greeted him. He ignored her as he put his boots on and walked out the front door.

"Ok – when he comes home, I'll try again," she thought dutifully and committed to following the format of this book she'd just read. She would have a fantastic marriage if she could stop causing him to feel like he had to ignore her.

CHAPTER 13

S unlight streamed through the windows of the living room where I'd slept and blinded me as I tried to open my eyes. I lay there quietly listening for the birds. I stared at the ceiling, squinting against the sunlight that still danced across my face, and silently asked God to give me enough strength for another day. I didn't even feel I had the will or power to get off the couch. If not for the boys, I would have pulled the covers over my head and continued in deep prayer for God to take my life. Then, I began formulating how I could end my own life. There had been a movie I'd watched. A murderer was injecting Potassium into the veins of their victims and causing cardiac arrest. I had Potassium supplements in the cabinet… I wondered how many I would need to take to cause my heart to stop. I could present as a person dying from a heart attack, and my kids wouldn't have to know their mother had killed herself. It seemed like a viable option.

Three little boys climbed on top of me as I was still figuring and formulating. They kissed me and asked why I had tears rolling down my face. I wiped at them, quickly removing all evidence of my silent crying, and hugged each child a little closer to me. I wasn't sure if I could leave them. I didn't see any other way to end this misery, but their untimely arrival into the living room just as I'd begun to figure out how to escape had foiled my firm resolve. I filed my thoughts away for another time and reluctantly got up to help them get their breakfast. Their chatter was just a distant-sounding noise in the background. I went through all the motions. I ensured they ate, dressed, and brushed their teeth well. We moved on to our school work, but I could not get out of my head.

I cut their assignments and lessons short and decided to take them back to the park for lunch. I needed to get the day to pass by quickly so I could escape this life by sleep, if not death, once they were tucked in and stories were read to them. We played tag. I looked like a normal mom at the park. I wondered if anyone could see through the fake smile and forced laughs, but I didn't care, anyway. I was alone. I was so very alone, and I couldn't stand it another moment longer, not a moment more than I had to.

Out of nowhere, there she was. It was her. Melody was dressed perfectly, with the lovely little baby boy, and was next to me and talking to me…

"Don't let this end," she said.

I looked up at her with a questioning look on my face. Was this woman reading my mind? Did she know what I was planning to do tonight?

"Can I snap a picture of you playing with your boys? Don't stop the game," she asked with her phone up to get a shot as soon as I complied.

"Give me your number so I can send it to you," she said happily.

I stood stunned, looked at this long-lost woman, and didn't want to lose her again.

"Don't you remember me?" the woman asked chipperly.

"Yes, of course!" I answered, trying not to look like the desperate woman I was or the stalker I might have been a week earlier.

I didn't know what to think.

"Can I get a picture of you playing and send it to you?" she asked with her phone up in the air again.

She held a bright pink flip phone in her hand. It was like one I'd had several years ago. I wasn't sure of the quality of the picture it would take, but I didn't argue with her. I thanked her for her generosity and did my best to look happy playing with the boys. I figured this would be our last picture together and wondered if God had sent Melody to get this picture just for the boys to keep.

Melody asked about homeschooling and kept chattering on and complimenting me about what an amazing mother I was. I had doubts about ending my life – and this was indeed drumming them forward. Maybe Melody was sent by God for me?

Phone numbers were exchanged as we talked for hours. I lifted Joey from the stroller. He fit perfectly in my arms like one of my own children.

"Look at what a natural you are. No wonder you're such a good mom to these three."

I looked at Melody's familiar face and wondered why she would appear today. Of all days to return to this park and foil the determination I had had to end my life.

Confused and feeling a small amount of happiness, we parted ways and went on to our own homes to cook dinner for our families.

When Peter came home from work, he dropped a half-drank cup of cola on the counter and told me, "I brought you that gift, even though you don't deserve it, because I'm the better man."

I didn't kill myself that night and instead felt the tingle of hope that I might have a friend in this world.

CHAPTER 14

Melody looked at the clock, knowing her husband would be home soon. She had dinner ready and on the table so he'd not have to wait. Taking her "Help Meet" book very seriously, she hurried off to the bedroom to straighten her hair, change into something fresh and what she hoped would be attractive, and ran around from room to room making sure everything was tidy.

She heard his truck door close, dashed to the kitchen to get Joey from his swing, and looked completely nonchalant as he walked in. Trying to tame her breathing to seem natural and not rushed, she greeted him with a big hug and kiss. He looked at her oddly and gruffly pushed her aside, claiming he needed a shower before she touched him.

She thought she smelled the faint hint of a perfume she didn't recognize but decided to ignore it like she was sure a good "help meet" would. Supper sat on the table, getting cool as she paced back and forth with her son quietly nursing. When he came in, he sat at the table, put a very small serving of the green beans she'd prepared for a side on his plate, and ate it before getting up without a word and going into his office.

Determined to win him over with love, patience, and service, she tidied the kitchen, washed dishes, and put the leftovers away without a word. When Joey fell asleep for the night, she quietly walked back to his office and softly knocked on his door. She waited for a moment for him to answer. Knocking again, with a little more effort, she heard his chair creak and knew he must have heard her and was getting up. Reaching for the knob, she was surprised to find it locked – but within a moment, he was there and answering the door. She tried to look as desirable as she could. Unable to pull off any sort of sexy voice or expression, she knew he was merely looking at her with annoyance. Remembering the book and what she needed to do to win him over took over all sense of insecurities as she mustered enough voice to tell him she was going to bed. Too many years of rejection pulsed through her veins to actually let on what her intentions were. She knew it had to be his idea, so she tried to wait for him to suggest he go to bed with her.

Instead of waiting any longer for him to make a first move, she turned around slowly and walked out of the room to their bedroom. She put on what she thought was the nicest nightgown she owned and hoped she might turn him on when he finally came to bed.

He was earlier to bed than usual. Hoping this was a sign that he was interested in her, she moved closer to him and tried to get into a position he could easily cuddle her in.

"If we're going to do this again, you'll have to make an effort to please me." Without shrinking back from the reproof, Melody moved closer to him, trying to do what she could to get him to want her… "to make an effort."

She felt his arm come around her. Warmth filled her heart as she felt, for a fleeting moment, what amounted to the mistaken feeling of success.

"Do you remember our first time, bitch?" he growled as he pulled her off the bed and bent her forward. He had her hair in his hand, felt her nightgown come up from behind, and her underwear pulled roughly to the side.

"I know you want it rough, bitch," he moaned behind her.

The slap to her rear cut through the quiet of the night before she even realized the impact on her own body. Her head was pulled back into an almost inhuman position as he commanded: "Arch your back and push your ass out further, bitch. You know you like it like this."

Trying to comply with the ungodly position with her head being pulled back so far, she felt her skin stretch taut on her neck and across her chest. She gasped as he sodomized her without warning and whispered into her ear that she was taking it like a champ... again.

Slapped again with more force than the last, "You know this is how you like it. You're a whore...."

Melody felt herself slip away to another place. She could see her body as if below her and knew what was happening, but she turned away and began planning her next outing with Joey.

When he was through, she smiled at him and walked quietly to the bathroom, where she turned the bath water on to scalding temperatures and stepped in, not even flinching at the temperature. With the water running, she cried the most silent wails of women lost and broken, but she was determined to win her husband over. Her face contorted with what should have been followed by deep guttural anguishing cries, but instead, she remained silent. She sat in the water, turning bright pink, scrubbing every part of her body, and washing her hair twice and her body once again while she let the conditioner set in. When her tears had expired, and she knew she'd been gone from their bed for too long, she rose to dry off and wrap a towel around her body. She quietly padded out of the bathroom and across her bedroom floor toward her dresser to get new pajamas and underwear.

Taking a deep breath and turning toward the bed after dressing, she plastered on a smile, gracefully got into bed under the covers, and slid in straight, careful not to touch him. He rolled over and grabbed her chest, telling her that he'd never felt so connected to her before in his life. He kissed her and licked her ear, forcing a shiver she couldn't control. He laughed before rolling back over and calling her a bitch before falling asleep instantly.

Melody remained on her back, holding her arms over her chest and staring at the ceiling. There were no tears left to cry, but it didn't stop her from weeping ever-so quietly.

"Lord," she prayed silently, "Can you ever forgive me?"

She was married to this man. He was her husband. She was trying to woo him to her, so why did she feel she had to repent repeatedly?

Her husband rolled over, grabbed Melody into his arms, and told her he finally had loving thoughts toward her. A sick knot rose from her belly to her throat as she felt his hot breath in her ear and his praise for her consideration of his needs.

Melody wasn't sure why she couldn't sleep and find peace. The book she'd been reading for guidance was written by a Baptist pastor's wife. She said to do just what her man needed and never feel as if anything was wrong with it. Melody chastised herself in thought as she realized how true her husband's words were. She really "wasn't sexy" and was "broken" regarding sex. She rolled toward her husband and whispered in his ear that she loved him too.

Tears wet her pillow as she softly cried herself to sleep, unsure why she kept asking if God hated her and if He could ever forgive her for what she'd just done when she was finally the wife He'd created her to be as a "help meet."

CHAPTER 15

Somehow, life had finally become more bearable. There were moments when I actually found myself smiling. I wondered if Peter had been right, and I'd been too hard on him, blaming him unfairly for my unhappiness. It seemed logical that since nothing else had changed except my friendship with Melody, I truly was the cause of our marital problems and distress. It seemed that all I needed was a friend to spend some time with to beat the depression I'd been suffering with.

Jonah and Gregory were sitting together at the kitchen table working out their own math problems for school when Peter came in from outside. I looked up and warmly greeted him, an uncommon gesture on my part. I looked at him, studying his face to see if he would respond. He made eye contact with me briefly before telling me that he would be working in West Memphis all day, beginning the demo for renovations and additions.

"Ok," I told him as I pointed at a blank problem on Jonah's paper that needed to be finished.

Peter looked at me with contempt. I looked back at him, stunned. How had I let my guard down so low and pointed out an incomplete problem on our son's worksheet right in front of him?

Peter was grabbing Jonah by the arm and pulling him off his chair. "He's coming with me today. There is no need for this type of treatment toward him…"

Silence filled the room just as Melody walked through the back door and into the room. Peter never even looked up to acknowledge her. He left quickly, with Jonah being dragged by the arm of his shirt.

I burst into tears as soon as he was gone, shaming myself for the error, and looked toward Melody with an apology. She only nodded and looked away. Melody had been over several times by then and had gotten in the habit of just coming in through the back door. Since I rarely heard her knocking, this had worked out well for us two friends.

If Peter were home, he simply wouldn't look at her. I couldn't understand why he didn't like her and could be rude. Still, honestly, the silent treatment was so familiar that it wasn't even that obvious to me except when Melody mentioned it. Melody sat quietly and looked over Gregory's math sheet. He didn't seem to notice and kept working on his sheet to show me how much he could do in math.

Melody broke the silence first. "Do you remember what it was like when you were younger and first married?"

I looked at the woman in my kitchen with an odd look. I wondered what Melody was getting at and answered, "Of course."

Gregory looked up from his work with a quizzical look on his face. I looked to see if he was stuck on a problem.

"What do you mean 'of course,' Mama?"

"Oh, I was talking to Melody," I answered warmly.

He looked at me even more strangely and went back to work.

Melody spoke up again. "Do you ever remember being so in love with Peter that you overlooked things or changed the way you did something to please him, even if it went against what you had always thought marriage would be like?"

The question made me feel ashamed and embarrassed. I had made many changes about myself and done things I never would have thought I'd do. In fact, often, I looked at myself in the mirror as a stranger, tainted, and too unlovable even to God.

I thought about the dreams of what I thought marriage would be like and who I would be. I thought about dreams long-since faded. I used to be talented. I'd written a children's book as a teenager. I wanted to be an author. I remembered the news piece done and the time I'd been on the local channel reading from my little story. I remembered the white top I'd worn, my favorite jeans. I remembered the time I spent putting makeup on and how proud I was to see myself on the television screen. I'd done a Levi's commercial for a cameraman's portfolio as a younger teen.

I had that video somewhere. I needed to find it and watch it for memory's sake. I used to even write music and create melodies and was a darn good pianist. I needed to start playing and creating again.

I was lost in thought thinking about who I used to be before I married. I recalled all the Christian love stories I'd read about and considered as I made plans to marry. I remembered how I thought I'd be treated as a Christian wife and what I thought my role would be and contrasted it to what marriage had ended up being. This brought me right back to the same question I'd had last time we were in church.

Were all of those Christian marriages like mine?

Suddenly, I wanted to know what Melody's marriage was like. I wondered if she judged my marriage based on what she saw and compared it to her perfect life.

Knowing that the boys would be listening intently, I motioned toward them, so Melody knew I meant to wait until they finished their work and went outside to play before I answered her.

Moments later, each boy handed their sheets to me and asked for a snack to take outside for their break.

"You've finished all your work for the day," I told them, pushing thoughts of their English assignments and spelling tests that I'd already had scheduled for the afternoon out of my mind.

We all went outside, the boys with bags of baby carrots in hand,

and they began playing in the gravel bed I'd put down under their slide for them to play in.

Melody and I sat in the shade on the deck and watched my three play as she passed her sleeping baby to me. I kissed the soft wisps of his hair and breathed in the sweet smell of baby, remembering when mine were so tiny.

I looked at Melody and asked her about her marriage. Her face flushed as though she were embarrassed, and she told me there wasn't much to discuss.

She wanted to know more about my marriage, so I figured she looked toward me as the elder in this relationship, as though I were a mentor, which I secretly found hysterical because she had saved me from my depression the very day I knew I was going to kill myself.

We chatted. She drummed up memories of things Peter had done to me that I didn't want to remember.

I finally had that kind of friend who fit, understood, and gave me purpose. She wasn't telling me that I was crazy or that I was supposed to love him more; she just listened and asked more questions. When I had exhausted myself and brought us to present-day marriage with Peter, she seemed satisfied with her questions. She told me she had to go home and get to her husband.

I wondered what she was thinking and immediately regretted telling her anything – yet still, she was so familiar it felt as though I were talking to someone I'd known all my life.

Peter was home earlier than I had expected that night. He even came into the kitchen when I called the boys for dinner. We sat together in silence except for Gregory's humming. Peter looked toward me, smiling. I wondered why. I grew increasingly uncomfortable as he stared until I looked up and smiled back at him.

His smile resembled the cat who swallowed the canary, but I didn't speak of it.

Instead, I asked if he needed anything to drink.

"No, I'm fine," he said with the same goofy smile and not once looking away from me.

"Did you get the demolition done that you'd hoped to get done?" I asked, trying not to look like his incessant staring bothered me.

"I didn't demo anything today," Peter answered without blinking.

"Was there a hold-up with the job?" I asked, wondering if this was why he was home so early.

"Hold-up with what job?" he asked incredulously.

"Didn't you plan to demo for the addition you're building in West Memphis?" I asked, trying not to allow my voice to raise in tone.

"I wasn't in West Memphis today. I was in Batesville all afternoon, trying to find parts for the van," he retorted as if there was something wrong with me.

"What's wrong with the van? Did that keep you from starting that job today?" I inquired.

"I didn't start a job today. I was looking for roof racks for my van. I told you I can't do any work until I get roof racks on my van."

I nodded as if I remembered he'd said that earlier. I went back to eating silently but could still feel the burn of his stare as I chewed my food meticulously so I had something else to concentrate on.

"What's in West Memphis?" he asked accusingly.

I looked up, confused. Jonah shifted in his seat and shot a glare at me. Andrew interrupted, asking for more milk, which I poured, glad for something else to do besides chew food.

Peter asked again, "What's in West Memphis? Why did you ask me about West Memphis? Do you have something to tell me about? Someone, maybe?" he said with his anger rising, his face turning red, and the veins in his forehead beginning to protrude.

I looked at him to ensure he was talking to me and not on the phone or something. He was talking to me.

"I mistakenly thought you'd said you were starting a demo today for an addition in West Memphis. I thought you'd told me you would be working all day. I just misunderstood, is all," I said quietly, trying to deter his anger and stop talking about West Memphis.

"How could you accidentally hear me tell you I was going to West Memphis when I'd clearly told you I needed roof racks or couldn't work on anything? What is wrong with you?"

I shook my head and apologized as Jonah glared at me and kicked me under the table. He mouthed the words "shut your hole" at me as I reached down to stop his foot from kicking me again.

Peter took Jonah from the table; they shook their heads and entered the den together. Gregory and Andrew were finished with their meals and wanted to get up from the table too. Still, I tried enticing them to stay with cookies so I'd not have to stay in the kitchen, clearing the table alone.

CHAPTER 16

Melody woke up with a pounding headache. The sun made it worse, but Joey was waking in the room next door, and she had to get up. Before going in to get him, she rushed to the bathroom and jumped into the shower to run hot water over her face. Melody stepped out quickly, dried off, and raced to get dressed, hoping the headache would soon disappear and sad that the shower had not removed the throbbing pain from her head. Joey was sucking his thumb when she walked in to get him. She gently picked him up and took him to the changing table, where she put a fresh diaper on and changed him out of his pajamas. She carried him into the kitchen and sat at the little table to nurse him. She desperately wanted to take ibuprofen or acetaminophen to calm the storm in her head but didn't want to take any chances with medication as she nursed.

She sat there for about forty-five minutes, feeding her infant before getting up to make breakfast. She had difficulty moving quickly as the pain in her head seemed to go down her back and into her feet. Still, she made coffee for her husband and breakfast for him, should he decide to eat it.

Sausage fried in the pan, and the biscuits sat by the oven, waiting for the oven to preheat. She moved toward the refrigerator to get a couple of eggs and cheese to make the sausage, egg, and cheese sandwiches he could take on the road if he was in a hurry.

She rubbed her temples, trying to relieve the pain that slowed her down this morning. Her husband came into the kitchen, noticed her rubbing her forehead, and smacked the counter with his open hands, laughing.

"Have you got a headache today? I hope noises don't bother you. I was thinking about staying home today and working on something that needs the nail gun and compressor running all day."

"Oh, what are you planning to work on?" Melody asked, trying to look interested.

"I'm not sure yet. I will have to tinker around until I think of something," he said, chuckling.

Melody left the room quietly, deciding if he was being serious or trying to be funny. Within a few minutes, she knew he was serious. She could see him taking the compressor out of his truck and bringing it toward the front of the house. She sat still, listening to the front door open and the machine loudly dumped off the floor. He yelled to her to come help him carry lumber in from the truck. With Joey in her arms and the pulsing of her head slowing her steps, she emerged from their room and into the living room.

She followed behind him, head down, grabbed two small pieces of scrap wood, and carried them back to the house still behind him.

She knew she'd have to get out of the house with all the noise. It felt as though her head would explode if he yelled to her again, and now he was plugging the compressor in and hooking up the nail gun.

She moved slowly and put together a sausage sandwich for herself to take along. Grabbing the stroller from the car trunk and setting Joey in his seat, she looked up, shielding her eyes from the mid-morning sun. She would walk toward the park again and be gone long enough for her husband to make whatever he was making and be back for Joey to take a nap. She walked, breathing deeply, trying to calmly will her pain to subside. She turned onto the main road and heard her husband call after her…

"Hey – Melody, you get back here!" he yelled.

Melody turned to look back at her husband, standing at the edge of their front yard and yelling for her. He had his eyebrows furrowed, and he was angry.

She walked back toward the house, unsure what the problem was.

"How dare you take my son on the road like that? A car could hop the curve and run him over with you walking like that," he growled.

"I was walking on the sidewalk… " Melody answered, shocked and unable to understand the problem.

"You don't even love our son, do you? How many times have you put his life in danger when I wasn't here to stop you? Have you done this before?" he spit at her as he sneered his disgust for her.

"We were just going for a walk to town. The sidewalk is safe. I'm not on the road…." she stammered as her elbow was grabbed, and she was moved toward the house swiftly.

Melody took Joey into his room. Her husband frothed for about an hour about how he couldn't leave the house and trust her with the baby anymore… she sat in the rocker, crying quietly. The pain in her head had intensified, so the darkness of the nursery was where she had intended to stay until she heard him leave. Instead, she listened to the compressor going off and on all morning and into the afternoon. She sporadically heard the nail gun popping nails out like a machine gun as she tried to soothe Joey to sleep. The nail gun stopped around noon, but the compressor kept going. She thought she heard his truck leave the driveway, but when she looked outside, it was still there. As the day went on and it got closer to dinner time, Melody left the solitude of their baby's nursery and went into the kitchen to prepare supper.

Her husband was nowhere around. She thought he might have gone to the neighbor's since his work truck was still in the driveway, so she prepared their meal, expecting him to come inside at any moment. She took a large pot out and filled it with water, constantly looking over her shoulder as if he'd sneak into the room without her noticing. Then, she put it on the stove to boil. Looking for large shells in the cabinet, she looked again toward the kitchen door, waiting for him to waltz in and make some more racket.

The compressor was still going on and off, so after finding the box of noodles, she went toward the sound and unplugged the machine. She boiled the shells in the kitchen and moved them to a colander to rinse and cool them off. Next, she pulled out a large mixing bowl from the cabinet beside the sink, poured half a container of ricotta cheese into it, cracked an egg into the bowl, and went to the cupboard to get a can of spinach. Setting the can onto the automatic can opener, then draining the excess water, she poured half of it into the bowl. Then, she added salt, garlic powder, onion powder, and Italian seasoning before mixing with a large wooden spoon. She checked the temperature of the shells as she heard Joey stir in the other room. She rushed to fill the hot shells with the cheese mixture, spooned sauce over each one, and sprinkled mozzarella and parmesan cheese over each before shoving it into the oven and running toward the nursery to get her baby.

She changed his diaper and brought him into the kitchen to nurse again. Half an hour later, the stuffed shells were finished baking; still, her husband was nowhere to be found. She kept looking outside, expecting to see him walking back from the neighbor's house, but he was not in sight. The evening turned to night. Melody ate a few bites of her meal and put foil over the rest of the cold dish to store in the refrigerator. It got later and later. Melody went to bed at ten o'clock, glad to end the day and rest her head.

The clock said 4:07 when she looked up and tried to figure out where she was.

Something had woken her. She immediately thought of Joey and went to get up from the bed to tend to him, but it wasn't Joey.

Lights shone in through the windows of their bedroom. Someone was in their driveway. She got up to inspect but could not see anything through the brightness of the high beams directed right into her window. She looked at her bed, going to wake her husband, but he wasn't there. The lights faded away as a car backed from the driveway and tires squealed away.

She went back to bed as she heard her husband come through the front door and into their room. Melody caught him off-guard and asked her husband who he'd been with. "Who was that?"

"Who was who?" he asked as he got under the covers.

"Who was that in the driveway? Where have you been?" Melody asked, trying to keep her voice level and inquisitive rather than accusing.

"I've been home all day. What are you talking about? There wasn't anyone in the driveway. You're crazy. Go back to bed. I will never be able to work again and leave you and the baby home alone with the batshit crazy coming from your mouth," he retorted, turning his back to her.

Melody lay there in silence. She tried praying, but the only word that would come to mind was "God." Nothing else would come to mind for her to pray.

She lay there awake until Joey woke in the morning. She went to his room to get him, unsure of herself, her sanity, or anything anymore. Her husband came in, watching over her shoulder, telling her he had to supervise her efforts with his number one son. He took him from her arms and carried him to the kitchen. Joey fussed for his mother, hungry after sleeping through the night, but he kept him in his arms and told his son that he'd protect him from his mother...

CHAPTER 17

I was in the kitchen, packing lunches to take to the park, when Melody stopped by. She seemed a little distant to me, but I didn't ask her about it. I let the day play out and tried to see if I just imagined things. She took over what I was doing and handed Joey to me to hold. Already, I figured I was reading her wrong. Maybe she was a little sad, not distant.

"You okay?" I asked.

Melody looked up at me with what looked like a tear at the corner of her eye but wiped at her eyes and claimed she must have a lash in one bothering her.

I let it slide. I figured she'd talk to me if she wanted to, and prying wouldn't help.

"Have the boys finished their morning schoolwork yet?" Melody asked me with a rejuvenated look on her face.

"They have. I'll bring their spelling words again and have them spell from the swings like last time. We'll also play the multiplication songs on the way to and from to help Jonah remember his multiplication. He's still struggling with that. His father showed him how to find the answer with the chart in the back of the journaling notebooks, and I can't get him to remember any of them anymore," I answered.

Melody looked at me with a knowing look. She knew I hated how their father interfered with their schoolwork, and it wasn't the first time he's seemingly sabotaged Jonah in his learning. He'd already told Jonah he wouldn't be good in school, just like dear old Dad, but that was okay. Jonah had taken that as permission to stop trying and an excuse for every wrong answer and unlearned skill. This multiplication thing would hinder Jonah from learning higher math, so I would work hard to get around the handicap Peter had placed on him.

"Have you packed a lunch for yourself, or do you want to make a sandwich here?" I asked Melody as I held Joey with one arm and packed up spelling lists with the other.

"I've got lunch packed in my car. We can all take mine to the park again. It's easier with the infant seat that way," Melody said as she helped my little Gregory wipe his wet hands off with the kitchen towel.

Before leaving, I sent my boys off to the bathroom and took Joey to my bed, where I changed his diaper for Melody. We all went out together and loaded up into her car.

"I'm glad to carpool with you, but don't you miss the walking?" I asked Melody with sincere curiosity.

"Oh, my husband doesn't like for me to walk with Joey on the sidewalk. He's afraid something could happen to us," Melody answered timidly.

"I understand; Peter said the same thing when Jonah was small. I haven't been able to walk since, except for a few rebellious attempts years ago. I guess that's the price of overprotective husbands, right?!" I asked, trying to make light of what I had always thought of as dominance. If her husband didn't allow it, and Melody had a much better marriage than I had, then maybe I'd been too hard on Peter for making the rule. Perhaps it was dangerous to walk to the park or on the sidewalk at all. Since meeting Melody, I questioned even more if it was my fault that our marriage was so hard. Maybe it was my mindset after all.

We arrived at the park, and all the boys took off running to play before they ate sandwiches and snacked on apples and popcorn

Melody had added to the lunch bags.

The two of us sat under the tree watching the oldest three play while taking turns holding the baby. It was my turn to pick Melody's brain. I wanted to know about her life. She'd been somewhat of a closed book; all I knew was that she had a happy marriage. She was over at our house several times a week, but I'd still not been to hers nor met her husband. The more I thought about it, the more I realized I didn't know about my best friend.

"What does your husband do for work? He must be gone a lot," I asked, thinking about how I'd never met him yet.

"He does stay busy," she answered lightly. "He owns his own business. He's got to do so much to keep it up and running…." she replied, trailing off.

"We should have a barbecue at my house this weekend. Bring your husband. He and Peter can get to know each other, and I'll finally be able to meet him," I said, realizing how much I wanted to meet him and see what a happy couple's interactions looked like.

Melody flushed. "Oh, no. He's not much for socializing. I don't think he'd come. He's always so busy with work, anyway."

"Well, maybe another time," I said, hopeful.

Melody looked at me with sympathy. "My old friends where we lived used to joke that I wasn't married to a real man. They said I probably had an imaginary husband or blow-up doll at home since they'd never met him. It's not you. He's just anti-social," Melody assured me.

The boys had come back for their lunches, and we all ate under the shade of the tree. It was time for Andrew to nap, so he stayed back resting on a blanket and fighting sleep. Eventually, the even breathing of the young boy notified me that he'd lost the battle and was sleeping. Melody had to feed Joey and offered to sit with Andrew while I went off to push the other two boys on the swings and give them their spelling words for the day.

As I called words and tried to keep track of which child was spelling which word and whether it was correct, I couldn't help but wonder if Melody was embarrassed to be friends with me. I wondered if she didn't want her husband to meet me. After all, we'd been friends for months now, and not once had I ever met her husband or come close to it while she was free to walk into our home without even knocking.

The boys were swinging opposite each other and getting high. They were yelling down the letters to their words at the same time, and I lost track of which word was which. I had to stop them and have them retake turns, but my mind was still on Melody and how she must be embarrassed to know me.

I said nothing more about getting our families together for a barbecue and thought I'd wait and see. I remembered thinking Melody seemed distant and then maybe it was just that she was sad, but now I wondered if it was distant again.

"No, that's ridiculous. She's over at our house almost every day. She wouldn't come over so often if she didn't like me. Right?!" I thought to myself, battling the feelings of being unlikeable.

Melody was flagging me over toward her. I left the two older boys swinging to see what she needed. Andrew was still sleeping and drooling on the blanket under him. Melody said she had to go to the ladies' room, so I held Joey and sat next to my sleeping boy. It seemed like yesterday the other three were as small as Joey. I was glad for the chance to hold him every time Melody handed him over. I missed the feeling of my little ones in my arms and was always surprised at how familiar it felt to hold her little boy. I sat watching Jonah and Gregory swinging. They were trying to outdo each other in height. Seeing them go so high was scary, and I wanted to stop them, but something held me back and told me to let them be. Let them enjoy the innocence of swinging so high they felt like they could fly and the freedom of going up until the chains pulled back down, and they went backward to matching heights.

Reaching down, I rubbed Andrew's back. His blonde hair was

slightly ruffled, and he still drooled onto the blanket below him. I looked at him, thinking about how I might not have been here without the miracle of Melody showing up just when I needed her. I wondered how I could have thought leaving them with Peter would have been better than living and being here with them, for them.

Joey had fallen asleep in my arms, so I had two sleeping boys. Melody waved to me as I saw her take a turn behind my oldest two, pushing them. They were already so high it looked like they would kick her, but she was somehow missed, and they continued to soar higher into the sky on their swings. The leaves blew overhead as they rustled in the wind. Playful shadows and light danced across the back of Andrew's legs and my own. I was mesmerized by the sight. The sun's warmth filled me with energy and gratitude for my life.

"Thank you for sending me Melody, my God," I breathed under my breath so as not to wake the youngest two boys napping under the tree with me.

Jonah jumped from his swing and landed on his feet. I worried the swing would come back and catch Melody accidentally, but again, it missed her. Gregory wanted to follow suit. I could see that he was nervous and unsure of himself. I could see Melody talking to him, coaching him, but his face was still mixed with worry and determination. I wondered if I should get up and tell him not to. He was still so young; he might get hurt. Before I could get up and put Joey into his stroller to continue napping, Gregory jumped. He soared higher than Jonah had. It was like slow motion watching him, hoping he'd land okay. His foot seemed to curl inward upon impact with the ground as he came down. Was he okay?

Was he going to cry? Melody was beside me, taking Joey from me instead of getting him into the stroller. I ran to Gregory. He was whimpering. His little ankle hurt. I carried him back to the tree, Jonah close at my heels, and set him next to his sleeping brother.

I wiggled his ankle, carefully looking and touching it to see if it seemed broken. I pulled the ice pack from our lunch back, set it on his ankle, and told him to hold it there for a while. Jonah was bored without his brother to play with and ate the rest of his lunch that was waiting for him. The day seemed to end with this injury as I watched for swelling and tried to decide whether I needed to take him to the doctor.

We packed our things, loaded into Melody's car, and headed to my house. It was a short drive; I didn't bother turning the multiplication on. When we got home, Melody came inside and offered to stay with Jonah and Andrew while I took Gregory to the pediatrician to check his ankle. It was sweet of her to offer, but I didn't know how long I'd be, and I knew she was typically punctual to go home and cook dinner for her husband. I told her no, thank you, and put the kids into our minivan. I dialed Peter's number as I drove to the doctor's office. He didn't answer, so I left a message for him to call me back, explaining that we were headed to the doctor's office to check Gregory's ankle out.

We sat in the waiting room for forty-seven minutes before Dr. Sawn called us back. He checked his ankle out and assured me that it wasn't likely broken, but he could send us for x-rays if we wanted them. One million thoughts raced through my head as I tried to decide what Peter would want me to do. He was against pain medicine and x-rays, but if his ankle was broken, shouldn't we know if it was? What if I didn't take him, and it was fractured or broken? Dr. Sawn saw my indecisiveness and gave me a referral if I decided to take him.

We paid our co-pay as we walked past the front counter and out to the car. I sat with the car running, trying to decide what to do. I tried calling Peter again, but he still wasn't answering.

I took Gregory for the x-ray, hoping it was the right decision, and waited with the boys for another half-hour. The technician took Gregory inside for x-rays and told us to remain in the smaller waiting room for him to finish. Gregory joined us there, and we waited longer. I tried calling Peter again, but he didn't answer. We waited another twenty minutes before the doctor came to us and assured us that Gregory's ankle was fine. No fracture, no break, and minimal swelling. He gave me a prescription for ibuprofen. I thanked him, went to the pharmacy to fill it, and drove us home to make a late dinner. We had ravioli with Texas toast and ate together at the kitchen counter.

I sat staring at the bottle of Ibuprofen, wondering if I should give it to my middle son or not. He was limping on his ankle some and still complaining of the pain, but Peter was always so against medication. I hadn't even been allowed to give Jonah iron supplements prescribed by our pediatrician when he was anemic.

I carried Gregory to the bathroom for a bath by himself,, then dried and dressed him before putting him in bed. I went to help the other two into the tub and asked Jonah to wash Andrew's hair so I could give him privacy.

Peter arrived home late. Everyone was in bed, including me, when I heard his keys at the front door. He entered our room, dropped his pants onto the floor, and went to the bathroom for a shower. When he returned, he climbed into bed, grabbing my chest and rolling me toward him. Disgusted and caught off-guard, I tried to roll back away from him to the safety of my side of the bed, but he pulled my pants down from behind and satisfied himself that way. I got up immediately and ran off to the shower, where I cried into the shower, spray scrubbing the filth off of my body.

In the morning, I waited for the boys to wake up and join me in the kitchen. Gregory limped in as Peter followed.

"What happened to you?" he asked Gregory.

"I jumped from the swing and twisted my ankle," he answered, looking his father in the eyes as he spoke.

"Is this his?" Peter barked, slamming the bottle of ibuprofen down onto the countertop.

"Yes, but I didn't give him any," I stammered.

"How did you get a prescription for it? Did you take him to the doctor? Did you get x-rays?" he snapped as his eyes bulged from their sockets.

"Yes, I tried calling you to ask what you wanted me to do…." I tried answering but was cut off.

The boys cowered behind the island in the kitchen, trying to inch their way to the door. Peter grabbed my hair as he stuck his thumb up under my jaw and pulled me closer to himself.

"I have to work… I've got to make money… you complain the most that we don't have any money… but this is what you do to our children?" Spittle swept across my face as he pushed me up against the wall in the kitchen. The boys had disappeared. He was lifting me up by my jaw now. Anger seared his eyes as they flashed with hatred for me.

"These are my boys! I can't go to work to make money for you if I can't trust you to take care of my boys!" he said, pushing me higher up the wall. I was on my toes, trying to relieve the pain inflicted by his thumb and forefinger pressing under my jaw.

I heard the back door open and knew Melody had arrived. Peter must have heard her too – because he let go and changed his voice calling the boys into the kitchen. They all came close behind Melody.

"Mommy was a bad mommy yesterday. Who says we should take her back to Walmart and return her for a younger model?" he asked them cheerfully.

The boys laughed and applauded, "Yes!" as they clapped their hands excitedly. Gregory and

Andrew both looked confused, yet chanted, "Yes! Yes! Yes!"

I looked in horror at my sons and then at Melody taking Peter by the arm and leading him away from me.

CHAPTER 18

Melody watched as her little boy took his first steps. He was nearly a year old and had been cruising around the furniture for months but was never quite ready to walk alone. She was delighted to see him go from one chair to another in their living room with a grin from ear to ear. She could tell he must also be proud of himself. The young mother whooped and hollered excitedly and danced around the room with her little boy in her arms. They both laughed and giggled as they swung around in excitement.

Melody wanted to call her husband and tell him the great news but decided to wait and surprise him. She envisioned the exciting scene in her mind of the excitement he'd have when Joey walked across the room toward him. Setting her son down, she stacked blocks for him to push over. They played this favorite game for several minutes before he moved on to another toy.

It was a beautiful day that she wanted to take advantage of to the fullest.

The sun was shining, and the southern winter felt more like fall to her. She longed to walk to town, stop at the library, and go to the park, but she dared not lest her husband found out about her defiance. The stroller stayed in the back of her car mostly now, and she felt guilty for even having purchased it as it sat unused.

She longed to stroll down the little town's roads listening to the winter birds and watching squirrels scurry to and fro. A favorite place to walk was down near the Larson's pond. There were ducks of a different assortment than she'd ever seen before, growing up in the North. They had funny red blobs on their heads that looked like exposed brains, and Joey always loved to see them swimming and taking off from the water or diving under to catch fish.

Melody looked out the front window at her car. She toyed with the idea of going for a short walk before her husband got home.

"He'd never know...." she thought, immediately consumed with guilt for entertaining such an idea. "In no way would that be honoring and respecting my husband as a 'help meet' if I went strolling down the road with Joey," she chastised herself. "Forget about it. He's right. You're an unloving mother to be considering putting Joey at such risk and a disrespectful wife at that," she thought ruefully. She turned away from the window, angry with herself for thinking her husband was wrong. "Whatever he says, it's what I'm to do," she chanted in her mind like the book had taught her months ago to do.

"Well, little guy, let's take a car ride to the pond and see the ducks."

"There," she thought. "Is it so hard to comply with my husband's wishes?"

She took Joey into his room and changed his diaper, grabbed his diaper bag and her keys, and headed out to the car. They lived in such a small town, with a population of 431, that while she was still in "city limits," there were no lines on the roads to divide lanes. In fact, that's exactly what she was on. A country lane. The town roads looked about the same with both large Antebellum homes and smaller ones that might have been considered Craftsmen style.

Melody drove slowly, staring out the side windows of her car to see all the beautiful homes, their well-kept yards, and their gardens. She enjoyed the scenery even though she couldn't walk it.

They drove the short distance to the pond and parked on the side of the road.

She took the stroller out so it would get some use and stood by the pond with her son, watching ducks play and swim in the water. She could still hear the sound of cardinals as they sang from their branches and felt so disgusted with herself for being such a callous wife, disrespecting a man who obviously cared more than she did about her and Joey's well-being.

She walked a little bit up the road to see the ducks with puff balls on their heads. They'd never seen this variety before and she wondered if they were wild or someone's pet ducks. The two were mesmerized by the wildlife on the water and didn't realize a truck had driven up and parked behind her car.

"What the hell are you doing?" came a familiar, stern voice.

Melody looked up to meet the green eyes of her husband glaring at her. He waved his hands wildly toward her as he cursed and yelled at her for the betrayal and lack of respect. He yanked Joey from his stroller, forgetting to unstrap him and being stopped by the buckle across their son's lap. The baby let out a cry as it caught him in the gut.

She stood helplessly as he unclasped the strap and pulled him into his arms. He marched toward his truck with Joey crying in his arms and swung into the driver's seat. He held Joey on his lap and squealed out throwing mud everywhere.

Melody stood in shock momentarily before getting it together and pushing the stroller toward her car. The Larsons had come out of their house and watched her from the porch. She could feel their accusing stares but didn't look up to acknowledge them at first.

Melody could feel her face red with embarrassment. Mrs. Larson had been so friendly toward her and even invited her to their church and Bible Study so many times. She rolled her eyes as she flushed a deeper shade of red, remembering that she'd already agreed to go to Bible Study with Mrs. Larson the next day.

She knew she'd have to acknowledge her, or she risked looking rude and unfriendly. She took a moment, breathing in deliberately with slow, smooth breaths.

Finally, she looked up and waved as if nothing was wrong. She plastered a smile on her face, straightened her posture, and walked forward. Slowly, she closed the stroller, opened the hatch in the back of her car, set the stroller inside, and quietly walked to the front to get in and drive away.

She drove slowly and on every road in town before she went home. She was ashamed and unsure how to approach her angry husband, so she hoped staying away would give him time to simmer down and make it possible to deal with her misdoings more calmly than they had started. With a heavy heart, she stared at the homes she passed, wondering what it was like in other people's families. She wondered if other mothers were scolded on the roadside or if they were kept from walking on the roads. She passed a neighbor walking their dog. She looked familiar, but Melody was unable to place her. They both waved; Melody forced herself to smile normally. As she stopped at the next stop sign, she saw a mother with a young child riding his little bike with training wheels. She pushed a stroller behind him and seemed at ease with the life of her preschool child at such a great risk. Melody remembered thinking she'd do just the same with Joey in a few short years. She planned to walk regularly to the main street with him to get library books and even do their banking with a branch situated at the end of the quarter-mile strip.

She was confused; her thoughts were tangled. She struggled to see the problem in walking on the sides of these little country roads and chastised herself for the irresponsibility of her own thoughts.

She loved Joey so much she couldn't imagine being able to live with herself if she'd let anything happen to him.

Pulling into the driveway, she looked for his truck, but it wasn't there.

How odd. He had Joey on his lap; surely, he would just drive straight home to not put Joey in any further danger.

But he wasn't home.

Melody felt frantic inside but acted as though she was okay. She parked her car and went into their house, waiting by the front door for him to come home. She saw Clara looking across her yard and the street to watch her out of the large window of their front door. Trying to gain composure, she went to the kitchen to start dinner. She knew he'd be hungry when he got home with Joey, so she had to get his meal prepared and ready for his arrival. That would help him see how sorry she was for disobeying him.

Hours passed as Melody tried to busy her mind with anything else to think about.

"Joey is his son, too. It's not odd for him to have him out for a while," she tried to tell herself as the sun had long since set, and it was getting past Joey's bedtime. It was hard for Melody to rest, as this was the first time he'd ever taken Joey anywhere without her.

It was eleven o'clock when he finally brought Joey inside. He was asleep, and his pants were wet from an overflowing diaper, but he laid him in his crib, covered him, and only looked at Melody long enough to give a menacing glare.

Melody knew better than to ask where they'd been. She'd wait until he offered and take whatever punishment he doled out.

She had to be strong enough to endure after hurting him.

She decided to plan a way into Joey's room to change him out of his wet diaper and clothes without being spotted.

Before she could devise such a plan and before her husband fell asleep, Joey had woken up and cried in his crib. She went to him timidly, afraid it would come across that she didn't trust her husband if she moved too quickly. Bending down over the crib, she could feel the sheet soaked through. She took her son to the changing table, got him changed and in dry clothes, and pulled the wet sheet from the crib mattress one-handed. She wanted to get the mattress wiped off and a new sheet on before nursing him because she expected him to fall asleep again and wasn't sure she could get the sheet on while holding a sleeping baby.

Melody was curious to know if he'd eaten any dinner and didn't know how hungry he was... or not, but she dared not ask his father.

She sat on the rocking chair, nursed him after getting his bed ready, and softly sang. He held tightly onto her index finger and seemed to nuzzle closer to her.

She sat there rocking her baby for more than an hour. He fell asleep but continued to suckle. Soon, he'd be a year old and not need her for milk. She was glad to soak in all their time being close like this. She thought of her foiled plans to show off Joey's walking and wondered if she could surprise him the next day. Around 1 a.m., she carried her child to his crib, carefully laid him down, and tiptoed out of his room. She went to her own room and silently got under the covers. She could hear her husband snoring and was glad that she'd gotten through the day without being reprimanded further. Maybe tomorrow he'd be more forgiving, she'd thought.

CHAPTER 19

The boys and I dressed for church, and I put together guaca-mole to bring for the potluck. We sat, as usual, in front of a public broadcast station documentary waiting for Peter to take his hand out of his pants and move from in front of his com-puter. We'd be late again, but I wouldn't act as though it bothered me.

When he finally got up, stretched, and left his half cup of coffee on the desk next to his keyboard, I carried the guac and chips to the car and set our Bibles on the passenger side floorboard where I'd be sitting.

He strolled out of the bedroom, towel wrapped around his waist, and announced in mock dismay that it was late and "we had to get going."

As he dressed, I led the boys to the car, where we sat waiting. Peter's grand debut from the front door had the boys sigh with relief. Carrying another mug of coffee and setting it on the con-sole between us, he put the minivan into drive and leaned over to kiss me.

"You're looking particularly clown-like today. Why did you put so much makeup on?" he asked coyly, as if complimenting me, as he backed out of the drive and coffee sloshed everywhere.

I apologized and looked straight ahead. He turned the car toward the end of our road and drove forward, still staring at me with what felt like menace. He drove toward the interstate and turned left to merge into traffic.

Stopped cars were as far as we could see, but Peter kept his foot on the gas as though we had clear roads. Just as it seemed there would never be enough room to stop, he lifted his foot from the gas pedal and pounded hard on the brake.

Everything went flying forward.

The container with guac tipped over as the boys yelled it would spill. He swerved off the side of the road and landed beside the car we should have stopped behind and laughed. He smiled cheesily at me and asked if it scared me.

I smiled back at him and reached for the bowl the boys fussed about. He hit the gas again and rode the shoulder until he couldn't get further and rolled his window down cursing at the cars in his way. Hand gestures were flying as I looked back to watch the boys all giggling because of their father. Still, I had to look as though it didn't bother me or it would worsen, so I folded my hands on my lap and prayed. I was not sure I knew what I was praying for – all I could do was repeat the name of God repeatedly in my head. I wasn't particularly coherent in the flow of words that went through my mind as I tried to string together a sentence of request. Still, I kept talking to Him in my head as if somehow that would make it better.

Before long, traffic was moving again, and we were on our way to church.

We were so late, I didn't know if we should just go home or carry on, but Peter drove. He weaved in and out of traffic jamming on his brakes and then slamming his foot on the gas to make up for the lost time. We made it to church in one piece. The kids thought it was so fun; it took longer than usual to get them to settle down before walking into the service, already halfway finished.

Tip-toeing across the back of the church to place the guac and chips, with three boys in line behind me, we quietly dropped our things off and walked silently toward our usual seats.

Elder Jerry looked up and smiled. It was his turn to preach this week, and he already had the familiar tears streaming down his cheeks. He continued crying as he held the Bible up and declared it the word of God…

"And in closing… the Lord made man in his image and woman from the rib of man. We are to love our God by knowing our place in the headship. God, Jesus, Man, Woman, Child. Let us pray." Jerry closed his eyes and began crying again. "Father, God, we come to you as lowly servants. We know you are the Creator, and we are made in your image with dominion over all the Earth. We don't take that job lightly. Help us men govern our homes and wives as you would want us to. Help our wives and children live in submission to their headship, the father and husband you put in their lives to govern them. We rebuke the proud and arrogant who try to live outside your will and pray all this in the precious… "

Jerry's voice cracked in the same spot every time he prayed. "Presh… squeak… sniff… us name of the Lord, Jesus Christ… sniff… sniff…. st," he finished as he lifted his head to look over the congregation. "Oh, yes, and Lord, bless our food and nourish our bodies. Amen. Ladies, please go to the kitchen and set up your dishes for our potluck while we men visit the sanctuary."

All the women rose as if on cue and went into the kitchen. It was set up like a cafeteria counter. Ladies were busy smelling, stirring, and peaking over the shoulders of the other women to see what they'd brought. When all the food was ready to serve, Jerry announced that the weaker vessels would partake and fill their plates. Jerry's wife was front in line and making her plate and his as mothers balanced their plates and their children's plates down the line and to their tables. The oldest children helped mothers set the younger children up, and all sat and looked merry. I looked on as if outside my own body and wondered what everyone else's lives were like.

Were these families actually happy?

Had I gained too much of a feminist spirit that kept me from marital bliss like these women and families seemed to have? Were all these men like Peter?

As the afternoon grew later, parishioners began to clear out. Women cleared the tables and wiped up all the crumbs while some older girls swept the floors. The men roared and laughed at their table. Peter looked very comfortable as they seemed to shake his hand and make him the center of attention. Jerry's wife came up from behind me. Jane hugged me from the side and asked if I'd heard that the church was hiring Peter to do the extension of their building.

"Eesn't thet gray – et?" she asked, smiling close to my face with her thick country accent.

"Oh, that's wonderful," I said, lying to this overly-excited woman. I fretted, and my stomach turned thinking about Peter being responsible for remodeling the church and adding to the space we already used. He was always so unreliable and irresponsible in his construction projects that I'd stopped recommending him within the first year of our marriage after several friends had grown mad at me for his lack of work, unmet promises, and excuses…

"Oh my," I thought. "They don't know what they have set themselves up for."

Jane was telling the rest of the women as they worked to clean up around the men, and many congratulations were given to Peter. My guts twisted within my stomach, and I wanted the ground to swallow me up. Then, something occurred to me.

"The church will find out first-hand what Peter is like. Maybe this isn't such a bad thing after all," I thought to myself.

Peter was animated and in a good mood the whole way home, talking about how they knew he was the best contractor in the entire state.

"They know I'm the only one who can do the job they want

done, and I won't be cheap," Peter smirked as his thoughts tumbled out of his mouth.

The excitement of his new job kept him from pestering the children or me for the rest of the evening. We were able to play outside undisturbed. As the sun began to go down for the evening, the boys and I cleaned up the toys and headed inside. I put together a box of macaroni and cheese for them to eat for dinner while they bathed.

Gregory cried out that Jonah had hit him while Jonah yelled at his brother and called him a liar. I could see a hand print on Gregory's leg that Jonah was adamant had come from the water toys in the water.

Peter came in behind me. His voice was booming a familiar chant. "WHAT IS GOING ON HERE?" he yelled.

Jonah looked up at his father with innocence in his eyes and told him Gregory was lying about him and said he'd hit him, but he hadn't.

I had Gregory in a towel, showed Peter the prominent hand print, and told Jonah to go dry off and get dinner from the pot; he would go to bed early this evening.

Peter grabbed my arm hard and told me that no such thing would be happening.

"Gregory, this isn't from Jonah. Tell your mother you're lying, or you will be the one to go to bed early."

I interjected that he was clearly telling the truth, and it was obviously a hand print that Jonah's hand fit perfectly.

"Were you in here?" Peter said, getting in my face.

"No, I was making dinner," I answered, skeptical of what he was getting at.

"If you weren't here, how can you know Jonah hit Gregory? You don't. Jonah is an honest boy, and he'd never lie. Gregory, tell your mother that you lied. This isn't from Jonah."

Gregory began timidly. "Jonah did hit me... "

Peter's face grew wild-looking. His eyes seemed to bulge from his face, and two veins stood out prominently from his forehead, making a 'v' shape up to his hairline.

"Jonah did not hit you," he hissed at our son. "You go on to bed without dinner for lying. I won't have liars for sons!" Peter spit as he yelled at him and swung his hand to catch his bare butt cheek.

Gregory jumped upon impact. He looked at me for safety. I took him into my arms and told Peter he was wrong.

Now, Gregory had two hand prints on his leg and butt cheek. Each looked the same except for size.

"Look! This is a handprint from Jonah like this is a handprint from you," I said with my voice raised.

Peter took one look at the child's bottom and called me a liar as well. "That's not a handprint on his bottom any more than a handprint on his leg. You're both liars."

Peter stormed into the kitchen and scooped dinner into a bowl for Jonah. He called him into the room and told him to sit and eat. He returned to his desk in the family room to work on our church's expansion plans. I filled a bowl with noodles for Andrew and Gregory. Jonah jumped up to get his father as he glared at me over his shoulder when he left the room.

Peter was back in the kitchen within seconds. Jonah had a smug look spread across his face, standing in the same position as his father. I shuddered more from my own son's behavior than my husband's.

Melody slipped into the house and grabbed a bowl of macaroni for herself.

She seemed to change the subject by raving about how delicious it was. "It's store-brand macaroni and cheese," I said.

Peter glared at me as if I was a lunatic to speak. Melody moved me from the room and whispered to me to put the two younger boys to bed. I ushered them to the bathroom, helped them brush their teeth, and tucked them in with an extra-long story. The house was tranquil when I left their room. Jonah was sitting in the family room with the television on and ignored me until I turned it off.

"Where is everybody?" I asked as Jonah looked at me, irritated for turning off the show he was watching.

"I don't know. I think Dad is in your bedroom," he said with annoyance.

"Time for bed, then," I said. "Go brush your teeth and get your pajamas on quietly."

He reluctantly and slowly walked out of the room, brushing hard against me to show his dislike for me. As he brushed his teeth, I heard the master bedroom door open. I expected to see Peter come out, but it was Melody.

"Oh, I thought Peter was in there," I said to my friend.

"I don't know where he is," she said as she led me back to the family room to sit with me for a while before returning home.

I was jealous.

CHAPTER 20

Melody had Bible Study early this morning and rushed to get herself and Joey ready for Mrs. Larson to pick them up. Mabel Larson had declared to Melody the week before that she would be taking her to her Bible Study this week and wouldn't take no for an answer. It was as though she knew, without her persistence, Melody would not go on her own, and after yesterday, she especially didn't want to go. The sound of a horn blowing meant she was waiting for her. She finished strapping Joey into his car seat and carried him outside with her diaper bag and Bible Study materials.

She was exhausted from lack of sleep from the night before but tried to put on a cheery smile for her elderly friend. Mrs. Larson looked at her sideways as she slipped into the front seat beside her after strapping Joey's seat into the car's back seat.

"Thank you for picking us up today, Mrs. Larson," Melody told the elderly woman.

"Please, call me Mabel. Mrs. Larson makes me sound old. So, how's it going?" Mabel asked.

"Great," Melody lied.

"Has your husband simmered down some since yesterday?" she asked. "You realize Bubba and I saw and heard everything between you two yesterday afternoon?"

Melody had known they had seen her but had hoped nothing

would be said, and it would soon be forgotten.

"Yeah, oh, yes. Everything is great. We'd just had a misunderstanding. Things are all worked out, now," Melody told her older friend.

Melody wanted to melt into the car's front seat to get away from the questioning.

Mabel seemed to notice but did not care about the discomfort she caused her young friend.

Melody sat there thinking up excuses to excuse herself from further Bible Studies as Mabel seemed to cross-examine her about the events of the day before.

"What had you done that got him so mad?" Mabel quizzed.

Suddenly, Melody realized she wasn't sure. Her husband had parked behind her car, so he had to have known she wasn't walking with Joey on the roads.

"I don't really know," Melody confided. "I wasn't supposed to walk with Joey yesterday."

She watched as the scenery zipped by. The land was flat with hay fields, soy, corn, and cotton for acres. Of course, it wasn't planting season yet, but the stumps and brush were being burned off in preparation. Smoke raised to the sky from one field to the next. She was watching and wondering how the farmers kept their field fires from burning up houses and other surrounding buildings.

Mabel interrupted her thoughts and told her there had to be something she'd done to have gotten her husband so angry.

"Well, I'm not supposed to take Joey for walks anymore because his father is afraid a car could jump the sidewalk and kill him while we walked. I took the car and parked across from your house so we could still see the ducks. I thought that was alright," Melody answered as she looked over, trying to see the eyes under her seventy-five-year-old friend's dark sunglasses.

"Well, I guess that wasn't alright with him!" she said with a bit of pep in her voice.

The car turned into the church's parking lot, and Mabel found a parking spot quickly. Fortunately, the ride was over, and there would be no more questioning. Melody hoped her friend would forget about it when they met back up at the car.

Melody unstrapped her baby boy and walked in with Mabel. She directed them to a children's room, and Mabel introduced her to the childcare worker.

Melody stood frozen.

"Nice to meet you," Melody said to the gray-haired woman.

"Darcy has been watching babies in this room since my children were small. She'll take good care of Joey," Mabel insisted.

Melody thanked Darcy for offering to watch her son but politely declined, explaining to Mabel and Darcy that she'd just take Joey with her.

Mabel looked confused. "Everyone leaves their babies in the nursery with Darcy," she said gently but with such sternness that Melody wasn't sure what to do next.

"If Joey's father finds out I left him with a sitter, I'll be dead," Melody thought to herself.

"I ca... can't leave him in here," Melody stammered.

Mabel took Joey from Melody's arms and handed him to Darcy.

"I'll just stay here with Joey, then. You go ahead to class," Melody told her dear older friend, who obviously didn't understand the danger it was to leave Joey with Darcy.

"You're coming with me. No 'buts' about it," Mabel said, grabbing the diaper bag, handing it to Darcy, and pushing Melody forward and down the hall.

"Are you prejudiced?" Mabel asked Melody in a harsh whisper.

"No! Why do you ask me that?" Melody asked incredulously.

"I can't understand why you wouldn't let Darcy take Joey, except for the fact that she's a black woman," Mabel retorted.

"No, no! It's my husband. He doesn't think Joey should ever be with a babysitter or in the church nursery. He says bad things can happen in there, and only parents who don't love their children would let their kids stay there," Melody explained.

"Well, my kids are fifty and fifty-one years old. Neither have ever been injured at church nursery or with a babysitter, so we'll leave Joey with Darcy, and that's final," Mabel commanded with authority.

Melody was a mess and couldn't stop praying that nothing bad would happen and her husband wouldn't find out she'd done this. She was only half paying attention when she realized that the Bible Study leader was complaining about taping the previous week's lesson several times.

"I was on the fifth recording. I was here with my husband after-hours giving the same lecture for the fifth time, y'all!" the instructor whined. "We finally finished, and I was sure it would be fine. I'd been praying it would be fine – but y'all, it wasn't. It had these dead spots in it, and I would have to record again. I stomped off this stage and went outside the back door of this church, and I yelled my head off. My husband came down from the recording room up there, y'all," she said, pointing to the balcony behind us. "He came out, and he gave me the biggest hug. He told me he'd figured out the problem. It was cellphones, y'all. Every time it rang, even on silent, it paused the sound recording. He wiped my tears, and we went inside together to record it for the seventh time."

Melody was amazed. This woman was a Bible Study leader, writing most of their material. Her husband was the local judge, and her father and brother were the local veterinarians. She was high class in their little community, and she was raising her voice. Her voice, just retelling the story, was too many decibels too high – and she went outside and yelled at the top of her lungs in frustration!

"How is it that her husband consoled her rather than reprimanded her? All of Batesville must have heard her scream; this town isn't much larger than ours. Why can she have emotions and feelings and act upon them like that, but I can't… ?" Melody wondered.

The large group broke off into smaller groups. Mabel took Melody to a side classroom with her group and introduced her to the other ladies. Melody was still in awe of what the main leader had just told them but hadn't paid any attention to the actual lesson she had given. A small woman with blonde hair and hot pink lipstick handed Melody a book. She told her the page to open to, and Melody quickly turned to that page. Reading quickly, she caught onto the lesson and sat listening to the women respond to the questions from the pages. A great worry still creased her brow as she hoped this would hurry up so she could get Joey. Every time the door opened, Melody jumped, expecting it to be her husband with Joey and a mouth full of curse words she knew these older women had never heard. The time dragged on as they each needed to give an anecdotal story of how their lives matched the text. Finally, someone rang a handbell, and all the women closed their books, stood up, straightened their clothes, and hugged each other goodbye.

Melody nearly bolted out of the room, but Mabel grabbed her arm and brought her down the hall to meet other women she knew.

She couldn't understand why Mabel insisted on introducing her to every woman they passed in the corridor, but eventually, they made it back to the nursery. Melody stood there tapping her shoe as she waited in line. Mabel elbowed her and pointed to her foot as she shook her head.

Melody stopped tapping and began shaking with anticipation and impatience for her turn to come so she could pick up Joey and go home. Once she had him in her arms again, she could relax and thank Darcy appropriately for taking such good care of him.

Mabel seemed to nod in her friend's approval as they walked toward her car.

At first, it seemed they'd drive back in silence, but that wasn't the case. Mabel spoke, breaking the silence. "I'm old-fashioned, as old-fashioned as they come, and I don't approve of going against a husband's wishes... " She paused to find the right words. "... but I don't think I'd be able to live with a man like your husband.

Something isn't right, Melody."

"Oh, well, he's much better now. I have to be a better help meet, and he won't have to be so strong with me if I do better… " Melody rambled on.

Silence filled the car again, except for the moving vehicle speeding along the highway. Mabel pulled into Melody's driveway, put the car in park, and stared at Melody directly in the eyes.

She looked into her friend's eyes, noting the brown irises surrounded by blue, and felt like she was trying to tell her something. Mabel firmly held Melody's hand and told her to be ready for her the next week. They were going to Bible Study again, and Darcy would watch Joey, too.

Chapter 21

Jonah was cranky as the day began, still angry with his brother and me. I tried to ignore him and act as though everything was normal. The marks on Gregory's leg and rear end had faded, as did the memory; it seemed that Gregory wanted Jonah to play with him and couldn't understand his brother's sour mood. Maybe I'd been wrong. With the way Jonah was carrying on with this grudge, I suppose I had to have been wrong, as was Gregory.

Schoolwork needed to begin, but Peter hadn't left the house yet. He was still working in the family room on the church plans. He was giddy with his ideas and bubbled over with excitement as he mumbled through all of his ideas. I'd never seen him so enthusiastic about work before. Maybe he'd do a good job on this and straighten his working reputation.

As it approached ten o'clock, Peter finally got up from his desk chair and headed out the door to his van. He seemed to be rearranging his tools and it left me uneasy, as he could walk in and disturb our studies at any moment.

Jonah continued to be grumpy and back-sass me with each new assignment.

He was angry that I'd given him a project on the water cycle and told him to create a diagram on a big piece of poster board.

"I've got about 5 different sizes and kinds in the front room you can pick from. Here, look at this page in your science book. This is a good example of how someone else has drawn the cycle. You draw it how you want, but make sure to include all the vocabulary words we've been working on. This is a list: evaporation, condensation, liquid, gas, sun, pond/lake... see them all?" I asked.

He was clearly edging his way to the front door to get his father, so I tried changing the subject and told him I'd give him his spelling words first. I hoped to buy enough time that Peter would leave and Jonah wouldn't be able to go out and complain to him.

Despite my best attempts keep him inside, Jonah slipped out the front door as I worked with Gregory on his subtraction problems. Peter came in with Jonah on his heels.

"What's this I hear about a 5-page report on the water cycle?" he charged.

With my best innocent smile, I told him it wasn't a report but a project.

"I want Jonah to make a diagram of the water cycle, is all," I told him, trying to express the ease of the project to my husband.

"Jonah, did your mother tell you to write a paper or make a diagram?" his father asked lovingly.

"A paper. A five-page paper!" Jonah retorted with his tongue sticking out at me.

"Jonah, I told you I have different papers in the front room for you to choose from. There are five different styles up there. You don't have to write five pages," I clarified.

"How dare you assign five pages to our son. He's not in college. Are you getting off on trying to make him feel overworked and hate school?" Peter sneered in my face.

"Peter, I want a diagram drawn on a poster board. That is all. I thought it was clear to Jonah that I was asking for a diagram. I showed him one in his science book to give an example..." I retorted.

"Don't lie to me, woman! Jonah has no reason to tell me lies. Why would he come outside to get help from me if it was just a diagram?" Peter yelled at me.

I was seriously beginning to worry about Jonah more than I was upset at the buffoon accusing me.

"I'm taking my number one son with me to church!" Peter commanded. "Come on, son, let's get out of this joint."

Jonah glared at me over his shoulder as he left. He was seriously falling behind in his schoolwork, but I was more upset at his attitude and behavior. I reminded myself I needed to talk softer to him and be more intentional about loving on him and giving him extra attention.

The week passed with regularity. Peter remained cold and aloof toward me, giving me the silent treatment I'd come used to getting. Jonah acted angry and distant toward me no matter how hard I tried to gain his forgiveness and affection. We were sitting at church again, eating our potluck. There wasn't much done to the church yet. I saw a pile of Peter's tools in the corner. I'd expected to see more progress for the week since he'd been gone every day, but maybe he was still in the planning and approval stages, I thought to myself.

I wasn't the only one expecting to see more progress. I heard the men talking about it at their tables, just as the women asked me about it. I could hear Peter answering the men. He had his special lisp in his voice that I only heard when he was trying to impress someone.

"Well, I had to take Jonah to work all week. His mother struggled with his school assignments, so I offered to take him with me," he said innocently.

Everyone looked at me, and I was sure I could feel the stares melting my back.

"How nice for you to get a break. I wish my husband would be so helpful. It's great for boys to spend the days with their father at work."

They all chattered at me as if I were the most blessed woman on earth and Jonah the most blessed son.

Peter beamed with pride as he was congratulated for being such a good example of a godly husband and father.

My stomach twisted and lurched as I swallowed my own vomit.

"Well played, asshole," I thought to myself.

Jane took me aside, patting my hand and offering to help me homeschool Jonah.

"I have a list of curricula you can use that would be appropriate for him, so you don't have to guess and make him hate school or push him behind," she offered kindly.

I smiled back with the most genuine smile I could muster and sat back down with the boys to finish eating.

Milly looked over at me with almost a compassionate look on her face. She was the wife of another Elder of the church, William. "You know, school isn't the most important thing. Letting your boys be raised to know how to swing hammers and work with their father is far more valuable. You should be so grateful that your husband is active in their lives."

I caught Sarah watching me out of the corner of her eye. She came over next and stood behind me. Sarah Willis put her hand on my shoulder and asked if I wanted to come by her house later that week. "We've got to let our husbands be the leaders. Don't fight him. Let your boy go with him, and you come by with the other two. I'll help you out with them. You're blessed. Remember that this is your blessed life. Being a wife and a mother and home-schooling your children is a blessing."

I hoped my emotions didn't show on my face as the most contemptuous wife of the whole bunch preached at me about not fighting my husband.

The boys were getting up and heading outside to play a game. Andrew and Gregory stayed beside me as Jonah went out with everyone else. I busied myself with the boys and having idle chit-chat with them to preoccupy myself lest anyone else wanted to congratulate me on my blessings.

Fifteen minutes had passed, and all the boys had come back inside. Some of the older boys were walking over to me with Jonah.

"Ma'am," they said, "He keeps cheating. He won't play by the rules, and we keep trying to tell him he has to. Our moms told us to bring him to you the next time it happened, and it's happening."

Peter jumped up, irate, and pushed the table forward, ordering us to get our things together to leave.

A hush fell over the entire room. "Hey, Pete, don't be too hard on him... " Elder William was telling him. The man's face was deep red and made his grey and white hair even more prominent as he tried to settle Peter down. Peter ignored him and grabbed my arm roughly as we were nearly carried through the door to our minivan.

All three boys loaded into the car quietly. Jonah sat behind his father as if to avoid direct eye contact in the rear-view mirror. I was ready for this man to start screaming at Jonah and was almost glad he'd finally decided to do something. This was not the first time Jonah had been accused of cheating, but Peter had nearly high-fived him. I was sure that was why Jonah was so confused. I figured yelling at him would be extreme but would finally let our son know that cheating would not be tolerated.

Peter broke the silence. "I will not sit in church and be disrespected with such accusations against my son!" he yelled at me angrily. "Jonah is not a cheater; he's not a liar and is honest! He's HONEST! Do you hear me?"

I tuned the rest of the ranting out as we sped home weaving in and out of traffic again. He screeched to a halt in our driveway, rammed it into park, and jumped out of the car, slamming the door behind him. Jonah got out first, smiling smugly. Then, the other two began to unbuckle. I unclasped my seat belt, turned the car off, and took the keys from the ignition. Gathering our Bibles, I got out of the car and made my way into the house. I could hear doors slamming and things breaking.

The boys were in their room with the door closed. I tried to make my way to them to sit with them until the rage was over, but Peter blocked me from going in.

"This is your fault," he hissed with a finger waging in my face. "If you didn't push him to go outside and play with the bigger boys, this wouldn't happen. If you knew how to be a submissive wife instead of always arguing with me, he wouldn't be caught up in this mess," he pushed me into the bookshelf outside the boys' room and told me to leave his boys alone.

Melody walked in the back door instantly. As if I teleported away from Peter, I ran to the back to see Melody in.

I could hear Peter ranting and raving in a rage. Melody took my hand and led me to the back deck. We sat for a while in silence. She passed Joey to me to hold. He was getting bigger and liked to walk and toddle by himself, but he still let me hold him more than he did for Melody. It was like salve on my heart to hold this little boy. He looked up and kissed my face, and then hugged me. His wisps of curls tickled my nose as he turned his little body around in my lap to sit and watch the squirrels Melody and I were watching. I could still hear Peter yelling at me, so I knew the boys were safe. He sounded like he was still in the hall where I had left him.

Melody wrapped her arms around me and told me it was alright. She was this friend I'd always needed. Just having her as a friend soothed my soul and made it okay.

The week went on as normal. The boys had their schoolwork, and Peter was gone all week long working at the church, so Jonah didn't have him to go for rescue from schoolwork. It made our week much more productive. We spent some time with Melody and Joey at the park, but it rained a fair bit, so our outings were curtailed.

Sunday morning, the sun had come back out. I had the boys dressed and eating breakfast, so I went into the bedroom to get dressed. Peter looked groggy and tired as he rolled over, reaching out to grab my butt.

"For a fat woman, squeezing your butt isn't that bad," he laughed.

I ignored him and finished dressing. Debating on whether I should mention the time or just assume that he wasn't going to church this week, I went into the bathroom, checked my watch as if it would give me a magical answer, twisted my hair into a French twist, and clipped it in a tortoise clip.

Peter came in behind me, reaching for my chest, remarking how small it was for such a big woman, and laughing as he pulled his underwear down in the front to pee.

Leaning forward and grabbing the wall to balance himself, he reminded me that we'd not had sex in some time, and he was a man with needs.

"You know, you're fat, and you lack in the sexual department, but I'd prayed for God to make me attracted to you, and now that I am, you really need to be putting out a little. Men have needs."

I walked out of the bathroom quickly and went to the kitchen, where I was sure such talk would be subdued by the children's presence in there.

Peter dressed and got out to the car in his usual late fashion. We sped to church, weaving in and out of vehicles, being thrown forward as the brakes were slammed, and squealing to a stop in front of the church, kicking up the usual cloud of dust we did every week.

As usual, we made our way to the kitchen before joining everyone in the sanctuary. I noticed again that there was really no work done. The same pile of tools sat in the corner in the same position as last week.

Pastor Craig was at the pulpit this week. He was the most tolerable of all the preachers to me. He was expositorily going through the book of Romans and explaining Paul and the historical context of his letter. I looked over to my boys, prayerful they would grow up to be good men.

I held my gaze on Jonah the longest.

He was getting older; he'd be a teenager before I knew it. I tried to imagine him as an adult and wondered how to help him change the hateful behavior his father didn't think he had.

We were dismissed with prayer, and the women were sent into

the kitchen to prepare the food. Like clockwork, the women set up their dishes and prepared the counter for buffet-style serving. Jane was always first in line getting her plate and Jerry's. Then, the rest of the mothers went before the men took their places at their table. I chose a seat near Myra and her nine children. I felt drained and needed some deep sleep, so I was hoping the conversation with Myra would be easy. I looked up at her and smiled.

"How did your week go?" Myra asked, smiling.

"It went well. Very productive," I answered, thinking back on how much nicer it was with Peter working at church full-time.

There was a commotion coming from behind me. I heard my name and Jonah's name.

Peter was sitting with the men, a smug look on his face, tipped back in his chair with his arms folded across his chest. Brian called out to me. He offered to send his wife to our house to help me with the kids so poor Peter could get some work done on the church.

Myra looked up at me as if I'd just lied to her. I turned around to face Brian. He was red-faced. He was coming toward me with his wife, Beth.

"Here, honey, sit over here; maybe you can help with homeschooling advice," Brian told Beth, pointing to a chair beside me.

Beth looked at me awkwardly. "Is there something specific you're struggling with?" she asked, almost embarrassed.

Jane came over, sat across from me and next to Myra, and asked if it was discipline. She went on and on about when spanking was necessary and how important it was to build a good bond with our children…

I sat confused and unsure of why these women were seemingly surrounding me until Milly sat on my other side and told me that while it was great for boys to go to work with their fathers, it was also important for women to do their children's homeschooling. She apologized to me for my misunderstanding her last week.

I sat in a daze, unsure of what to say. Then, I think it was Brian or William's voice telling another that the church couldn't get done because I'd had Peter home all week teaching the kids, as I had a bad episode and had needed him.

"Peter couldn't leave her home alone with the kids; it was so bad," I heard him whisper.

I looked around at all the parishioners looking at me. Peter had leaned forward in his chair and wasn't tipping it anymore, staring at me as if willing me to defy him.

I excused myself to the bathroom with Andrew, as if he'd said he needed to go and needed my help. We stayed there for some time until I felt they must have moved on to another topic and went into the nursery to play with my youngest child.

I could hear the women cleaning up, clearing the men's plates, and sweeping, but I stayed in the nursery with Andrew. Peter came to get me about half an hour later and told me the boys had been looking for me.

Silently, I followed him to the door and went to the car.

CHAPTER 22

Melody had managed to spend some time at the park with Joey. He was big enough to climb on some of the equipment and kept his mother busy following after him, ensuring he was safe and not about to fall off a platform.

He enjoyed the swings and asked to be pushed most of their time there. He was growing up so fast. It seemed time went so slowly and yet so fast. Melody looked at his little feet clad with sneakers. She had to put his little leather booties away months ago as he outgrew them. She was so proud of how he was growing and making his milestones. He was a happy little boy. Going to the park had become a solace for Melody. It was where she could chat about kids, development, and even the weather. Sitting under the tree to eat lunch with her friends made the week seem more bearable.

Once she'd gotten over the paranoia that her husband would know she was leaving Joey in childcare at Bible Study, even this weekly excursion helped her feel human. She had a friend and knew she could stop over with Joey whenever she needed a change of scenery. She was glad they'd moved to their small town and grateful for the friend God had put in her life.

Glancing down at her watch, Melody realized it was time to go home. She said goodbye to the other children and their mom, told them how glad she was to see them again, and packed Joey into her car to go home. Melody was making corned beef and cabbage in the crock pot for dinner and needed to make time to bake the bread that went with her favorite meal.

She knew her husband could get home any minute and wanted to be sure all the dishes were dried and put away so he wouldn't have to see what she'd used to create the meal. The smell of soda bread baking wafted through the house, making Melody's mouth water. It was finished baking, the table set, and she was sitting in the kitchen with Joey, waiting for his father to get home. She'd freshened herself up and put on a pair of pantyhose hoping it would entice her husband to notice her and appeal to his sexuality. Still, he was taking forever to get home. She was starving and couldn't wait to eat this Irish meal she'd always loved, but she waited. The evening turned to night, and it came time for Joey to sleep. She brought him to his bed, softly sang, and patted his back until he fell asleep. She walked out into the hallway into the empty house. Except for the kitchen light being left on, it was dark, and Melody suddenly felt very alone. She went into the kitchen, checked the time, and saw that it was after nine o'clock.

Dinner was cold, so she served herself and put the plate in the microwave before eating it. She sat at the counter with her hosed legs crossed, hoping her husband would come in at any minute and find her outfit and position sexy.

By eleven o'clock, Melody put dinner away and went to bed. Bright lights flooding their bedroom window woke her at about four in the morning. She could hear a woman's voice – "No, maybe that's the radio," Melody said, comforting herself. The lights were moving. Wondering why her husband was backing back out, she went to the window and saw a sedan leaving the driveway. Her husband's work truck was parked in the circle drive and dark inside. She could see the dark figure of her husband moving toward the house.

"Maybe I'm just not awake and seeing things," she told herself to cover all doubt she had.

Melody spoke first as he walked into their bedroom. She seemed to catch him off-guard, as his voice was shaky when he answered.

"Go back to sleep; I'm just getting up to go to the bathroom," he told her.

"Where were you? Who was just in our driveway? Was that a woman?" Melody asked.

"What are you talking about? A woman? I can assure you there was no woman in the driveway! Actually, I've been here all night long. I'm getting up to go to the bathroom. Now, shut your hole and go back to sleep," he retorted. "Crazy-ass woman is off her fucking rocker," he mumbled loud enough for Melody to hear as he went into the bathroom.

She could hear him drop his pants on the floor and get into the shower.

When he got out, dried off, and came to bed, Melody asked him why he was showering at four-thirty in the morning.

He called her a loon, said she acted like a patient and that he'd just gone to the bathroom, and told her to shut her hole again. He rolled away from Melody as she reached out and touched his wet hair to see if he was lying. In the morning, her husband slept in late. When he awoke, it was after one in the afternoon. She'd dared not go anywhere but played with Joey in the living room instead. When he finally came out, his hair was standing up from going to bed with it wet, but he wouldn't answer Melody when she asked about what had happened in the wee hours of the morning.

She prepared leftovers that evening for supper. He vigorously ate it and told her she was finally learning to cook.

Melody was pleased with herself and blushed at his compliment. He smiled at her and made her giddy with that one gesture.

She offered second helpings to him, hoping to get another smile. He obliged and turned his lip up just ever-so slightly like Elvis did.

He leaned forward toward her. Melody leaned in, expecting to be kissed, but he grabbed for the salt instead.

"It's a bit bland but so much better than usual." She moved away, trying not to look disappointed. He laughed at her. "Did you think I was going to kiss you? You've got meat stuck between your teeth – you look ridiculous. Go to the bathroom and fix yourself, woman."

Melody hurried from the room to the bathroom but didn't see meat between her teeth. Leaning closer to the mirror and reaching for floss, she studied her teeth, trying to see what her husband had seen. She flossed her teeth, brushed them, and then gargled them with mouthwash. When she walked back into the kitchen, Joey sat alone in his high chair. She unstrapped him, removed the tray, and embraced him. She went to the living room, looking for her husband, but he wasn't there. She looked out the window and saw his truck was gone. She looked at her son in her arms and set him down on the floor. He went straight to his pile of trucks and started making motor noises as he pushed the yellow pick-up forward and backward. Melody tried to stay focused on her son, but she fought off a deep sadness creeping into every corner of her heart.

Joey looked up at his mother, smiling. He seemed to sense her need for human connection and brought his truck over to her.

He handed it to her and said, "Tuck."

Melody smiled at her little boy. He was a tender and loving toddler. Tears streamed down her cheeks as she thought about how sweet her baby boy was and how blessed she was to have him for her son. She scooted off the couch onto the floor with her son and pushed the yellow truck beside him. She made her own motor sounds, and Joey joined in, taking the truck and pushing it harder and faster.

The sounds of Joey's giggles filled the room and salved a part of the sadness stirring in Melody's heart.

It was getting near his bedtime, so Melody picked up her little boy and carried him in front of her like he was driving in a go-cart. She made the motor noise loudly, pressing her lips onto his head, and told him he had to steer their way to the bathroom for a bath.

The little boy held his hands out as if holding a football-shaped steering wheel and wiggled his wrists wildly.

Melody pretended to be steered toward the hallway wall, then to the other side. She made a screeching noise as if to signify brakes squealing and told her son with a laugh that he better steer better or they'd get into a crash.

He laughed and wiggled his wrists with even more action and movement – howling with laughter. Melody pretended to be scared and made gasps as she whisked him past the wall, going back and forth, lifting him higher and lower in the air to make it as fun as Joey seemed to think his steering made it.

She put him down carefully and took his clothes off to prepare him for a bath. She turned the water on and set the rubber ducky with the thermometer patch into the water to test the temperature. Once the water was run and ducky-approved, she lifted her toddler into the water and started cleaning him with a soapy cloth. He splashed and looked at his mother for a reaction. She set a towel up to keep from getting too wet and gave him the face and response he sought. His laughter echoed in the tiny bathroom.

She let him splash and play a little longer than usual that night, then took him out, dried him off, and put a clean pair of pajamas on him. She gently combed his hair and brought him to his room where she laid him down, turned on a soft lullaby, and kissed his forehead good night. She paused momentarily and prayed for her sweet little son, asking that God protect him and bless him to grow up loving the Lord.

She went into the bathroom, turned on the water, and sat down in the hot water. She sat staring at the faucet as she soaked and hummed her favorite hymn. She stayed in the water until it grew cold, dragged herself out to dry off, and put her nightgown on. She didn't know if her husband would be home that night and almost didn't care…

CHAPTER 23

The weeks dragged on. Peter was home more often than usual, so I brought the boys to the park for schoolwork and playing almost every week. We stayed for hours, working at the picnic tables, having lunch, and then playing on the playground equipment and their bikes. I was glad for Sunday when it finally came. I'd made a sugar cookie pizza with the boys this morning for the potluck.

We loved this recipe and enjoyed arranging the fruit across the cream cheese frosted top.

As our ritual predicted, the boys and I sat in the car, waiting for Peter to come out with us and drive us to church. We made the familiar walk to the kitchen and the sanctuary where we found our usual seats and sat quietly. The sermon was unusually long as Craig preached through Gregory MacArthur's footnotes in his Study Bible. I paid little attention to the details as I was sure it would only annoy me to hear the gospel according to this church's favorite Bible commentator.

As Craig closed and led us in prayer and grace over the food, I licked my lips in anticipation of our good food today. Our cupboards had been getting bare lately, and with no money for groceries, I'd let the boys eat ahead of me and only ate what they hadn't.

I sat with Myra again and lightly chatted about vitamins. I kept my well-practiced smile plastered across my face.

There had been some progress done on the church by now but not nearly as much as one would expect an experienced contractor to have completed by now. The pastor's wife came and sat near the two of us, and it looked like she had some tea to spill. Bubbling excitedly, she said she'd heard we'd had quite an exciting week.

Still with the fake smile dancing across my lips, I looked at Janice and asked her what she meant. Janice was Pastor Craig's wife. She had four children spanning from three years to fourteen years old. She usually played the piano for their hymns and had joyful yet opinionated mannerisms. I liked her very much. I thought she was the perfect mix of spunk and submission, actually.

"Well, I heard you had to come to get Peter and drive him all over the county trying to find the right floor paste with him since his van had broken down. I guess you might not have thought that was so exciting?" Janice said, prying.

"Peter's van didn't break down this week, and I didn't go anywhere with him to find paste. I'm not sure what you mean?" I said quizzically.

"Both Tuesday and Wednesday, Craig, the kids, and I stopped by to see the progress of Brother Peter, and he wasn't here, but his van was. He said it had broken down, and he'd had to leave it here to get parts for it and the floor, but you had come to get him…?" she trailed off.

"To my knowledge, Peter's van has been running fine. He's come home with it late every night. He said he's been working here non-stop," I said, trying to remember to smile again.

"Peter was definitely not here on Tuesday or Wednesday. When he wasn't here, I stayed here to practice the piano for this week's songs, and Craig worked on his sermon. If he'd been here, we definitely would have seen him. Our church is basically one room plus the kitchen, but you can see right into it.

There isn't a door," she said as if speaking to a child.

"I don't know where Peter was. If his van was here, I have no idea where he could have been," I said without trying to smile any longer.

Janice got up, looking puzzled, and sat back with her family. I watched her look back and forth from me to her husband's ear as she whispered ferociously to him.

Myra changed the subject immediately. She told me about her new Jersey cow and how milking was going.

I half-listened as I wondered why my husband had been missing this week. I glanced back toward Janice, wondering if she thought it bizarre.

I looked down at my plate, reminding myself to enjoy dessert and put my mind on simple things like this sugar cookie crust. I didn't want to wonder, think, or speculate this afternoon.

I just wanted life to be simple.

Peter was rarely where he'd said he would be. The confusion over his being in Batesville while I thought he'd said he would be across the river in Arkansas came to mind. The lack of work and his excuses about having to be home with the boys. His telling Janice and Craig his van broke down. I couldn't understand why no one else saw the obvious problem with Peter and why they were so willing to pin it on me.

Jonah had gone to play with the other kids again, and Gregory and Andrew were playing with the large church cardboard blocks on the rug near the nursery area. I could sit and listen to Myra talk about Jersey cows and milking all day if I didn't have to go home too early with Peter.

Sooner than I liked, the women went to their tasks. I cleared the tables, Sarah asked her husband, Elder Willis, to sweep, and Beth wiped down half the tables as her eldest daughter did the other half.

Jonah came in angry and red-faced just as I'd finished tossing the last of the trash.

He'd been called a cheater again, and he was stomping his feet with anger nearing rage. All the men looked at me as the women seemed to scurry to collect their children and move them away. Peter yelled from the back of the room for Jonah to go to him. Jonah sneered at me as he walked past me and toward his father.

The two walked together hand in hand, with their faces up in what I could only describe as pride. Peter angrily motioned for me to follow, which I dutifully did, collecting the younger two as I hurried behind him.

Peter was angry, driving recklessly, and cursing at me for setting Jonah up in the position. He told him he wasn't to play with the other boys because they'd gotten to be lying about him, and he didn't want him around such bad children. Gregory chattered on and on in the seat next to Andrew as if nothing was going on, and Andrew seemed to be entertained by the incessant speech of his older brother. Jonah sat sulking. We arrived home quickly. Peter got out and slammed his door shut. Jonah reached for me, slapping my arm as he grunted, "thanks a lot," and stomped off.

I composed myself and helped the other two boys out of their seats before grabbing the dishes and Bibles we'd brought back from church.

Peter and Jonah spent the rest of the afternoon next door with the elderly neighbor. I kept watching for them. Barry was an older man rumored to have killed his brother in his youth, and his wife was quick-tempered and always complaining. I wasn't sure if it was okay for one of the children to be there so long and feared he'd get the old lady angered. Hours later, the two came home, Jonah describing the Tom and Jerry cartoons and how he'd watched them with Nona, the old lady, while his father and the old man talked about guns and being patriotic.

CHAPTER 24

Melody stood outside on the back deck hanging diapers as she did every morning. Joey was napping, and the days were getting much warmer. Summer was coming, and she wanted to soak up every warm ray of sunshine. She watched the bluebirds as they landed in nearby branches and sang to her. The mockingbirds were busily divebombing the neighbor's cat as it tried to get to their nest of babies, and the robins were all around, pecking the ground for worms.

She breathed in deeply, enjoying the solace of the perfect morning. The sound of her husband's truck interrupted the medley of bird songs she swayed to. The robins flew into the branches, the mockingbirds flew into the oak with their nest, and the bluebirds seemed to vanish. He came around the house stomping his boots and mumbling under his breath. She could tell he was angry, so she quickly grabbed her basket of wet diapers and slipped into the back door before he got to the backyard.

Her husband followed in through the door faster than she anticipated. He growled his disapproval of wet diapers sitting in the basket.

"Hang those before they mold up," he told her in a huff.

He followed her outside again and paced the deck she stood on as she clipped diapers to the line.

She wondered if she should ask him what was wrong but feared the response, so she kept clipping diapers one at a time. She had a system for using one clip to hold two diapers and worked quickly to finish and retreat to the house's safety again.

He grabbed her by the back of the arm and spun her around. The basket of diapers fell from the ledge of the railing, but it didn't matter. She was more concerned with what would happen next.

What was he going to do?

She tried to keep her balance as she looked at her husband, searching his face for answers.

"Where were you? I've been calling you all morning. I got run off the road by some maniac and skidded into an embankment. The truck's front end is all beat up, and I needed you to come with money, but you didn't answer the phone. I gave you a cell phone to use it. You need to answer the phone when I call. I have to go back to Memphis now – because you couldn't manage to answer your fucking phone."

He released her arm, and she dashed off the porch to collect the diapers and then headed toward their driveway. She could see the front right headlight was knocked out, but other than that, the damage was minimal.

"What do you need the money for?" she asked. "A new headlight?"

He retorted angrily, "I don't need to take your crap. Where is the money I gave you yesterday for the bills? I need that."

"I put it in the bank to pay the bills and paid the bills," Melody said, afraid of how he'd react.

"I give you cash to pay bills in cash. The government is watching everyone's money. It's not supposed to be in the bank," he said, spitting in her face. "How much is left?"

"I can't pay the mortgage in cash, and the government isn't watching money," she retorted.

He got into his truck and sped out of the driveway toward Main Street. Fifteen minutes later, he was back and angrier.

He had the window down on his truck and was yelling out the window at his wife.

"I took nine hundred dollars out of the account. You said there was only a hundred fifty. You lying bitch," he told her.

"There are only a hundred fifty dollars in the account. I mailed the mortgage check yesterday. It wouldn't have cleared. Once they get it, they will cash it, and the account will bounce. There isn't enough money for the check I wrote, now," I said in a panic.

"There were nine hundred four dollars in the account. Not one fifty. LIAR!" he fumed at her.

Melody tried to explain again. "I wrote a check to the mortgage company. I paid them seven hundred fifty dollars, but they didn't get the check yet, so the bank wouldn't know that. According to the bank, nine hundred dollars are in the account because they don't know I wrote a check out for the mortgage."

"You lying bitch. You're trying to keep money from me. The bank said there were nine hundred four dollars. I'm taking it with me. From now on, I'll give you cash for the bills, and you pay in cash. You don't get to keep the rest hiding in the bank from me."

Melody didn't know how to explain it to her husband, but she didn't know what would cover the check she'd written for the mortgage. She sighed before realizing it.

"Sorry, bitch – don't get to take my money this time. Sigh," he mocked.

He left the driveway in a hurry, spinning gravel in various directions and squealing his tires as he pulled forward and left again.

Melody fought off tears of anger, frustration, incredulousness, and emotions she didn't know the names for. She walked toward the house, realized the front door was still locked, and went off through the backyard to go inside that way. She had to rewash the diapers and knew Joey would be awake soon enough.

A deep sadness was settling in and consuming the joy Melody struggled to hold onto. She aimlessly walked around the house trying to sing to God. Obliviously, she began pacing the hallway. Back and forth, up and down the hallway, she tread. She thought about all the advice her "Help Meet" book had offered and felt like a complete failure. She'd tried everything. She thought she would win her husband over, but she couldn't.

As depression tried to creep into the depth of her soul, she moved into the bedroom and pulled back the curtain.

Staring out the window, she found the words to beg God to help her. She saw the mockingbirds, this time fighting off a blue jay, and the robins tenaciously searching out worms and bugs from the lawn, but she felt nothing. The monster had taken her joy. She stood in shock, trying to feel elation at the sight of her favorite creatures – but she had died inside and could only feel a failure.

Melody searched her mind, trying to figure out where she'd gone wrong. She backed away from the window and went to her bureau, fingering the dried flowers she'd picked the year before and had set in a vase on her dresser top. The corner of a white card caught her eye. She reached for it and found it was a card she'd seen in her things after returning from the shelter. It had the name and number of an LCSW. In complete abandon, she jogged to her phone and punched in the number on the card.

The voice of a young woman answered. Melody almost hung up. Her heart was beating ferociously in her chest. She could hardly hear her thoughts over the quick-paced thump of her heart.

"How much is it to talk to a therapist?" Melody almost whispered into the phone.

The receptionist answered her, "We are a ministry. There is no cost to you."

"Can I come in?" Melody asked with more uncertainty and almost slammed her pink flip phone shut.

The voice on the other end of the line told her that there had been a cancelation, and she could get in that afternoon. "Can you come in at 2? she asked.

"Where are you located? I'm not sure where your office is," Melody said, realizing she had no idea where she would have to go for this appointment.

"We are located in Southaven on Stateline Road between the

First Pentecostal Church and the Citgo station. We are in a small building with a red roof. Can you be here at 2? Actually, 1:45, so you have time to fill out paperwork," she answered.

Melody pulled her phone from her ear to look at the time. She had two hours to get there. She could arrive by 1:45. "Yes, I can be there then. Thank you."

"Great. Let me put you down. What's your name?" the young woman asked.

"Melody. My name is Melody Timbre."

Melody packed Joey's diaper bag, snacks, and a cup of water.

She put together a peanut butter and jelly sandwich for herself and cut up an apple to go with it. While filling her water bottle to take along, she heard her son waking up in the next room. She turned the tap off, picked up the lid to her bottle, screwed it on, set all of their food into the diaper bag, and set it by the front door to grab on her way out.

She could feel anxiety in her veins and tension in her shoulders. She walked into Joey's room to get him from his crib.

He smiled at her as he saw her come in.

The usual wave of relief that flooded her when her child smiled at her didn't come. Melody knew it was right for her to go to the therapist's office. She smiled at her son, a forced smile that didn't feel natural.

She changed his diaper, combed his hair, changed his clothes into her favorite onesie and a pair of shorts, and took him into the kitchen for lunch. She set him on the floor and let him walk around while she washed her hands. She grabbed the towel beside her to dry them and neatly hung it on the stove handle before picking Joey up and setting him in his high chair to eat yogurt and toast.

She took a bib from the back of the chair and fastened it around his neck before feeding him.

As usual, Melody tried to stay focused on feeding and interacting with her son, but she felt far away. There had been a horrible change inside her; she couldn't get herself to feel normal anymore. Joey seemed to sense her anguish and looked at his mother intently. She tried smiling again. His eyes locked with hers as if he were looking past the façade and into her soul instead. The little boy blew a yogurty kiss to his mother. She smiled for real, and his eyes softened. He returned to eating his lunch, munching on toast while Melody spooned yogurt into his mouth.

It was 1:39 when Melody pulled up in front of the little building with the red roof between the First Pentecostal Church and the Citgo station. Her stomach hurt, her shoulders were tense, and her veins felt alive with a nervous tickle. She felt as though she might throw up, and her chest tightened as she put the car in park and got out of the vehicle. She went to the back door and opened it to get Joey. She took her sandwich out of the bag and put it beside Joey's seat, as she had been unable to eat like she'd planned to on her drive there.

She unsnapped the buckles. Joey helped her remove the straps around his body and scooted forward for Melody to pick him up and take him from the seat. She swung the diaper bag over her right arm and her little boy onto her left hip, closed the door with her free hand, and took a deep breath before walking toward the front door of the therapy building.

She walked in and was immediately met with the smell of an old house. The paneling dated the waiting room, and the chairs were mismatched but neat and clean.

A young woman sat behind a glass window. She reached up to slide the window open and welcomed Melody.

"Mrs. Timbre?" she asked.

"Yes, I'm Melody."

"Here are some forms to fill out," the receptionist said as she handed a clipboard through the open window.

She was a pretty young woman. She looked to be in her mid-twenties, maybe a year or two younger than Melody. Her blonde hair was neatly tied back in a ponytail. She had a short-sleeved sweater on with a necklace and earrings to coordinate.

Melody looked at the woman with envy.

She felt as though she looked like a frumpy old woman compared to the well-put-together woman sitting behind the glass.

Melody took the clipboard and brought Joey to sit in the waiting room. She sat him on one leg and balanced the clipboard on the other. He kept trying to take her pen, making it challenging to complete the forms. Melody set her little boy down on the floor where he could stand near her. She pulled a baggie with his favorite freeze-dried pear bites from the diaper bag and offered him one. She also grabbed a toy truck from the side of the bag and handed it to him. He was happy to drive the truck back and forth on the chair seat beside her and asked for bites of pear every so often as Melody finished filling the pages before her. When she finished, she brought the pages to the window and handed them to the same petite blonde woman.

Melody went back to her chair with Joey and sat with him until her name was called. An older woman, slightly heavy around the middle, called to Melody from the side door.

She looked over multi-colored half-reading glasses as she said Melody's name and waved for her to come with her.

Melody quickly grabbed Joey and his truck and hurled the diaper bag over her arm as she swiftly followed the woman through the door.

CHAPTER 25

I was awake before Peter, as usual. I slipped out of the bed and room undetected. Padding through the house to the den, I sat in the glider with my Bible open. I read from Proverbs 31 to match the date. It was the infamous chapter about the excellent wife. I reread the chapter wondering if I could ever be an excellent wife. I had no skills, my husband rarely ate what I cooked, and I avoided having sex with him at nearly all costs. My oldest was heading down the wrong path, and I was his homeschooling mother; I had no excuse for his poor raising. I could hear the annoying sound of a crow outside. I looked up to see if I could see where it was coming from. For a moment, I sat thinking about how I used to love the sound of crows.

I was as angry and bitter as Peter said I was. I felt lost and wondered where the woman of my youth had gone. She used to be so cheerful and happy.

I hadn't heard Melody come in with Joey, but she was sitting beside me on the sectional. She put Joey down to play on the carpet before her, and I pointed out the noisy crows.

She, too, confided that their caw had become a racket to her, and I no longer felt so inadequate. Joey walked over to the basket of toys by the edge of the couch. He pulled a few items out before getting to Andrew's favorite truck. It had been Jonah's and passed down through the boys. It brought back fond memories of my oldest child. I thought about the little boy who would drive trucks around with me on the floor and the sound he made to pretend the engine was running. Joey matched him identically, from his curly brown hair to the outfit he wore that I'd passed on to Melody for him. I almost forgot he was Melody's boy for a moment, lost in time and remembering what my boy was like before he had gotten old enough to cheat at church games with the others. Joey brought the truck to me and held it up, spraying as he "*brrrrrrrrmmmed*" the truck on my lap. I picked up the toddler to snuggle him and salve the wound in my heart.

I whispered to Melody of my concerns over Jonah. I confided in my complete inadequacy and the feelings of failure I had succumbed to. Melody put her hand on my shoulder, comforting me and trying to cheer me up with thoughts of what she knew I'd been doing to work with him and that I was not a failure. I looked at my friend. Her tanned skin nearly glowed. She wore a blue tank top that brought out the blue in her eyes. She was stunning. Her hair was always in place; beautiful blonde wisps framed her face and highlighted her brown hair. Her long, tan legs were crossed as she leaned back to her spot on the sofa.

We got up and moved to the kitchen, Joey toddling behind us.

I began making breakfast for all four boys and three adults. I pulled a large mixing bowl from the cabinet to the left of the stove and began cracking eggs into it. I went to the pantry for canned mushrooms and the freezer for frozen peppers and onions.

I was glad I'd precut them before freezing them. I had picked them from the garden a few weeks earlier on one of our many trips out there to keep it weeded for Peter. I returned to the cupboard over the stove to get some garlic powder, salt, and pepper and grabbed a heavy cast iron skillet to fry the eggs in. I set the pan on the stove, turned the gas on, and put a large pat of butter in to melt. I went back over to the counter and whipped everything up well before returning to the stove, where I smeared the melted butter all over the bottom and then poured the eggs in to cook.

Melody looked up from the spot she sat at the counter. "I hear the boys coming."

Three boys made their way into the kitchen. Jonah had a scowl; the other two didn't seem to notice.

They climbed onto chairs at the counter next to Melody and began chattering. Gregory told every last detail of his dreams while Andrew listened, waiting for a turn to tell about his. Jonah sat with his head turned down and angrily told his brother to "shut his hole."

Melody and I exchanged glances. I never knew how to handle Jonah anymore. I didn't want to conjure Peter from the bedroom any earlier than he would already come out. If I was too harsh in my correction, Jonah was sure to make enough noise that he'd wake his sleeping father, and who knew how the day would end up going? He'd probably take Jonah to work on the church again, and I'd never hear the end of it from the church family.

Melody spoke first. "Hey, buddy, I don't want my Joey saying those things. Can you keep that sort of talk away from him, please?"

Jonah looked at her as if he were looking through her and didn't acknowledge she'd spoken to him. I was on edge and looking out the kitchen door toward our bedroom, afraid Jonah was about to wake him over this.

Gregory had not even slowed down as he went on with the details of his dream, and Andrew was trying to get a word in edgewise.

"Shut your faces," Jonah growled at them.

Gregory's face immediately crinkled up, and he told his brother not to say that.

Jonah made a face at his brother, called him a baby brat, and hopped off his seat.

I stood petrified as I whispered after Jonah not to wake his father. He either didn't hear me or didn't care to listen. The next thing I heard was a door slamming, and moments later, Peter rushed out of our bedroom.

"WHAT IS GOING ON IN HERE?" he bellowed as he sauntered into the kitchen in his tight white underwear.

Gregory was the first to speak. I was so ashamed and looked toward Melody to see if she was trembling as much as I was.

"Jonah told me to shut up!" Gregory said with anger.

"Jonah – git in here!" Peter called.

Jonah came in cross-armed and asked his father, "What?" It looked like a challenge, and I feared for Jonah.

"Did you tell Gregory to shut up?" Peter asked Jonah.

"No, he's lying!" Jonah said, sneering and cutting his eyes at Gregory.

"He did tell me to shut up!" Gregory insisted.

"I did not, you baby brat liar!" Jonah shot back at his brother.

Peter reached for Gregory. The anger flashed in his eyes as he yanked him by the arm out of the chair. Melody and I both jumped. She grabbed Peter by the arm and took him out of the kitchen.

I sat with Gregory, holding him as he cried. Joey toddled around and came to offer condolences to Gregory as he cried into my chest. Andrew climbed down from his chair to get on my lap too. He cried and told his brother it was okay, parroting after me.

I held them both tightly and nuzzled my face into the tops of their heads. Joey climbed up, too. With my lap full of curly-haired boys, I sat with tears dripping into their hair. My heart broke for them, and it broke for Jonah.

I didn't know where he'd gone off to or how to stop him from turning into his father...

CHAPTER 26

The older woman introduced herself as Mrs. Winters and told her to sit in whichever seat she liked. The office was brightly decorated and neat but crammed with bookshelves, plants, and a small desk on the back wall. There was a large, colorful, braided rug on the floor between the entrance and the desk and a leather loveseat against the wall adjacent to the desk.

Two wooden chairs with matching cushions sat opposite the loveseat in front of two tall bookshelves seemingly looming with books.

"Have a seat. What is this little guy's name?" she asked sweetly.

Melody looked over at her son. "I hope it's okay that I brought him; I can't leave him with a babysitter. He has to come. Is that alright?" she rambled to the therapist before her.

Mrs. Winters assured Melody that having Joey with her was fine. Melody handed Joey his truck and gave him pieces of pear as she settled in to talk to her new therapist.

"What brings you here? You left that part blank on your intake forms, I see," Mrs. Winters asked.

Melody looked down at her hands; she didn't know how to answer. She delayed long enough for her therapist to ask again.

"I am trying to fix my marriage, but I've failed… "Melody stammered to Mrs. Winter.

"What's wrong with your marriage that you must fix?" Mrs. Winters returned.

"It's just that my husband doesn't like me much. I'm trying to be a good wife but can't get it right," Melody told her.

"How long have you been married?" she asked her.

"We've been married for about 4 years," Melody replied.

"And when did things start going badly for you two?"

Melody thought for a moment. "I think it's always been like this."

"That's unlikely. Why would you have married, then?" the therapist said with a smile.

"No, he says I'm fat, not sexy, he doesn't like my cooking, he doesn't seem to trust me… and I can't think of a time when it wasn't like this," Melody answered, knowing how crazy that sounded. "Why had I married him? There should be something I can think of pointing to a logical reason to marry a man who doesn't even find me attractive – " but Melody could think of nothing.

The two women talked for forty-five minutes. Melody told her about the bank account and her money problem with her husband earlier that morning. Still, besides sympathy, Mrs. Winter had little to offer. She felt frustrated. Going to therapy was supposed to help her.

"It's only the first time, though," Melody chided herself. "I need to come back, and then it will help."

Melody continued to see Mrs. Winter for several weeks. By her sixth appointment, she was feeling reluctant to go.

So far, she sat telling this therapist about her troubles within her marriage and only got sympathetic looks and shallow statements about how hard it must be. She had gone for answers. She didn't need someone to tell her, "Yes, I see," and not tell her what to do differently.

She asked Mrs. Winter why she hadn't given her things to do at home. She told her about the "Help Meet" book and that it hadn't been working, so she needed advice for her particular type of marriage.

Mrs. Winter looked at Melody empathetically. "You've got to be ready to change."

"I'm ready!" Melody said with a tear in her eye and her voice cracking. "What do I need to do to change?"

Mrs. Winter answered frankly, "You must change how you look at him and your reactions. It takes two to be married. You can't expect to change everything on your own if he doesn't budge. Everyone wants to think marriage is fifty-fifty. It's not. It's one hundred-one hundred. You can't put more than your own one hundred in and expect there to be a solid marriage if your husband isn't putting in anything."

Melody needed clarification. "So, what do I do then?"

"It's not your place to do anything, Melody. You either take it as it is or get out of it."

"But I'm married! I can't get divorced! I can't break up Joey's family," Melody clamored.

"Then you might want to go to your doctor to see if you can get a Zoloft prescription. You will either have to accept this as your marriage or leave it. Nothing will fix it or change your husband unless he wants to," Mrs. Winter told her.

Time was up, and Melody was glad about that! She couldn't believe what she was hearing. She'd wasted a month and a half of her life going to see this woman. She picked Joey up, thanked her for her time, went out to the same pretty blonde receptionist, and canceled her next week's appointment.

With a quizzical look, she did as asked, and Melody thanked her before leaving the little red building with the red roof for the last time.

Melody felt more depressed than she had when she started this therapy. She had no idea what to do. She drove aimlessly toward home but turned off several times to add length to her trip home. Joey had fallen asleep in his car seat, so she used it as her excuse for driving and driving instead of heading straight home.

CHAPTER 27

Autumn had arrived with another heat wave. It was an Indian summer, and our church family was planning their annual fall camping trip. The debate was whether to delay and wait for cooler weather or take advantage of the heat and lake for swimming on this trip. Peter was voting for the swimming and looking at all the older teen girls. Beth seemed to notice his awkward stares and moved to put herself between him and her daughters. There was a scuffle. Beth's face was red, and Peter's lip was tilted upward as he did when trying to impress someone. She took her family to the back of the church sanctuary behind us. I sat dumbfounded and oblivious to what was happening. It was only a short time before a decision was made to wait for the weather to cool down. Families began filing out of the church building.

Peter sat in the driver's seat of our minivan with a smirk on his face. I tried not to look in his direction not wanting to give him any satisfaction of wonder. My lack of interest annoyed him so much that he began talking to me.

"Did you see Beth's face?" Peter said, laughing as he reached down to scratch his crotch.

I answered him briefly with a shoulder raise and a slight head turn.

"She caught me looking down at her blouse. Man, she is such a fox. I was trying to guess the color of her nipples, but she saw me looking," he said, laughing as if he'd just told a hysterical joke.

I sat mortified, wondering how I could have married such a pervert.

"Come on!" he laughed, grabbing at my knee. "It's funny!"

Jonah laughed from behind us, and my anger soared. I looked at my son with the mom stare, trying to quiet him, but he raised his arm and sneered at me as he reached forward to tap his hand on his father's shoulder and laugh more exaggerated than the first time.

I sat watching the fog line as we sped down the road. Peter and Jonah were discussing a fishing trip.

"I know how to get to Hickahala Creek from the interstate. We'll have to park under the bridge, but we can go in the morning," Peter told our son.

"Great, he's teaching him to trespass now," I thought, rolling my eyes but unwilling to say anything.

"Can I go too?" Gregory asked, joining in from the rear set of seats in the minivan.

"Sure, buddy. We will have to get up early to get there when the fish are biting. You think you can get up early?" Peter asked with unexpected love in his voice.

"Yeah! I can! I can!" Gregory squealed with excitement.

Andrew didn't seem interested which I was glad about because I wasn't sure Peter would keep him from falling into the creek and drowning downstream, and I wasn't sure I was invited to this fishing and trespassing adventure.

True to his word, Peter woke early and got up to get the boys from their bedroom.

I watched Jonah sleepily go into the bathroom and put clothes on that Peter handed him. They went toward the front door, both whispering and tiptoeing.

"Where's Gregory?" I asked.

"He'll be too noisy, and I'll have to watch him too much. Tell him I tried to wake him, but he wouldn't," Peter said as the two opened the front door with fishing poles in hand.

Before they closed the door, Gregory came barreling out of their bedroom, hopping on one foot as he tried to get his croc on the other. His hair stood up from where he slept on it, and his clothes were wrinkled as if he'd slept in them. Peter and Jonah quickly slammed the front door and ran for the van.

Gregory stood at the front door, trying to get the latch undone. He ran to the edge of the porch as he watched his father speed out of the driveway.

Tears flooded his face. He cried for hours that morning, unable to understand why his father had left without him. I held him tightly, rocking back and forth with him in my arms, crying into his hair because I didn't know how to console him.

I looked into Gregory's tear-stained face and told him he, Andrew, and I would take the day off from school and go fishing ourselves. "I know of a duck pond not far from here that I used to take Jonah to when he was a baby. We can bring our own poles and see what we catch."

I didn't have a pole for Andrew, so I tied a string with a paperclip securely tied on. We went outside, hunted for worms, and packed ourselves some snacks.

We drove over to the water and parked on the side of the road. It had been many years since I'd last been here.

Darkness washed over me as I tried to push thoughts of Peter and Jonah speeding away in his work van out of my mind.

Gregory and Andrew were excited to get the worms on their hooks, so I looked down quickly and set my mind to the task. We spent about two hours fishing. Andrew caught 3 small fish on his little paperclip hook. Gregory caught four fish with his Mickey Mouse fishing pole and begged to keep each one for cooking. Unable to say no to him after Gregory's devastating morning, we took all the fish home.

Two happy boys helped me load the minivan with their fishing poles and seven little fish. I was relieved that the two of them had gotten to fish. We drove home, chatting endlessly about fish and how to cook them.

They skipped into the house not caring that Jonah and Peter were still not home. We took the fish into the backyard with a fillet knife as I attempted to clean, gut, and fillet these little fish. They were so tiny that it was nearly impossible to remove the bones, so I did my best to remove the guts and clean them so we could take them inside to fry them up for a snack.

We were all sitting at the counter swinging our feet and smacking our lips at the good-tasting fish when Peter came inside with Jonah. Gregory and Andrew still had an extra fish on their plates.

The sweet boys offered their catch to their father and brother, only to be turned down. Peter glared at me as if I'd gone against him by taking them fishing. He slammed his fist onto the counter, causing all of us to jump in surprise. His eyes flashed with anger. He railed against me for taking his kids fishing when it was for fathers to do. He pulled Gregory to his side and ruffled his hair, apologizing for leaving without him.

"Your mom said you wouldn't wake up and that we should go without you," Peter said, looking down fallaciously apologetically at his son.

Gregory hugged him back and told him it was okay. Jonah stomped away, calling over his shoulder, "He's just trying to get attention. Gregory is a baby!"

I moved toward the doorway to follow him, but Peter put his hand out to stop me.

"You caused this!" he hissed at me. "He's my number one son; I'll go talk to him…."

Peter spun around and moved swiftly down the hallway toward Jonah.

Gregory sat back at the counter, looking pleased as he and his brother ate the last two pieces of fish their father and brother had not wanted.

Jonah spent the next several weeks stomping through the house, elbowing Gregory at every opportunity, and feigning innocence.

I punished Jonah, took dessert away for the week, forced him to apologize to Gregory, and pleaded with him to understand what he was doing wrong.

Peter grew increasingly furious with me each time his son ran to him, crying that he was hungry, but I'd not let him eat, which was only true for desserts, not meals.

The weather cooled enough for our annual church campout. I spent the week making lists and packing up supplies to take with us. I had an old two-horse trailer from my training days and loaded it into our makeshift camper. I collected the boys' bikes and put them inside the trailer to take with us.

Using dollar store table clothes, I cut curtains for the open slats to keep bugs out when we slept and packed up our things.

The boys were so excited even Jonah seemed to forget to be angry. We were waiting for Peter to get home so we could head toward Arkabutla Lake, but he was late coming home. I tried to keep the boys preoccupied as we waited, but the day was getting late, so I called Peter.

"I'm too busy working on the church. I've got a helper now. He's going to partner with me on some of my jobs. He's a good guy, a worship pastor. Everyone knows him and likes him, so I'll be able to get jobs in homes like the Change Pointers."

He was referring to the Change Point Church we'd attended when we'd first moved here. I'd become a member, but we'd left after an argument Peter and I had had that I'd asked them to get involved in. He'd never forgiven me for "airing our dirty laundry" and claimed they didn't like him because of my lies and crying.

"I won't be able to make it. Go without me," he told me.

"Okay…" I stammered. "Will you be coming later?"

"Yeah – yeah. I'll be there later tonight," he said.

I told the boys we were ready to load up into the truck.

"Where's Dad?" Jonah asked. "Did you make him not want to come?"

"He's going to be there later. We'll set up without him, and he'll be there tonight."

We drove toward the campsite singing – except for Jonah, who sat with his arms crossed.

I backed the trailer into our spot and put the truck in park. The first thing we did was take the bikes out so the kids could play while I unpacked. Jonah seemed to loosen up some as he rolled down the driveway of the campsite with the other kids. I was relieved to see him playing well with them and relaxed as I made beds and set up our campsite.

Everyone wanted to know where Peter was. I was so aggravated at his last-minute ditching us that I didn't feel like listening to everyone "*ooh*" and "*ahh*" over how wonderful it was that he was working on the church while we had fun. I told them he had a partner helping him now, so he should be finishing the project faster now.

We all went our own ways as the kids played so we could get our fires started and meals cooked. Beth and Brian had a table and lights strung up around their site. They had a double-burner camp stove and a delicious pot of stew. Others were heading toward their camp area to sit and fellowship together. Once our hot dogs and baked beans meal was finished, I served the boys and myself and headed over to be with everyone else.

Craig and Janice arrived late and were offered food from everyone else so they didn't need to worry about cooking.

Their children ate quickly and joined the others riding bikes down the driveway.

"Sorry, we're so late. We had a lot of cleaning up at the church from construction, and it was our turn for cleaning," Janice offered as she sat with the rest of us while her husband set up their tents.

"What was Peter working on today?" Brian asked.

"He wasn't there today. He said he had another job to work on this week," Craig yelled from the back of his car to answer Brian.

All eyes were on me. I'd just told them he was working at the church with a helper, and now Janice and Craig were telling them he wasn't there THIS WEEK. I wondered where he was, then. Peter had clearly told me he had been working at the church all week. I excused myself from the group, mentioning all the tea I'd drank going through me quickly, and headed off toward the bathrooms. I stopped halfway, realizing I needed to get the boys with me so I didn't just leave them alone, so I moved my way along the outskirts of our sites to get to them.

They were reluctant to go with me, and the other kids thought it meant they had to return the bikes, but I assured them they could keep playing. I washed the boys up so they'd be ready for bed and returned to the campsite on the backside again while the kids ran ahead to play with the other kids again.

CHAPTER 28

After putting Joey down for his nap, Melody laid down on her neatly made bed. She felt so alone. "Mrs. Winter thinks I need medication," Melody said to the empty room. "Maybe I am the crazy one." She had finished her Bachelor's Degree with zero fanfare. She held a degree now that sat in a box on the top shelf of the bookcase in the hall. Her husband had not acknowledged it and deflated any remaining excitement by reminding her that she was Joey's mom, not a teacher. She had begun her graduate degree in Education with a full scholarship from Western Governors University. Her first class was to start the following day, and her books had arrived that morning.

She wondered why she was going through the trouble of getting these degrees. She wasn't even sure she would be able to actually teach anyone anything.

Melody didn't feel confident in anything about herself at this point. She was low, lonely, and desperate for time to pass. She'd not attended church since her mistake in going to the shelter. She felt uncomfortable being around the Pastor or his wife, Glenda.

She got up slowly from the bed. It was getting chilly now that it was December. The heat didn't need to be put on yet, but she wanted to wear a sweater. Heading toward her closet to grab her favorite sweater, Melody passed her reflection in the mirror over her dresser. She saw dark circles under her eyes and a bulge at her belly, and she stopped to stare at her own chest. She wore a full B cup, but she'd been called flat-chested for so long that she could only see the same flatness described. She looked at her lifeless hair and undid her hair clip to see if she could add any appeal to her appearance but failed to. She grabbed her sweater and entered the living room to check on her portal. She wanted to be sure she knew how to get onto her school platform to be ready for her class assignments.

Tears sprang to her eyes as she couldn't focus on the task at hand and instead went back to the failure of a wife she was. A failure at life. She grabbed her Bible from the coffee table and tried to read for comfort. She found nothing to console the emptiness inside of her.

Mabel would be coming to get her for Bible Study that coming Thursday. She reached for her Bible Study material to complete the assignments required until she heard her son waking from his nap.

She got him from his bed, changed his diaper, and brought him to the living room to play. She felt bored and trapped in the house. She wanted to go for a walk or to the pond to see the ducks… she wanted a friend.

The afternoon dragged on. She forced herself to make dinner, a simple Alfredo sauce to go over spaghetti.

She smiled at her son, who played in the kitchen beside her, banging pots and pans with wooden spoons. He'd be two in a few short months. Where had the time gone?

Melody heard her husband come through the front door.

Unexpectedly, he came straight back to the kitchen with a large bouquet. She was so surprised that she stood frozen and unable to speak. Her husband was standing before her with flowers and offering them to her with a big smile. He reached for and held her, whispering how much he appreciated and loved her in her ear. Joey grabbed onto her leg and gleefully bounced.

"Up peas!" he said as the three huddled in the kitchen. She watched her husband bend down and tenderly pick their toddler up.

He laughed, looked directly into Melody's eyes, and mouthed, "I love you."

The three ate dinner together while Melody listened intently to her husband tell her about his day working at the Luwfolk's kitchen. He described cabinet door styles, which walls he had to remove and rebuild, and the colors he'd suggested they used. He was animated as he described the hardware for the cabinet doors and how Mrs. Luwfolk loved all his choices and suggestions.

"I got in good with her. They have a bathroom that needs to be renovated, too. I gave them a great price, and Mrs. Lufolk is enamored with me, so I can bang her on the next project."

Melody hated it when he told her of his plans to "bang" someone but overlooked it because they were having a wonderful family dinner and evening together.

As they finished their meal, Melody was shocked to see her husband take his plate and hers to the kitchen sink. He washed them both while Melody picked up their son and took him to the bathroom to clean his face and hands off. The three retired to the living room to play with Joey together until it was his bedtime.

"Are these new curtains?" he asked.

Melody looked up quizzically. She was sure he was making a joke, but to her astonishment, he looked serious. She didn't want to do a thing to change the ambiance of the room, so she just nodded and smiled.

"Do you like them?" she asked gleefully as he got up, fingering the tassels as if he'd never seen them in the nearly two years they'd been hung there. He complimented her on the skill she had as a seamstress. Melody blushed and pulled Joey close to kiss his head and hide behind the soft curls on his head.

She watched her husband smile at her from the windows and return to the couch near her and their son. He slid to the floor beside Melody and put his arm around her. Chills filled her body, exciting her in ways she'd not felt in a long time.

After he helped her brush Joey's teeth, dress him in his pajamas, and tuck him in, he walked out of his room hand in hand with Melody, led her back to the living room, and cuddled with her on the couch. He kissed her ear and told her she smelled good. The movie played in the background as he leaned in to kiss her passionately. His kisses were wet, overpowering. For whatever reason she couldn't understand, he encapsulated her lips with his and slobbered on the skin surrounding her lips.

She didn't like kissing him like that, but he loved her, and she wasn't about to stop him. He moved his hands to her breasts and tenderly touched her. She could feel his excitement next to her, something she had longed for for so many years.

He pulled her shirt up and explored her chest as if he'd never touched her, groaning as he nearly suffocated her with his ridiculous effort to make out with her. It didn't matter. Her skin was electric. She moved with his body and worked her hands under his own shirt. His chest lacked muscles, and she wasn't to touch too close to his neck or get anywhere near his nipples, so she concentrated on trying to be sensual and stay in the safe spaces.

The credits were rolling at the end of the film as they laid on the couch together wrapped up in each other's embrace. By the time they'd actually made love, he was very quick, so she missed out on her own finish, but that was okay with her. She didn't want to hurt his feelings or make him feel less manly, so she laid with him, acting as if she had been satisfied and not turned on so hot just to be let down. He was snoring lightly.

She woke up around three in the morning stiff from laying in the same position for so long but smiled at the memory of her husband loving her. She moved, trying to get up without disturbing him, to stretch and work the cramp in her neck that had formed. He grabbed her as though he didn't want her to leave.

The sweetness of his gesture overcame even the pain in her

neck, and she laid back down, entangled in his arms and legs.

The following day, she struggled to get up and walk straight. Hobbling a little and unable to turn her neck to the left, she went to the kitchen to make coffee and breakfast. He followed her in once the bacon was sizzling, filling the house with the savory scent. The three sat and ate breakfast together just like the night before. Melody couldn't help but smile. She really did have a good husband.

CHAPTER 29

Morning dawned. I could hear other church friends getting out of the tents by the sound of zippers and cracking sticks and leaves. I looked around our little horse trailer at the boys. Jonah was moving around. I expected him to wake first, followed by the other two. The space next to me was empty, as Peter had never arrived the night before. With chores to do and a bathroom to hike to, it gave me something to look busy at. I stayed behind our trailer, making breakfast for the kids as more church families woke up and started puttering about.

Beth and Brian had their makeshift outdoor kitchen in full swing. They had a griddle set up this morning and were making pancakes. Their oldest son, Benjamin, asked the rest of us if we wanted to share pancakes with them and invited everyone to come to their campsite for morning devotion.

Slowly, we all gathered at their site. I set my chair up in the back so fewer people could look at me as they wondered where Peter was. Myra set her chair next to me and sat down with a smile. We said good morning and nothing else. Brian started with prayer. Elder William and his wife, Milly, sat up front in our little group.

William got up and stood beside Brian as he finished his prayer and took over what would be our corporate devotion for the day.

The rest of the parishioners raised their heads as they said, "Amen." I quickly parroted them, realizing I hadn't prayed or bowed my head and didn't want to be found out. I was relieved to see Elder William lead even though I paid little attention to his message. Peter had rolled up in his work van. He was making a huge scene as he made his way to the front row, sat on a log, and interrupted the outdoor service to tell everyone how sorry he was for arriving late; he'd been up late working at our church.

I was glad to be in the back. He had no idea Craig and Janice had already told everyone he wasn't there.

I watched as Janice shifted in her seat, and Pastor Craig looked as though he were about to say something but stopped before uttering a word.

Elder William went on, glancing toward me several times. I looked away, unable to meet anyone's direct eye contact, and found myself wishing the earth would open up below me and swallow me.

At the end of the service, most people hung around, and several encircled Peter. He looked pleased with himself to have such attention. I could hear him telling Craig he was mistaken.

"I must have been out back in the swampy area, making some cuts on the tile, or out to Subway to get some supper when you came by. I was there all night long," he said, looking as though he believed his own lies.

"Who's your new partner?" Jerry asked.

Peter caught my eye before answering. "It's James; you know the guy you and Jane introduced me to at Visco?" Peter said, looking pleased with himself.

Jerry looked pleased too. "Oh, he's a good guy. Good guy!" Jerry said as if he'd just overstepped his bounds and was backtracking.

I wondered if our friends were starting to realize what was going on.

Did they believe him? How many times would they excuse him? Milly had made her way back and stood beside me.

She reached over and touched my arms, looking into my eyes with sympathy. Immediately, my eyes stung with tears. Myra put her arm around me as we stood silently, each speaking volumes to me through their gentle touch. And yet, I couldn't be sure they even thought what I thought.

The group disbanded, and the kids went to their playing. The women helped Beth clean up the makeshift kitchen and took their chairs to create a circle they could talk in and watch the kids play from.

I sat quietly. Peter left again, claiming the need to work more at the church.

I wondered where he was actually going.

With Peter gone, Milly and William took the opportunity to sit and chat with me.

We moved our chairs off to my campsite and began with small talk about how much fun the kids were having with the bikes we'd brought. The two seemed to look at me as if I had something to say. I sat quietly. They looked away for a moment and then back again.

"Do you want to talk?" Milly asked.

I heard myself tell them I did. "If I start, though, it feels like Pandora's box. Once it's said, it can't be unsaid," I told them.

They nodded and sat quietly.

"We're here for you if you want to try. It will just be between us, and we won't hold anything you say against you," William said, offering a sympathetic look matching his wife's.

Within a moment, I poured my heart out quietly to the couple. I told them about Peter's rage and anger, how he treated me and the boys, his computer tucked away in his office, the unexplained absences, his lying about his whereabouts, and anything else that came to mind at the time.

William told me there was likely a porn addiction with the rage he displayed and the secretive computer time. They offered book titles and said they would loan them to me, but I interrupted them and explained that I'd already tried to be the best wife. I didn't need books…

Both looked at me with empathetic bewilderment. "We'd like you to read about the symptoms wives see when their husbands are secretly addicted to porn."

"He said he'd had a porn addiction when I first met him but had gotten rid of all his movies when he knew we were getting married," I said, being as forthright as possible. I didn't want them to believe anything that wasn't true.

"You don't just get rid of a porn addiction so easily," William assured me.

"We've had some women come to us, telling us that Peter has been inappropriate with them, and they thought he might be a predator… " William said, looking me in the eyes as if to see if I was about to go crazy from this information.

I remained calm on the outside as my inner voice had a grown-up temper tantrum on the inside.

"We're sorry to tell you this," Milly said as she reached to pat my knee.

"There's a nouthetic counsel in Memphis the church will pay for you and Peter to go to. We've already spoken with Craig, Janice, Jerry, and Jane, and they are willing to babysit for you to go weekly," William told me.

"So, the church is all talking about us?" I asked.

"NO – it's not like that. We have had the complaints, though, and Jonah has been causing trouble with the other kids, so parents have been coming to us. We had to get together with the church Elders to decide how to handle this," William assured me.

Milly handed me a card and said it was the counselor's phone number. "We've already arranged to pay him if you decide to go to him, but as members, we strongly advise it – church discipline would be our next step."

I took the card and shoved it into my back pocket. William got up to leave, excusing himself, while Milly continued to sit and chat lightly about the pretty colors of foliage as if that would take my mind off of what they'd just told me. Still, it was nice of her to sit with me.

It took me a few days after the camping trip to approach Peter with the counseling idea. I didn't let him know I'd spoken with William and Milly or that the Elders had gotten complaints about him. Instead, I told him I needed help and that his being with me would help the counselor better understand what I was doing wrong. I was shocked to hear him say yes.

"But we'll need a sitter, and you know how I feel about that, so we probably wouldn't really both go," Peter said as he tried to back out.

"I could call Janice and Jane and see if they wouldn't mind babysitting. They've both offered to help me with homeschooling, so they might be willing to babysit. Is that alright?"

Quite unexpectedly, he said yes.

CHAPTER 30

Melody smiled at her husband as he greeted her in the kitchen. Her husband smiled back at her and kissed her before patting Joey on the head and heading off to shower. She was working on a special dinner for them to have that night. She had a surprise to share with him and wanted the evening to go perfectly.

About thirty minutes later, he was back in the kitchen and ready to eat.

They had been sharing family meals together for several weeks by now. Melody was elated and couldn't help but anticipate their shared joy.

She dished out lasagna to her two men and sat down, eager to get to her news.

He smiled as he took his first bite and told her how yummy it was. Melody bubbled over with joy at her happy little family. She thanked her husband, licked her lips, and nervously began.

"I took a test today," she said, about to explode with excitement.

"Which class?" her husband asked as he looked up.

Melody was so excited that her husband was paying attention to her now.

She hardly remembered the days she couldn't get him to listen to her.

"I'm pregnant!" she said with anticipated joy.

"WHAT? YOU WHORE! Whose is it? I know it can't be mine. We don't have sex often enough for me to get you pregnant," he barked at her across the table, right in front of their small son.

Melody struggled to her feet. She helped Joey down from the table and brought him into the living room to play. Her legs felt jiggly beneath her, so she carefully looked down with each step to be sure she wouldn't fall.

He followed her into the room and begged to know who the father was.

"It's you! You're the father. I promise!"

Melody said in a low voice, trying to shield Joey from the conversation.

"You're always off doing who knows what with who knows who. There's no telling who the real father is. If it's mine, you tricked me, then, BITCH! How could you do this to me? I don't believe you!" he yelled as he stormed away.

Melody was mortified. Her heart broke into more pieces than she imagined possible. She sat on the floor sobbing and heaving with each breath.

She was ignored for the next three weeks. She lay in bed sobbing uncontrollably. She was so broken over her own husband's response. The pain she felt inside her heart was so intense she felt as though she could die or wished she would to relieve herself of such pain.

"Lord, I'm so sorry! This baby doesn't deserve to be born into this family," she prayed. She shook the bed with her sobs. Her husband hadn't been home for the last three nights. She had no idea where he had been but supposed that was best because he'd come home as she slipped into bed and had nothing but hatred to spew at her. He called her a slut and a whore. He told her he knew she'd cheated on him. She burned with anguish and aching so fiercely. It was a pain she'd never felt before.

She lay in bed listening to him snore. She kept from touching him as she rolled over and away from him, trying to find some relief from the agony. By morning, she felt even more pain. Her stomach hurt and twisted far worse than she'd ever felt before, and she began to bleed.

He laughed at her as she sat on the toilet and cried. She told him she was scared she was losing the baby and had to go to the ER. He just laughed at her and walked away, leaving her on the toilet trying to clot blood and find thick maxi pads to put in her underwear.

She hurried to get herself and Joey into the car to get herself to the doctor.

She waited in the ER, doubled over in pain, with Joey beside her asking if his mama was "Otay." She sat waiting for hours before a nurse called her back. By then, she'd bled through her pads and was a mess. The nurse comforted her as she helped her clean up and set her up in an open bed in the ER.

The doctor came in and confirmed what she'd expected. Melody had had a miscarriage. She was immediately consumed with guilt. She'd prayed for the baby to be born to another family.

She'd caused this. She'd caused her baby to miscarry. The nurses were in no hurry to discharge her until the bleeding was under control.

Joey sat on the bed with her for hours, looking at books and coloring with crayons and paper the nurses and staff had provided.

Once she was discharged, Melody put Joey into the car and got into the driver's seat. Never had she felt so alone in her life. She picked up her phone looking for a number for someone to call – but there was no one she could confide in. No one to put her head on their shoulder and cry. She was alone. Getting pregnant had caused her husband to go back to hating her. She didn't know how to go back home. She wasn't sure if he'd be there or what he'd say to her if he was.

Melody had nowhere to go, though, so she headed toward home.

Her husband paced in front of the living room door as she walked in with their son.

"How dare you take Joey away from me like that again. How can I trust you if you're taking him away from me for hours with no idea where you are?"

Melody stared at her husband in disbelief. She'd just miscarried their second child, driven herself to the hospital, and entertained Joey. At the same time, she felt like she'd bled to death, and now she came home to his ludicrous accusations.

Overcome with guilt, shame, and loss, Melody grieved alone. Her husband did not mention their lost child, as if it had never happened. She bled for several weeks and tried not to look mopey as she navigated through a grief she'd never encountered. Her husband couldn't believe she struggled.

"You care about that kid? I'm sorry, but I don't see how this counts as a loss. You're being so dramatic like you just want attention," he told her.

She felt numb. She felt absolutely nothing! She wondered how she could have married such a heartless man, had a child with him, and just weeks ago thought they had a happy marriage. It was as though a switch had been flipped.

She didn't hate her husband, but she felt nothing but disdain for him. She felt weak from losing blood and went to her room to lie down.

Joey followed after her, chattering to his mother. He was unaware of the change that was taking place within the heart of his own mother.

Bitterness crept in as she thought about the years of her life wasted, mixed with the loss of her unborn child. She looked at their son with resolve. She'd get away from his father. She'd escape the man who made her life a living hell. She'd never again look at herself in the same way. She was fierce with a silent rage that would remain burning for some time.

She began secretly planning with even more tenacity than

she knew she could have. She'd go on, finish her degree, squirrel money away, and get away from him. She'd teach to support both of them and live without this torment. No one could know of her plans. She'd have to act as though everything was still normal so he didn't suspect anything was going on. Even those closest to her would think she had a happy marriage until she was ready to leave.

CHAPTER 31

Peter announced his need for a new work van. He said his had worn out, and he couldn't keep it running any longer. He sat night after night in front of the computer screen, searching through an online auction site to find one. Months dragged by. Each night was the same ritual. I had no idea where he would get the money for a new van, even at a used price, but he watched and scrolled through this site like he had an addiction. As February ended, just after celebrating Andrew's fifth birthday with cake and balloons, Peter announced his excitement. He'd found a van in North Carolina's correctional facility and would be bidding on it that night. Three days passed before his bid was accepted, and now he was looking to me for the money.

In my mind, one day, I'd escape. I was done having all the loans and bills in my name. I refused to get a loan, give him my PayPal information, or any other ridiculous idea he had to get money out of me for this prisoner's van. He raged for the first day, then gave the silent treatment I'd come so used to.

He came back begging but making it sound more demanding because he had until the end of that day to get his money together or lose the bid and whatever down payment he'd made with it.

It was the eleventh hour when he figured it out and angrily told me about how I'd screwed him, PayPal had screwed him, and our bank had screwed him. Still, he'd gotten the money and paid for this van sight unseen.

Now, he had to go to North Carolina to get it. I ignored the entire process thinking the whole thing was a fiasco.

If that auction was accurate, this van was a 1991 Ford Econoline with one hundred seventy-four thousand miles that he'd just paid thirty-five hundred dollars for. He was spending six hundred eleven dollars on a one-way ticket and planned to drive the van home from North Carolina.

I was angry that he could come up with the money to buy this stupid van while his regular work van was newer with fewer miles. I was angry that we lived hand to mouth and spent summers eating cucumbers and squash because we couldn't afford groceries. We wore our coats inside all through January and February because he couldn't afford to give me money for the gas to heat our home. However, now he had over four grand to spend on a van I still didn't think he needed.

I kept my mouth shut and agreed to drive him to Memphis the first week of March so he could take a Southwest flight to North Carolina to get this thing.

The kids and I got up early and loaded into the minivan to deliver their father to the airport. They waved goodbye to him as we idled in the drop-off zone, and I unloaded his small suitcase for him. Once he was out of sight, I drove away, watching the signs for Jackson South I55.

We made it back to Mississippi and down the interstate in about thirty-five minutes and went inside to eat our last box of cereal.

Peter called that evening, angry and cursing. He'd never coordinated a pick-up time with the prison to pick up the van.

"That guy is on vacation and can't get anyone else to do the transaction for me. I'm so pissed. I own the van. I paid for it with my money, and they are holding it until next Tuesday," he said.

My stomach twisted, and I wondered where he'd get the money to stay in a motel for the next four days. I considered him an idiot for not coordinating the pick-up time with the man he bought it from.

Myra and her husband Chris had just moved to North Carolina. He was an Army Sergeant Major and had been relocated around Christmas. Myra had kept in touch by letters and had excitedly told us about their in-laws' living quarters in their new home, to be used for guests, and offered an open invitation for us to visit; actually, all of the church family received the invitation.

I called Myra, told her of Peter's predicament, and asked if Peter could stay in their guest quarters. She was so happy to help. I got Chris' phone number and called Peter back with the information. I was relieved to think he'd be able to save at least four hundred dollars staying with them. Myra said her oldest son would go to the airport, pick Peter up, and even bring him to the prison on Tuesday before work.

Peter sounded less than thrilled but took the number. He called later to tell me that he was at Chris and Myra's new home, had had dinner, and was going to go to sleep. The call was quick, just as I liked it.

In the morning, Peter called again. Never had he kept in touch so well, but he was calling to complain. He didn't like the smell of his suite, so he'd rented a car and a motel room to stay in until Tuesday. I had no idea how he could have gotten the money to afford any of it and accepted that it meant the electric bill would most likely not get paid that month.

By Wednesday, Peter was calling again, complaining that the van had broken down, and he would have to stay overnight in Tennessee while it got fixed.

That evening, he cursed in my ear as he blamed the mechanic for ruining his life and delaying the repair.

"I'm going to be here until Thursday," Peter said, sounding less reluctant than I would have expected.

The boys and I had been relaxing for the days Peter had been gone. Jonah seemed more like his old self lately and had gotten his schoolwork done without issue all week. Andrew had started reading and loved to curl beside me with a book to practice this new magical skill he'd acquired.

Melody had gone away for a week on vacation, and I hadn't heard from her. I imagined she and her husband were on the beach enjoying each other and the warm Florida winter, building sand castles with Joey.

She said they were visiting her husband's mother and celebrating Joey's birthday late since her mother-in-law hadn't been able to visit them. Melody used to keep her marriage private but had been going overboard telling her about his romantic gestures, flowers, and everything I wished my husband would do for me again. I was jealous of her but tried not to let it get between us and our friendship.

But Peter's return home scattered my own emotions enough to forget about my jealousy of Melody.

The van looked like a piece of crap. It hardly ran, and I wasn't even sure how he managed to get home.

It sat in the driveway with its prison name fading from years of use as he drove away in his regular van to go to church and finish the renovations. James was supposed to meet him there and finish the mother's room that week. I wonder if anyone even paid attention to the promised completion dates as they loomed on and were never done as described or on time. They were only denied with poor excuses and angry outbursts.

I made meatloaf from deer meat Clara had brought over from her grandson's previous years' hunting trips. She said he needed room in the freezer for this year's bounty, and I was welcome to all of it. I appreciated it and happily took every last pack of meat. I worked the meat into the shape of feet and told the boys I was making "feet loaf" for dinner. I sliced onions and set two slices on either "ankle" of the feet to make it look like I'd chopped off someone's feet from the leg. I felt proud to be a boy mom and willing to go to such lengths to entertain them, even with food. Peter had gotten home just as I pulled the red and white speckled pan from the oven.

"Smells good!" he said. "I'm starving and can't wait to eat."

I looked after him, surprised that he would eat with us. I brought the meat to the table and placed it between the mashed potatoes and green beans. Peter came in, drying his hands with a paper towel, and sat at the head of the table where I hadn't seen him sit in years, at least that I could remember.

Gregory chattered on as and on like usual. He asked his father about the trip to North Carolina to get the new van.

They hadn't been allowed inside it yet, but all three thought it was cool to have a van prisoners had ridden in.

Peter seemed overjoyed at the attention and told them how nasty Myra and Chris' house had been and that he couldn't stand the smell, so he had to move out in a hurry. He described the motel and told the boys how much he'd missed him as he drove around…

"Where were you driving around to?" I asked, wondering if he'd gone sightseeing while waiting for the van.

"We ate at this great fish place a few times," Peter answered.

I didn't let on that my heart skipped a beat at the word "we" and hoped the kids would ask him more questions as I sat speechless and afraid I'd give away my shock.

"What else did you do?" Gregory asked.

"Well, he didn't like fish as much as I did, so we drove around looking for something else to eat the third day. The town was a dump. They didn't have anything good there, so we were mostly bored and watched TV at the motel," Peter answered.

I tried to find my voice and swallow the lump in my throat and the anxiety in my chest. "Who is he?" I asked, afraid he'd answer and afraid he wouldn't.

"Oh, I helped this guy out. He needed a motel room, so we split the cost and ate together," Peter said, as if that was a perfectly logical answer.

"Where did you meet him? How did you… ?" But I couldn't find the words to finish the question.

"What do you mean? He was just a guy who needed help. I helped him. I don't know where I found him. We split the cost of the room. Weren't you the one who didn't want me paying for a motel? I thought you'd be happy to hear I hadn't paid the full price. Isn't that why you tried to have me killed by staying in a moldy room at Myra and Chris'?" Peter retorted angrily.

He got up quickly and shoved his chair into the table. I watched a shadow cast over Jonah's face as he glared at me.

After Peter left the room stomping away, Jonah spoke up. "You had to make him angry again?"

I swore I heard my son call me a bitch under his breath, but I couldn't be sure and said nothing to him about it. He mirrored his father, slamming his chair into the table and trying to stomp away.

I called after him to come back and bring his plate to the sink, but he only stopped long enough to look at me angrily before spinning and stomping down the hall after his father.

The other two boys looked at me with bewilderment. I wondered if they, too, blamed me for getting Peter angry but asked nothing of the sort.

Melody had gotten home from her vacation and was helping me clean dishes that evening in the kitchen with me. Joey and Andrew played on the floor in the dining room with trucks that had once been Jonah's. Melody put her arm around my shoulder and let me lean my head on hers. I whispered to her about this man he'd been with and how absurd it seemed to me that he'd share a motel room with a total and complete stranger. I dwelled on it, playing his words repeatedly in my head. Melody offered to talk to Jonah while I sat defeated at the dining room table, looking after the two youngest boys. Gregory came in moments later, looking for dessert, but I had nothing to offer him. I suggested more mashed potatoes, but he declined and took the truck Joey had been playing with to push beside Andrew's. Joey took another truck from the basket of toys, and the three sat on the floor, driving their trucks around and making loud motor sounds with their flapping lips, making my nose itch.

Jonah came in to apologize, and I was grateful for Melody. She was such a huge help to me. I figured Peter had gone to the bathroom and would be back to sit with us soon, but half an hour passed, and it was getting late. The boys needed baths and to brush their teeth. I put Joey and Andrew into the tub together, bathed them, and then the older two took turns. After drying the youngest two, I looked for Melody since she was obviously away from the bathroom. She came out from behind my closed bedroom door and blushed as she saw me approaching.

"I talked to Peter. He's sorry for how he slammed the chair into the table, but he said there was no man at the motel," Melody said sheepishly. "He said you made that up."

I was offended by my friend. She seemed to believe him and had a hint of defensiveness in her voice. It took my concern for finding her in my bedroom with Peter behind a closed door again away as I focused on my own defense.

I knew Peter had said he was with a man.

He'd specifically said they shared a motel room, and he accused that I should have been happy about it since I didn't want him spending the money on a motel.

Melody picked up Joey, and I noticed her skirt was tucked into her underwear as she bent over. I fixed it for her and felt betrayal sting through my veins and questions raised in my mind.

In a daze, I put the boys to bed. It was past everyone's bedtime, but Jonah argued that he was the oldest and shouldn't ever go to bed at the same time as his baby brothers.

I had no patience for him and snapped at him to lay down and go to sleep like I'd said and briskly walked out of the room, closing the door behind me.

I immediately felt bad and turned back to apologize to him. I blew him a kiss, told him I loved him, and walked out of the room again.

CHAPTER 32

Melody worked hard to complete her graduate degree. She still met with Mabel and her other friends as though everything was the same old, same old. She threw in a few tales about how her husband had brought flowers home to her to keep anyone from suspecting anything. Her husband remained aloof and ignored her. The silent treatment suited her just fine.

No longer was she the weak woman pining after his affection, attention, or even eye contact. She didn't want him to look at her, touch her, or want her in any way. Her eyes turned a shade of grey as the menacing cold that filled her soul took over.

She was a woman on a mission who would be free from this man once and for all.

Her classes all seemed easy as she focused her efforts on them rather than pleasing her husband. She finished classwork in record time and was given permission to add more classes each semester. She was on her way to finishing within a year. Between Joey and schoolwork, she kept busy. Dutifully. she did her Bible Study and rode with Mabel to class.

Putting Joey in the nursery didn't twist her gut any longer. She was not going to be a kept woman. She would be a free woman and didn't care if her husband even discovered her and Mabel's secret.

She walked with Joey to the pond across from Mabel's house

again. She walked to the park to meet her friend there.

She rebelled from the confines of her crazed husband until that afternoon when he brought home half a coke from the gas station uptown.

He offered it to her as "an olive leaf, a peace offering." He told her he didn't want to live like that any longer.

He was sorry for being such a jerk, and he was going to change. He wanted to go to a new church. His friends from Visco had spoken so highly of their church in Coldwater. They had invited him so many times, and he wanted him and Melody to begin attending.

"We can renew our marriage. I have come to the Lord again. I thought I was a saved Christian but realized I wasn't. I've been listening to sermons on the radio and can't tell you the exact moment I knew I got saved, but I know I am now. I know the Lord. I will get baptized, and I'd like you to be by my side through this," he said, smiling with his lip tipped up.

Melody didn't know how to answer or what she felt. She didn't want to come across as unsupportive. Still, he'd been saved when she met him, rededicated himself at the church they'd met in, and was baptized, then again when they had moved to Mississippi a couple years earlier. Now, he was planning his third baptism.

She smiled at her husband. He frowned.

"Why can't you ever support me? I'm the man of this house. You're the woman. We're going to this church, and I've already scheduled to meet with the pastor about getting baptized. I'm so happy to know the Lord. Praise God!" he said.

Still smiling, she nodded her head. She'd missed church. She'd missed having a church family and friends she could see regularly. The church was small. It had once been a little store in a plaza, but now the only thing in it was this church and a small mechanic shop next door. It was one room with a kitchen in the back. There was no nursery, which was a big plus for her husband. Joey sat with his parents until it was time for the baptism. She watched her husband stand on cue and grimaced as he motioned for her and Joey to go up with him. He walked forward as Melody trailed behind him, Joey on her hip. The pastor welcomed them and visitors and told the congregation that he'd had the pleasure of meeting with her husband and was convinced he needed to be baptized on the right side of his conversion.

"We like to get testimonies from our new members. Tell us about yourself and how you came to know the Lord," the pastor asked him.

"Well, I used to be a very hedonistic man. I liked girls, and they liked me. I spent my life chasing tail," he said, smirking.

Melody looked down at the floor. She was so embarrassed by what this man had just said in front of the entire congregation and all the kids.

"I've always been a good guy, but I've had my issues with sin as I'm only human and prone to sin and need a Savior just like y'all," he continued. "I don't pretend to be perfect, and I know my savior is. Hallelujah," he sang.

Melody looked at her husband, wondering why he was talking like that – and singing...

"Do you believe in Jesus Christ as your Lord and Savior and repent for your sins?" the pastor asked.

"I do!" Melody heard her husband say proudly.

She expected the pastor to pronounce something as it sounded so much like a wedding at the end, and then the pastor interrupted her thoughts as if he could hear them.

"I pronounce you part of the bride of Christ, Brother!"

Melody choked at the pastor's words. She watched her husband climb the stairs into the baptismal and sit on a bench under the water.

"Oh, it's cold!" he said with added enthusiasm she didn't recognize.

"I baptize thee in the name of the God, Jesus Christ, and the Holy Spirit, Amen!" the pastor said as everyone in the church echoed. He dunked her husband under the water and watched him come up animatedly. It was a blatant display of grandiosity for the crowd. He climbed out of the water, hugged Melody, laughed at her now dripping-wet dress, stepped back, and told the church he was so proud to be part of the body of Christ.

They stayed for the potluck, although they had not brought anything to eat themselves, and met their new church family. Melody played along as the happy housewife and chatted easily with the other women.

It would take more than this display for Melody to trust the church people and her own husband, but she analyzed quietly so that no one could read her thoughts again like it seemed the pastor had.

After their lunch, the family drove home. Melody put Joey down for his afternoon nap and sat in front of her computer.

She was finishing another class in record time and hoped to get another class lined up the next day. At the rate she was working, she'd have her graduate degree in the course of six months.

Her husband locked himself in his office for the rest of the day, and even though she was deeply immersed in an essay when Joey woke up, she was the one to go get him and spent the rest of the day with him. They went outside, glad for the spring weather to be back.

Melody heard the commotion of mockingbirds fighting off the neighbor's cat again. She watched the robins sitting in the branches of the large oak tree in their backyard and looked for where the sound of the mourning dove came from but couldn't tell.

Joey had a hand-me-down bike from her friend's son. They'd met at the park, and she was glad to get the things her sons had outgrown. They chatted regularly and enjoyed each other's company. Still, Melody was quiet about her own life, making the relationship seem a little awkward at times.

The blinds were open in her husband's office. She looked inside to see his head in front of the screen and what looked like a man's penis and a dark nipple. Surely, that wasn't what she saw; she chastised herself for such a thought and for having her mind in the gutter. First of all, the man was nearly asexual. She didn't even believe him that she was the twentieth-something woman in his lineup or that he was hedonistic at all. He was probably autistic. That was probably their problem. She'd heard of an uncle on her father's side who was autistic and uninterested in sex. The special education courses Melody had been taking painted a vivid picture in her mind of the possibility. He was probably high functioning autistic. She would bet he made that garbage up because he thought that sounded normal.

After all, she'd met her husband's father and had heard countless stories about the man telling his son that he'd never perform like his old man, his dick was too small, and he'd been circumcised. He, therefore, would never be able to satisfy a woman like his father did. Melody reasoned that with such huge shoes to fill, he must have felt inadequate, and with a tendency to dislike sex, he had to borrow his father's life like he was living vicariously through him. Melody spent the afternoon feeling like lightbulbs were going on over her head. Of course!

It was all making sense to her now.

Melody felt relieved to have named it and was suddenly more forgiving. He would never be normal if he was on the spectrum, so she needed to spend more time focusing on herself and accepting him with his disability. Moments later, she saw him heading toward the back door as he came outside to join them.

She had moved to the side yard where she had been working on a garden and asked him if he'd mind making a raised bed box to add to her garden plot. He declined politely, and she found herself running through passages of information about autism in her mind to accept his answer rather than grow angry with him for it.

She wondered why she hadn't thought of it earlier.

For weeks, she grew stronger in her unofficial opinion that the man she was married to had a handicap and was most definitely on the spectrum. It explained so many things to her. Satisfied with her diagnosis of him, she went back to chastising herself for all the years of trouble she'd caused because he hadn't realized what was wrong with him and had treated him and expected him to treat her as if he were perfectly healthy.

CHAPTER 33

For whatever reason, I could never understand why Jerry and Jane hired Peter to work on their house even after the debacle with the church renovations. I wasn't sure how Peter had pulled it off, but he was set to work on their addition.

Jane sat with me regularly at church, discussing colors and patterns and showing me pictures from magazines of what she would have Peter do for them in their home. Week after week, I listened to Jane gush about Peter's fantastic work.

We brought the kids to their home to be babysat as we went to see our nouthetic counselor for the first time. The two of us sat in a small room with an older, heavy man who gave a quick synopsis of the difference between nouthetic counseling and ordinary counseling. His hair was grey, what was left of it, and his brown pants were held up with suspenders over a bright red button-down shirt.

He had a five o'clock shadow and a mustache that was neatly combed. He sat in an antique wooden desk chair and spun to his computer to read from it.

This was supposed to be a biblical approach with biblical boundaries and parameters.

"When I start with couples for marriage counseling, I always want to let them know that I've been happily married for fifty-seven years. My wife is in the bedroom next door in a vegetative state. I am her caregiver and have been for the last eleven years. Her accident has left her unable to live a normal life."

Peter ignored the tragic story, as if he'd said nothing about a vegetative wife in the room next door, and agreed to counseling. However, he began by telling this counselor we were there for me, not marriage counseling.

Dr. Daniel White, our counselor, said, "I see," then looked at me to see if I agreed.

I remained still. It had been the reason I'd given to him.

Peter spoke up and began telling the doctor that I was always angry.

"She doesn't laugh; she doesn't smile. She's just angry. So angry that I'm afraid to come home at night. The kids are upset with her. Jonah, my oldest son, especially. It's like it's too much for all of us. She's so aaangry!" he said, dragging the word out with emphasis. "I even miss work regularly to stay home with the kids because of her anger."

Dr. White looked at me. "You're having trouble with the kids?"

"Yes, Jon..." I started but was cut off by Peter.

"That boy loves his mother so much. He used to have nothing bad to say about her. He'd stick up for her and defend her. But it's so sad; now, he doesn't. He is so ashamed to have her for his mother. He is getting messed up because of her...." Peter said as he dramatically shook his head.

The rest of the session was spent mainly with Peter repeating those exact words.

He added that I was a perfectionist and couldn't imagine doing anything wrong – but I needed to learn to apologize to Jonah and the other boys for messing up so frequently. That would be a start to healing our marriage and family.

"They respond to that. I screamed at Jonah the other day at the job site. Then, after I cooled down and he told me what had happened, I said, you know what? These kids need to hear their parents apologize. So, I apologized. They don't get that from their mother, though. They just get an angry, bitter woman! An angry, bitter woman who won't put out sexually for me and keeps them from being able to make friends. Jonah is struggling at church to even get along with the other kids because of how angry his mother is all the time. It's affecting all of us. It affects me and my work. I can't even go to work most days because I have to be home with the kids, protecting them from their angry mother," Peter claimed.

Every time I tried to defend myself, Peter spoke over me, repeating much of the same.

After forty-five minutes of this torture, we left his office and drove straight to Jerry and Jane's to get the boys. I said nothing the entire drive there or while we pretended to visit before bringing the boys home.

Jane called the next day and asked what had happened. She said I looked like I'd been beaten down while Peter looked satisfied.

I started to explain – but Jane stopped me.

"I like Peter. I don't want to hear anything bad about him."

I hung up, beginning to feel this anger Peter had been talking about.

A week had passed, and we were dropping the boys off with Janice and Craig, this time to see Dr. White again. He welcomed us into his home again, brought us to his bedroom door, and introduced us to his wife, Sarah, before escorting us to his office again. He wore the same trousers and suspenders over a hunter-green button-down this time.

Dr. White seemed to have a specific agenda this time and steered the conversation away from me. He asked Peter about his past. Peter was happy to answer and give the same testimony I'd heard the last three times he'd been baptized.

"I was a very hedonistic man. I loved my girls. I was monogamous, but I had lots of girls and few long-term relationships," Peter said with his lip turned up like when trying to impress someone.

I sat quietly next to him, studying the rug below my feet. It needed to be vacuumed and cleaned because it was full of dog hair and stains. I made faces and other shapes out of the stains like some of the clouds.

Peter was not amused that I wasn't giving him my attention as he went on again in his long-rehearsed soliloquy about his sexual prowess.

"She won't have sex with me – which, I'm a man, and I can only go for so long without… well, you know all about that, don't you, Doc?" Peter said, winking at him.

Dr. White looked as though he were about to speak but stopped.

"You know, men have to take things into their own hands," Peter said, laughing at his pun. "I wasn't even attracted to this woman," he said, gesturing to me and holding the word attracted out for effect.

"I prayed to Goood that I would want her, and now I do – but I get nothing in return. She pretends to be sleeping when I go to bed; she pushes me away," he said with added drama.

Dr. White looked at me and back at Peter. "You had to pray to be attracted to your wife?" he asked incredulously. His eyes mirrored the shock in his voice. "Look at her, man! She's beautiful." It was the first time in forever that anyone had ever said I was beautiful. I looked at this man with the same shocked look he had.

Our session seemed to drag on for hours when it had only been forty-five minutes again. Peter shook Dr. White's hand, said good-bye, and winked at him. He grabbed his black leather jacket and swung it around his shoulders as I got up behind him and put my coat on. Dr. White caught my eye, and he mouthed the words to call him. I nodded and said nothing else, putting my head down as I walked out behind my husband. He'd just called me beautiful and was now mouthing for me to call him… it made me worry. I debated until the next day when my curiosity won out, and I decided to get the card William and Milly had given to me with the doctor's number on it.

I called Dr. White the next day while Peter worked on Jane's house. I sat in the dining room, listening to the man tell me that my husband was a porno addict and had all but said he had no intention of stopping it.

As the doctor spoke, a long-ago tucked-away memory came to mind. I didn't know why, but I'd not remembered this until Dr. White spoke about the porno. I'd walked into the office years back and found porn pulled up on Peter's computer.

There were dozens of pages of lesbian lovers open and an assortment of other violent-looking sexual videos.

"Why had I forgotten this? How had I forgotten this?" I wondered, horrified as I remembered finding this when Jonah was around four years old and easily could have sat in front of the computer to play his Sesame Street computer game and found it.

I clearly remembered screaming at Peter now and being enraged. I'd threatened to leave him and expose him… and… and… my memory was blank after that. I couldn't remember what had happened next or figure out why I hadn't remembered it happening for all these years.

The awkward silence between us as I drummed up parts of these painful memories was interrupted as Dr. White cleared his throat.

"I can't see you two together any longer. I will refer you back to your church so they can apply church discipline to him. You should spend time away from him. The church may have a place for you and the kids to go while he is rehabilitated. You can come to see me alone if you need support, or you can call. I'm sorry. If you were my daughter, I wouldn't be able to keep from beating the life out of him. Be blessed," Dr. White said before saying goodbye and hanging up.

I was still numb from the recollection of Peter's porn. Had Dr. White just told me that he'd beat the life out of the man if I were his daughter?

I sighed heavily. By noon, Brother Jerry had called to tell me that he'd been assigned to meet with Peter for church discipline and would start by having breakfast with him and trying to chat while he worked on his house.

I failed to see how breakfast and chatting fit into a biblical version of church discipline, but I said nothing.

Peter came in more chipper than usual. "I had a good talk with Jerry today while I worked," he said. "He has the same extracurricular activities that I have!" My jaw dropped to the ground. Was he talking about porn? "It was initially a problem with Jane, but once she realized what men needed, the problem resolved itself. We're meeting for breakfast tomorrow morning, so I have to get my ass up early."

In the following days, Peter called me at least daily to ask me for prayer.

He'd tell me, "Satan is attacking! He's bringing images of the college girls I used to peek in on from my apartment window and watch dress to my mind to torture me and tempt me. I need you to pray for me against these attacks."

He'd call and describe two Asian girls in great detail as "they touched each other and licked the others' dark nipples contrasted by their light skin" and cry into the phone that Satan was torturing him with old images of porn.

The details sickened me and drudged even more images of porn that I'd found on Peter's computer. I was so angry with myself for forgetting such horrific details. I'd even defended him when William and Milly addressed this porn use.

"How did I block this from my mind? Why did I block it?" I wondered silently as I listened to my husband giving more putrid descriptions of his "attacks from Satan."

"He won't stop running all the images I've seen through my head like a movie reel that I can't stop. Please pray for me… " Peter sobbed into the phone.

Daily, I'd get vivid details of the trash he was most likely currently watching in the guise of his need for prayer – but I knew it was to remind me that I'd never measure up to his fantasies or be as good as his porn or his own hand.

I'm not sure there is a name for the emotions these calls drummed up. When I didn't answer his calls, he'd come home, take me to the bedroom, close the door, and tell me. He'd cry and whine about how he needed me to help him. I had to fulfill his lusts to make the images and desires he had go away.

He'd grab me and try to throw me to the bed or push me over the side of the clawfoot bathtub. Still, every time, I managed to get away and leave him breathless, sticking out of the front of his dirty pants and cursing in my wake. I found it easier to answer his calls than deal with this.

My life had become so much of a nightmare it was hard to do anything but breathe. I reminded myself to breathe.

"Inhale, two, three, four, exhale, two, three, four," I'd repeat in my mind as if I'd suffocate if I didn't keep it going.

I went through my days numb to the sounds of the boys chattering. I felt like I was almost watching myself go through the motions of parenting, homeschooling, cleaning, cooking, and running errands. I was there, but I wasn't there. Melody filled in for me regularly. She'd take the list of spelling words I had to give to the boys and recite each word listening for them to spell it back correctly. She'd sit with Jonah and help him with his math, pulling out cubes and drawing pictures to explain his problems best to him. She'd sit and listen to Andrew read to her. Melody helped Gregory with his grammar and made cards to build funny sentences he could easily diagram with shapes and popsicle sticks. I felt like I should be doing all this, but I was weak and too broken.

The world seemed to go by in a blur, and I couldn't trust that I'd teach the children anything. I felt all my energy had depleted, and I needed to depend on her. She seemed pale to me – less vibrant than she used to be. I hoped the pressure of helping me so much wasn't too much or causing her distress, but I couldn't get up and change anything. All I could do was sit with Joey, his wisps of curls against my lips as he sat in my lap playing with Jonah's old trucks, and just breathed.

When schooling was finished, she'd get up and make dinner; she'd make homemade bread, pick the boys up to sit on the counter, and help her. They made cookies and decorated them for dessert.

She built soups from ingredients I had in the refrigerator and cupboards that she must have purchased because I didn't remember going to the grocery store.

Sunday was the only day she didn't come over anymore. I had to prepare food and often brought leftovers Melody had made from scratch the week before.

I had to appear normal for my church family, though. I smiled and laughed when they did so I didn't look aloof.

I got up when the women were cued to the kitchen and mindlessly prepared food Melody had made, and I was taking credit for it.

I noticed a difference in both Jane and Jerry. Jane regularly sat at the end of the men's table next to Peter, looking over magazines or bragging about his outstanding work at her house. She'd tell them how talented he was with his hands and wink at my husband as if no one could see. The awkwardness wasn't lost on our friends as I watched them exchange glances with their wives and steer their daughters away from my husband. Jerry seemed not to know what to do. He tried sitting across from his wife and joining in on their discussions on color choices. He reminded Peter and the rest of the men that he'd not finished the church yet and said maybe they should pause their home renovations to let him finish up there.

I stopped paying attention and went back toward my sons. Jonah didn't play with the other kids anymore, so he sat near his brothers listlessly and was ready to leave. The other two used those stereotypical cardboard bricks that every church seemed to have and stacked them with Beth and Brian's youngest sons.

Beth came over and quietly sat beside me, neither of us speaking to the other. It made it hard to fake normalcy when I didn't have her to lead in a conversation or chuckle. We both just sat silently looking at the boys playing. Two of her oldest daughters also came to sit with us. The four of us sat silently, none knowing what to say to the other and hoping our young kids would do something we could be impressed with or that they would need us for to break the deafening silence between us. Jerry came over toward me. He sat with the rest of us and contributed to the silence. We could hear Jane's cackles and Peter's laughter as they continued sharing stories of their renovation project.

Beth and her daughters got up to leave. We looked at one another as they departed but still said nothing.

They motioned toward Jonah, and he got up and left with them. I watched him walk off with Beth and her daughters until Jerry spoke.

"I told Jane she's not allowed to be at our house alone with Peter. When she first met him at Visco, she'd go on and on about how wonderful this Peter guy was. I thought I was a jealous husband, so I ignored it. I started working there with her when I retired from FedEx, and we both started talking to Peter together. I thought inviting him to church would be the best thing," Jerry said, as if he were speaking to himself as much as he was talking to me. "I think he's been inappropriate with my wife, and Jane likes him too much," he whispered through tears.

Jane made her way over toward the two of us. Peter remained at the table, pushed back as if he was quite satisfied with himself.

Jerry turned away and wiped at his tears.

"What are you two up to?" Jane asked with what may have even looked like contempt toward me.

"I was just telling her about the beautiful job Peter is doing at our house," Jerry lied.

Jane smiled. "Isn't he amazing?"

Both Jerry and I mustered smiles so fake I was sure she'd notice and nodded in agreement.

I couldn't understand why Jerry had excused Peter's porn and failed to incorporate any of the church discipline Dr. White had said he would instruct the church to do.

"If Jerry feels this way about Peter, why is he creating this "breakfast club" with Peter and telling him he had the same problems?" I wondered.

My disgust for Peter grew. I couldn't stand to be around him. His porn, his disappearing. Even Jerry was scared for him to be around his own wife. All the church family went behind our backs, acting as though they liked us while secretly reporting his lude behavior and thinking him a predator.

I was furious with everyone and wanted to leave the church and never see another person again. I was revolted and consumed with the very anger I'd been accused of having by the man who tried guessing the nipple color of our friends' wives' breasts. I could have vomited right there but swallowed hard and made a feeble excuse to be excused. I gathered the boys and sat with them in the minivan with our belongings packed at my feet until Peter was ready to leave, and I could go home, heave, and spill my lunch into the toilet.

CHAPTER 34

Melody found her husband much easier to get along with now that they'd started attending their new church. Coupled with her realization that her husband might be on the spectrum, she found herself much more forgiving of him. She struggled with selfish thoughts, though, as she battled lonesomeness. She wanted to be caressed, loved, and thought of… and a husband with autism wouldn't ever fulfill that void. She found herself going out more and spending more time with her friend and her family. She felt as though she were living vicariously through her. They'd been married for so many years, making it look easy to still be in love.

Melody wondered if she'd die not knowing what it felt like to be loved. He was home for dinner regularly again. He occasionally complimented her on her cooking but regularly locked himself in his office. She tried to busy herself with her schoolwork and Joey, but with each passing month, the solitude grew more unbearable.

Melody made an appointment to get her hair done. It had been years since she'd allowed herself such an indulgence, but she hoped a new fresh cut would snap her out of the depression she was avoiding. Frank called her to his chair; he was stout with hair that looked like it used to be blonde. He looked her in the eyes as he spoke. His unwavering and soft eye contact stirred something within her. When he ran his fingers through her hair, asking what she wanted to have done, butterflies flipped inside her stomach. She lacked physical touch from her husband.

Her body craved and burned to be held.

She was ashamed as she discovered her own frailty and curiosity and suddenly noticed other men noticing her.

At first, it was the man at the gas station pumping gas next to her. Then, it was her friend's husband. The desire to be noticed and have attention paid to her filled a cavity so deep she didn't know if it would ever be filled.

She began daydreaming. She tried to imagine what it would be like to have a lover who loved her. She pictured herself on her own front porch, sipping lemonade with a man – any man and no man in particular. He was just a man who cared about what she had to say, listened to her, and told her about his own day, thoughts, and love for her.

She regularly imagined what it would be like to be touched often by a man who loved her.

At night, she cried silently until she lost herself in her own imagination. It was an escape from the constant ache of solitude as her husband lay beside her, snoring, moving away from her even as he slept and driving stakes into her devastated heart. She had tried snuggling up next to him just to feel him and imagine he loved her back, but he'd move away so abruptly she didn't have a chance to even pretend.

Melody fell into despair, realizing it was far lonelier to be lonely when one wasn't alone. She'd roll over and return to her front porch, sipping lemonade, laughing, and smiling with the faceless generic man she'd conjured up in her imagination to dull the pain of loneliness.

She lost herself in caring for Joey and helping her friend. Staying busy was all she could do to pass the time and keep her mind off her own life. As sadness inflicted her with a disease she could not cure alone, she continued as if she was fine. She carried on as Joey's mother, taking him to the park and to play with other friends.

She helped her friend as much as she could, but in the back of her mind, she was always looking at how her friends' husband looked at his wife and wondered what that would feel like.

She got along fine with her new church friends, though they hadn't gotten close enough to visit with one another yet. It seemed like her husband had had a true conversion as he continued attendance, too, and was often found sitting around the house with his Bible open and glasses slid down his nose. He ignored Joey and Melody as he licked his fingers and turned the pages.

He took calls outside in his truck, answered texts on his phone that he denied even getting, and disappeared suddenly to get a part or a tool he had "just realized he desperately needed."

He'd be gone for hours and come home with a musky scent which made Melody feel like she'd go insane. She was sure he had another girlfriend, but what for? He didn't like sex. He continued to push her away in the bedroom and lay beside her, gratifying himself in his own hands instead.

Melody was trapped in a loveless, sexless marriage. She was ignored and lonelier than she knew was humanly possible.

She felt desperate for love.

She stood in front of her friend's sink snapping beans and tossing them into the nearby colander after having had dinner with them. Her friend sat at their kitchen table playing with Joey and singing songs.

"Pat a cake, pat a cake, baker's man…." her friend sang loudly.

It was getting late, and Melody knew she needed to get home soon. She excused herself from the kitchen and padded down the long hallway toward the bathroom. She looked into the master bedroom and saw her friends' husband changing into clothes after a shower. She looked away quickly, knowing she should not have even looked toward the door. She knew that he regularly seemed to dress and undress without closing their door. He knew she knew it. Had he seen her? What would he think?

Chapter 35

Peter ambushed me in the bedroom. "Damn it! I prayed for God to make me attracted to you, and NOW I am. You withhold sex from me while I ACTUALLY look at you and WANT you." He grabbed my arms. Fear gripped my heart. I could feel my guts twist in my belly, and I fought not to vomit. He was running his hand up my shirt. My arms tingled, goosebumps rose, and the hair on my neck stood on end.

"You bitch! You know you want some!" he hoarsely whispered into my ear.

Pushing me to the bed, he gruffly lifted my shirt and thrust his hand over my left breast. He was breathing heavily in my ear. His sparse scruff scratched my face and tickled me at the same time. I tried to get away from him. The more I wriggled, the more he held me down firmly.

"The kids. They could come in any minute," I said, grasping for anything to get him off of me.

He covered my mouth with his and stuck his tongue so far down my throat that I couldn't breathe. He pulled at my clothes, trying to get them off. I tried to free myself from him. He pushed me down with more force. His weight was crushing my chest – or maybe I was having a heart attack.

I couldn't get a breath. The room was getting darker. Bursts of light sparkled around my head like fairies taunting me and laughing at me...

Peter rolled me over and around like a rag doll. His hot fingers touched my stomach as groans escaped from deep inside him.

I kept trying to free myself. I reminded him of the boys again. I tried to push him off. I couldn't get him to budge. His tongue was down my throat again as his lips cupped over mine. I could feel the inside of his lips over my mouth making a seal with his saliva. I was panicking. I needed to get away from him.

"Stop squirming, mine love. I want you. I'm hungry for you. God has given me a strong desire for you," he murmured in a low growl...

The moonlight shone in through the window. I could see our shadows cast on the opposite wall. I wiggled enough to escape him as he pushed me further to the top of the bed, trying to roll me over and get my pants down. He had me by the arm again, thrust me backward, and slammed me on the bed. The mattress caught me mid-back. I gasped from the pain as I bent in an arch on the bed. He was pulling me up from under my arms. The pain of his fingernails in my armpits was sheer, and I let out a yelp. His hands were on my throat as he pulled and pushed me back onto the bed. His hands were everywhere, trying to take my shirt off.

I could hear fabric tearing or seams ripping; I wasn't sure which. He didn't stop. I kept trying to cover myself and keep my clothes on as he fought me harder. We scuffled. I put up a good fight. I thought he'd quit after enough time – but he was still going after me with as much intensity as when it first started.

"Stop fighting me. This is your wifely duty." His mouth covered mine again. The taste of rotten teeth and garlic overwhelmed me and made me gag. I thought I was going to throw up.

The sharp noise of a slap across the face echoed in the room before I realized the pain of impact on my cheek.

"Stop moving..." he commanded.

I stopped fighting. Instead of trying to get away from him, I grinded back. I pushed harder, faster, and with rage he seemed to mistake for passion.

I chanted, "I hate you! I hate you! I hate you!" with every thrust. Tears sprang from my eyes as I watched him below me, gloating that he'd gotten what he'd come for. At some point, the chanting became louder and louder in the silence of the night! "I HATE YOU!

I left the room, focusing on a moonlit night. The silence was now defeaning. I thought I should hear some night sounds, the melody of cicadas, something outside, but there was nothing. I moved through the house to the back door and went outside. It was still silent even once I stood in the middle of the night surrounded by nothing but dark sky, stars, and the glow of a full moon.

I watched moths flutter by the street lamp. I was straining to hear crickets or tree frogs, but I couldn't. I was afraid I'd gone deaf. Maybe that slap had made me momentarily deaf. I listened for my own footsteps. Right, left, then right again. I should have be making noise in the grass. I suddenly realized I didn't feel the wetness of the dew on the grass, either. I hugged myself with my arms to warm myself from the chill that felt bone-deep, but I couldn't feel my arms on my body. It felt like a dream. Before realizing I'd returned inside, I was in the boys' room looking over their sleeping bodies. It was as if I floated, hovering above them. I could see their bodies rising and falling with every breath, but I still heard nothing. Their bedroom door was closed; I didn't remember opening it or closing it. I was losing my mind. I couldn't think straight.

I couldn't remember. Why was I in the boys' room? Had I heard one of them stir? I needed to get out before waking them. I still couldn't hear anything. What was wrong with me?

I made my way to the kitchen to make tea. I put a pot on the stove to boil water but turned back, and it was gone.

I went to the cupboard to get another pot and found the one I'd just filled. But it was empty and stacked with the other pots.

I lifted it again and filled it with water to boil. I felt so tired. My vision seemed so cloudy. Where had I put the pot? Where was the stove? How did I get into the living room? I wanted tea. I tried walking back to the kitchen, but my feet felt like lead. I had to go check on the water. It would be boiling soon. I needed to get to the kitchen. My feet. I felt so heavy like pressure was weighing me down. I couldn't get out of the living room. I felt trapped. I couldn't breathe. I needed air.

I had to get to the kitchen to get to the stove. What happened to my tea?

I woke up cold, covered in sweat, and naked. It was dawn. I was freezing. I tried to slide my legs off the bed and not disturb my sleeping husband. For once, he wasn't snoring. My legs shook like I couldn't trust them to carry my weight, so I lay in bed. I was so tired. I needed to get up and wash my hands. They were sticky.

"Why are my hands sticky?" I wondered groggily. Not just my hands – the bed and my body felt sticky. A faint, familiar aroma of metal filled my nostrils as I tried to raise my head to look down and see why I was sticky, but I was so very tired. I closed my eyes just for a minute. I needed to sleep.

CHAPTER 36

Melody shook as he startled her. She felt his hot breath on the back of her neck. "Is he kissing me?" Melody wondered. "When did he even get in bed with me?" Melody wondered. "When did I get in the bed?" she pondered. Her head hurt. She felt fuzzy. She tried thinking harder to remember. Looking around, she tried to figure out where she was. His hands were all over her, wrapping around her body and up her shirt.

His hands made her body tingle.

He pulled her close to her like he wanted her...

"He wants me!" Melody thought incredulously. "Does he think I'm sexy? Did I do something to turn him on?" Melody squeezed her eyes shut, trying to make the dizzy spell leave her. "I've got to remember. Why am I here? Think, think, think," she told herself as if she could will her head to stop pounding and the room to stop spinning.

His hands were wandering down her legs and back up. It made her skin tickle. He made his way to her inner thighs and tried to spread her legs. She protested, unsure of how to respond. She couldn't remember the last time her body had turned a man on. She was frozen in fear and amazement. His hands were moving up under her shirt again. He cupped her breast, whispering to her.

"I want you!" he groaned. "You tease me with your little flirty body. The way you bend over to pick up the toys on the floor. I know you're doing that to get my attention. You little slut. You have me so turned on! You follow me into the bedroom and try to take my arm into yours. I know you want me! I know you've wanted me!" he purred into her ear.

Melody squirmed under his touch. She felt him tickle her as parts of her body, desperate for touch yet ignored for so long, responded to him. He squeezed too hard as he leaned over to kiss her. Moving his tongue into her mouth as if they were connected, he pushed her legs apart again and tried to climb on top of her.

She was so lonely. She'd wanted to be loved – to be desired for years. She wanted her husband to notice and touch her, but he hadn't except for rare occasions when he told her she wasn't sexy and she should just get it over with.

Now, she was lying in bed being touched and fondled like she'd dreamed her husband would touch her. It was as if she couldn't make her body stop reacting. Starving for affection, she clung to him. She kissed him back. She matched his tongue with her own strength. She moved with his body. She was so desperate to be loved and needed, wanted and held. He moaned with pleasure. He held a smile on his face until she leaned down to kiss him hard on the mouth. She tasted blood on his lips, and still, he moaned beneath her. She was finally sexually pleasing. Her mind exploded with thoughts and her soul with emotion as they moved in sync giving pleasure to the other. His hands touched her in places she'd never been touched.

It felt like she imagined it would feel to be loved by a lover. All this time focusing on her marriage, trying to make it better to be a better wife, lover, cook, and mother – the help meet her husband needed, and now she found herself here.

Pushing thoughts of her broken marriage aside, she leaned down to tenderly kiss him and rolled off to her back, where his touching and fondling grew more intense. The elation of being loved, eradicating loneliness, and the spontaneity of what was happening sent a buzz through her veins. She didn't care about anything or anyone else at that moment except for the exhilaration of being loved.

The light of the moon illuminated the room through the sheer curtains flowing in the breeze let in by the open window. She watched the shadows. At first, it was just the two of them – but then, a body rose above him. She could hear her name being called.

"Melody."

"Melody."

Who was calling her name?

"How dare you?!"

"Peter! What is this?"

"Who is interrupting us? Who is in the room with us?" Melody thought, frantically trying to sit up, but was suddenly paralyzed and unable to move.

"How dare you sleep with my husband!"

Melody looked at Peter. He was oblivious to his wife calling them out.

Light flashed off something in her hand. Melody could see a blade. She couldn't move to protect herself. She couldn't hear anything and heard everything all at the same time. There was a struggle. Peter lurched forward but not to protect her. He fell off of her like a rabbit after breeding, leaving her vulnerable and alone to fend for herself. The blade sliced down the first wrist with precision. Scarlet blood ran from the wound. She watched in both horror and awe as the right wrist was sliced with a jagged line. It wasn't cut as well as the first like two different people had been doing the butchering.

The room spun. Melody felt so weak as she bled all over the bed.

"I'm sorry! I'm so sorry!" Melody cried into the dimly lit bedroom. "I was so lonely." Melody's eyes grew heavy. She couldn't keep her eyes open as she whispered into the night. "I'm sorry! I'm so sorry! Can you ever forgive me? I just wanted to be loved," she repeated nearly inaudibly until there was no sound – only silence.

CHAPTER 37

A bright light shone down the dark corridor, luring me toward it. "Who's calling me?" I needed to know. It was so hard to see anything except for the light. The sound of people all around frightened me, but I was too weak to open my eyes. I could hear voices but didn't know what was said. Something stabbed my arm. I felt like lead blankets weighed me down. I think I was floating. No, not floating, but I was moving.

"Where are we going? Who are you?" I wanted to know, but the sound wouldn't come from my mouth.

I didn't think I could make my lips move, either. What was wrong with me? Why was no one telling me anything? Was I sick?

"Am I blind?" I thought, tumbling one question into the next, yet unable to make my mouth cooperate. I tried to kick free, but my body didn't respond, either.

I wasn't floating anymore, but I was rocking. "Am I in water?"

"We're losing her!" I heard someone say.

"Who are they losing? Are we going to drown?" I wondered. I was being suffocated. I felt someone holding something over my nose and mouth. I couldn't breathe. I couldn't move.

I woke up. I was floating again. I still couldn't get my eyes to open. Voices clustered over my head. I was dumped off. Falling… fear gripped me, but I couldn't catch myself. The ground was soft. It felt warm.

Hands touched me everywhere. The constant sound of a beep began taunting me with its regular beat until I was nowhere and heard nothing.

I lay in the solitude of darkness and silence. I was present and absent at the same time. Time dragged on as I lay aware of the nothing for what seemed like an eternity. I couldn't think in words. I saw colors, scenes, and faint images of my children's faces, but I couldn't remember their names or why I knew they were mine. I thought in smell and felt comfort when my mind offered the scent of baby shampoo like I'd used on my babies and smelled on Joey's head. And then, it was dark and silent again for more eons of time.

Slowly, I began to hear around me. I didn't know what the sounds meant, but there was a soft tone that made my body feel warm and a deeper tenor that shocked me with cold. It took too long to warm back up, but I only knew I didn't feel good; I didn't have the words to know warm or cold.

Time went on. Words returned, but I couldn't make my body respond to my commands. I couldn't make my voice work or even my lips move, but I could hear. The beeping was back, but it didn't bother me as it did initially. I was glad to understand the sound and repeat the word "*beep*" in my head, if not with my lips. I could hear and understand words. Warmth was a woman. Cold was a man.

And then one morning, I could see warmth. She was a short woman with blonde hair. She was older than I was and dressed in violet scrubs. She saw my eyes open and looked excited but left immediately.

"I must have upset her," I thought sadly. Unable to move except for opening my eyes, I was frustrated and hoped warmth would come back. Moments later, she did. She and cold spoke to each other at first and then to me.

"Do you know where you are?" warmth asked.

I tried to answer, but nothing came out of my mouth. I wanted to answer her with my eyes, but they closed too soon for me to get her to hear them.

"Dr. Lamb?" I heard warmth say softly.

That bright light was in my eye, and my eyelid was open against my will. I tried to close it but had no strength to fight it. Then, the next one. The light burned, but I couldn't defend myself.

Warmth took my hand into hers. "I know you're in there, sweet one," she said with such tenderness in her voice.

"I'm Adeline, your nurse. This is Dr. Lamb. You're in the Baptist Memorial Hospital in Memphis," she said softly.

As the days turned to weeks and months, I regained strength and could finally move a little and speak.

Adeline came in with another woman and wished me good morning. I could speak now but only in a whisper, though.

Adeline stepped closer, took my pulse and temperature, and put my index finger back in the holder. She introduced me to the other woman, Dr. Gray.

"Good morning," she said, walking over to me with what I think may have been my medical chart.

Adeline looked at me with concern.

"Do you know why you're here?" Dr. Gray asked.

"No, I don't remember anything except silence and darkness before waking up," I thought but couldn't answer.

"Okay. Adeline, I'll come back to see our patient again tomorrow," Dr. Gray said before telling me goodbye and patting my knee.

Adeline looked at me with what looked like pity. I thought we'd be happy I could talk and that I was progressing.

"Your PT will be here in half an hour. Let's get you all ready for him," she said warmly.

I had tuned Adeline out as I thought, considering for a moment that I didn't know why I was there. I didn't know who was caring for my kids or where they were, and I was beginning to fear the worst.

"Did we get in an accident? Did they drown? I remember water. I remember not being able to breathe. Were the kids with me then? I don't remember them. Are my kids still alive? What aren't they telling me? Why haven't I seen Peter in all this time? Does he not want to visit, or is he in a different room fighting to get well like I am?" I thought with increasing agitation.

"Okay. Okay. What's got you so upset, Missy? Your vitals are starting to act up. Let's calm down some. Deep breath in, two, three, four, five, six, seven, eight, nine, ten. Hold, two, three, four. Now, blow it out… " Adeline instructed.

I was surprised at how quickly I complied and saw my stats get back to normal.

I couldn't remember what had distressed me any longer as Adeline moved around the room and the bed to get me ready for my next appointment. Still, I couldn't remember what that was for, either.

CHAPTER 38

It was suppertime, and cafeteria aids were bringing around meals. "Good evening, Miss; we've got your favorite color jello today, and it's meatloaf and mashed potatoes day. I gave you extra gravy, too," the aid said with a wink. I thanked her as she set it on my tray table. I pulled the cover from the plate and saw green beans next to mashed potatoes drowned in gravy and a fat piece of meatloaf sitting in between. I pulled the jello cup off the plate, set it on the napkin I'd saved from lunch, and started eating. I was so glad to have solid foods again. Adeline had been pleased with my progress and the work I'd been doing to get well and be able to walk out of there.

I sat with a furrowed brow, twirling my beans through my gravy like Gregory always had when I made this meal.

Suddenly panic filled me, and all my machines started beeping. Adeline came in quickly with another nurse close at her heels.

"Where is Gregory? Who's taking care of him??? ...And Andrew and Jonah? Where are my kids?" Adeline tried to soothe me and reassure me. "How long have I been here, and where are my kids?" I shrieked as I remembered my children for the first time in I didn't know how long. I was not consolable. I needed to know if my kids were alright and why I was there. "What happened to me? And my family? Why am I here?" I asked, nearing hysteria.

"You were brought in unresponsive more than four months

ago," Adeline said as she pulled her cell phone from the pocket of her scrub top and typed something onto the screen. Within moments, I heard Dr. Gray's name being paged on the speaker system.

Adeline stayed with me, soothing me, petting my hair back from my face, and whispering that everything was going to be alright.

When Dr. Gray entered, Adeline jumped up to meet her at the door and spoke to her too softly for me to hear.

Both women came to my bedside.

Dr. Gray looked at me with kind eyes as she asked me, "Do you remember what happened before you got here?"

I didn't and shook my head, wondering what they weren't telling me.

Suddenly, I remembered! The color drained from my face, and I lurched forward in my bed. "I killed Melody!"

Both Adeline and Dr. Gray looked at each other, exchanging unspoken words.

"I killed her, didn't I?"

Dr. Gray rubbed my arm, assuring me that I was alright and I hadn't died.

I pushed her off me and said, "I know I'm here. But I killed Melody! I killed my best friend! I killed the only one who understood me... but she was... she was in bed with my husband. She was sleeping with my husband. I'm married. Where is my husband? Where is P... Pete... Peter? Where is he?" I asked, suddenly remembering everything. "Does Peter have our boys?" I fired questions too quickly for anyone to answer.

Dr. Gray looked at Adeline as if asking something. Adeline moved away from my bed and sat in the empty chair at the end of my bed.

I began crying uncontrollably. "My best friend. I killed my best friend. What have I done? No wonder there's no one visiting me. I'm a killer."

Dr. Gray touched my arm again. She looked me square in the eyes and spoke sternly to me. "You haven't killed anyone."

She paused as if summoning the words to continue.

"You tried to kill yourself, but you survived," she said after an incredibly long silence.

"No, I cut Melody's wrists to kill her when I found her in bed... with Peter."

Adeline bowed her head as if she couldn't face me. Dr. Gray tried to explain again. "Honey, you were found in your bed, unconscious, by your husband. You tried to commit suicide by slitting your wrists." There was a long pause. I tried to tell Dr. Gray that I'd cut Melody, but she was taking my arm into her hands and holding it in front of me. "Look at your wrists, honey. You slit your wrists."

I traced the scar on my left wrist. The skin was still pink, a fresh scar. Then, I looked at my right arm. The scar was jagged, not a smooth line like the one on my left side. I looked up at Dr. Gray, unable to understand why I had scars on my wrists. I knew I'd cut Melody.

Adeline told Dr. Gray she'd sit with me for a while. They discussed setting up my psych eval for first thing the next morning and that I needed to be on twenty-four-hour watch. I watched as Dr. Gray left the room.

"How could I have cut myself?" I asked, mostly rhetorically. "Are they sure I didn't kill Melody? Did I cut us both?" I didn't remember a struggle with her. A flash of a memory leaped into my mind for a brief moment. I remembered Peter. He was naked and forcing himself on me – but then I saw him and Melody in bed. "Could all three of us have been in bed?" I wondered. "No! No!" That was impossible. "I'd never have done anything so... so... " I didn't know what word to use. But I knew we couldn't have been having a threesome. "Why did I remember Peter forcing me to have sex? My memory must still be very fuzzy. I must be mixing memories up. Putting two events together in my mind."

"Adeline," I asked, looking at the chair at the end of my bed. "If I didn't kill Melody, where is she?

Adeline didn't answer. She just rubbed my feet and told me everything would be alright.

I spent the night thinking about how angry I'd felt when I found the two together in our bed. I could vividly recall every moment and feel my emotions as I remembered trying to kill my only friend. Melody looked like she enjoyed it. She was on top of him. Was Peter in love with her? Did he leave me for her? Was that why everyone was so closed-lipped about the details?

"Where is Peter?" I asked my nurse.

She smiled and shrugged her shoulders as if in sympathy.

"I knew it!" I thought, both angry and accepting at the same time.

"He left me, didn't he? He's got Melody and my boys and doesn't care about me…."

Adeline still didn't answer.

CHAPTER 39

It seemed like I had just gotten to sleep when they were waking me to get into a wheelchair. "We're heading downstairs for brain scans, Miss," the orderly told me softly as she pushed me through the door into the brightly lit hallway. It was the first time I'd been out of my room. The halls were clean and bare. The usual nurses' carts with all their apparatuses were not in sight. Each door was closed tightly. I'd not ever been in a hospital that was so empty before. I began wondering which hospital I was in.

"I don't remember anyone ever telling me where I am," I thought to myself. We came to the door at the end of the ward. My orderly flashed her ID card at a scanner and punched in a code. I'd never seen anything like this sort of high security. "Maybe they've taken me to a bad part of Memphis, and this is for security purposes to protect everyone." It figured.

We rolled down another bare corridor with each door closed tightly. We approached another set of doors, and out came the ID card and a secret code. I watched curiously as she fumbled to hold the door and pull me through at the same time. "Too bad they had to have such high security," I thought ruefully.

We came to the elevators, and my orderly had to wave her ID card at it and punch in a code before the doors would open. Inside, she did the same thing. I was getting very suspicious of where we were. I couldn't understand the need for such high security at every set of doors. The doors closed, and I could feel us go down. I watched the numbers four, three, two, one… I was beginning to feel dizzy and was glad I was in a chair instead of walking.

Finally, the elevator made a dinging noise, and the doors opened. I was pushed forward into another stark hallway. We rounded a corner and went through a set of double doors that didn't require the same ID scan and passcode, which was slightly confusing. Still, we went through another door quickly, and I forgot all about my worry.

Inside this room, I was passed off to a technician who checked my armband. He seemed to hesitate for a moment, looking at the jagged lines on my right wrist, and looked away before I could be sure. I felt shame, but I didn't know why. He wheeled me to a long tunnel with a bed hanging out of it. He told me he would scan my brain in this machine, and it wouldn't hurt.

I felt like he was talking to me like a child. I wondered if he was used to pediatric cases. He helped me onto the bed and told me how to lay still and what to do with my arms before leaving and going behind a glass window.

I could hear him by speaker right in the contraption. He told me to breathe and would slowly move me inside the tube.

"Now, look up at the image above you. Focus on that and breathe until I tell you to hold your breath and be still," came the voice in the tunnel.

I closed my eyes for a second and must have moved because he was back on the speaker, telling me to focus on the image above and to stay still.

Before long, he had finished and told me I could breathe. The picture above me disappeared, and I was being moved out of the scanning machine. I was helped into my wheelchair and told to wait for a moment. He went back behind the glass wall for a few minutes and looked intently at the computer screen in front of him.

Adeline came in and offered to bring me to my room. The

technician obliged, and I headed back through the bare halls toward the elevator. Adeline waved her ID pass at the elevator sensor and waited for the elevator to come down to our floor. She pushed me inside the small space, waved her ID badge again, and typed in a passcode before hitting the number four on the panel. I looked straight ahead at the double doors. I could hear Adeline fidgeting behind me.

"What are they looking for in the scan?" I asked curiously.

Adeline was delayed in answering. "The doctor just wants to do a full evaluation for treatment."

"What are they treating? My arms are healed, and I'm sure I could walk if anyone would let me. When will I be discharged?" I asked just as the elevator dinged, and the doors opened on the fourth floor. Adeline moved me out of the elevator and down the stark hallway.

We got to the first set of doors, where Adeline waved her ID badge and typed in a series of numbers again. We repeated this at the next set of doors and returned to my room. Dr. Gray walked into the room with us and told Adeline she could be excused.

I made my way back into my hospital bed and looked up at the doctor. She was looking at her computer screen, analyzing colorful blobs. She seemed particularly interested in measuring distance or length like how the ultrasound tech measured my babies while I was pregnant.

She looked up at me before taking a seat in the wheelchair beside the bed that I'd just been wheeled into the room in. "What was your marriage like?" she asked.

I wasn't sure why she asked in the past tense form. But I answered anyway. "It's bland, I guess you'd say," I answered using the present tense.

"Bland, how?" the doctor asked gently.

"I guess we don't really like each other," I said tentatively.

"Have you ever felt scared of him?" she asked carefully.

"Peter… um, Peter… he's… yes. I've been scared of him," I told her.

"Has he ever harmed you?" she asked, prodding me for answers I wasn't sure I should give.

"He's got a temper," I said briefly. There was a dramatic pause as the doctor looked at me like I was supposed to continue. "I left him once, but he promised to go to counseling. I went back to him and tried harder to be a better wife. I read this book about being a godly help meet and doing it so well that a wife makes her husband want to change. Our church got us marriage counseling, but that didn't last long," I stopped again, looking at Dr. Gray to say something, but she just sat patiently waiting for me to go on. "I thought about leaving again but ended up pregnant with Gregory and Andrew and thought I'd better stay. Mostly, I've spent the last several years avoiding him as much as I could," I said, afraid of her reaction.

But she was calm and didn't defend him.

Dr. Gray seemed ready to speak. She moved to the edge of the wheelchair and leaned forward.

"There is a part of your brain called the amygdala. It's enlarged on your scans," she explained, but I cut her off.

"Do I have a tumor? Or a brain disease?" I asked, afraid she was going to tell me I was sick. "Am I crazy? I've heard about people with brain tumors changing their entire personalities. Is that why I killed Melody? Am I insane?" I asked, wondering if that was why I hadn't been arrested yet.

"The amygdala is a collection of cells near the base of the brain. This part of the brain is where emotions are given meaning, remembered, and attached to associations and responses. This is commonly enlarged in trauma survivors. It tends to mean that your signals are hypersensitive. When you perceive danger, whether real danger or something that reminds you of a traumatic event, your response probably tends to be more dramatic in a fight, flight, or fawn. Meaning you're hyperaware of things around you, and your brain responds to them. Basically, what I'm telling you is that your brain scans confirm trauma or abuse," the doctor told me.

"Oh my gosh! I overreacted. I killed my best friend because I'm brain-damaged?" I looked at the doctor, trying to understand. "Is this why I killed Melody?" I asked. "Did I have an overreaction to finding her in my bed? Was she not really in my bed?"

Dr. Gray cut me off. "Let's talk about that night. Is that okay?" Dr. Gray asked, shifting in the wheelchair. "What do you remember happening before coming here?"

I thought for a moment. I could picture Melody in my bed, but then a memory flashed, and I remembered being held down under Peter. It was a foggy memory, but I recalled a deep sense of fear and disgust rising inside me as I remembered Peter had forced himself on me that night.

"I tried to get away from him. He was too strong. He overpowered me, and I fought. But then, I gave in and left the room after that. I went outside and I checked on the boys. I tried to make tea but ended up in the living room and couldn't get to the kitchen to finish making it," I said, knowing that didn't make any sense out loud. "Then, Melody – she was in my bed when I went back into our bedroom. She was with Peter and… and… she was on top of him. She was smiling and telling him, "I have you." She repeated it over and over again. He had a grin on his face. He was enjoying her… and… and… I snapped. I couldn't take it anymore. "I hate you! I hate you! I hate you!" I told him as I grabbed a pocket knife from – I don't know where," I said, looking at Dr. Gray as if she would know. "I sliced her wrists. I just wanted it to stop. I didn't want her to be in bed with him. I wanted to get away. I was so lonely. So lonely. So much pain! I couldn't stand him and what he'd been doing to me. I needed to get away. I had to die… " I said.

"You felt as though you had to die?" Dr. Gray said, repeating what I'd just said.

"No, I mean, Melody had to die," I answered with a look of bewilderment on my face.

"You went to bed with Peter and were forced to have sex… but you didn't leave the room, Melody," Dr. Gray said, looking me in the eyes for a response.

"Melody didn't leave the room. She wanted to have sex with my husband. I killed HER. She was my best friend for the last couple of years, and I killed her… ohh… ohhh… I'm so sorry. I was so lonely," I said to the doctor.

"You are Melody," she said softly yet firmly.

"I'm not Melody! I'm… I'm… who am I? I'm not Melody. Melody is my best friend. What is my name? Why can't I remember my name?"

I sat for what seemed like an eternity staring at my doctor, afraid to remember what I remembered. "I am Melody. I didn't hear her tell my husband, "I have you!" It was my voice… I told Peter, "I hate you" – It was 'hate' not 'have.' It was me – Not Melody. I was on top of him. I was angry and…" but I couldn't finish. I cried. My body heaved. Each time it seemed to begin to subside, the heaving and tears came in another wave. I didn't even recognize my own crying. It had been so long since I'd cried – more than just tears. All the control I used to have was gone. I couldn't stop. "These scars on my wrists… I did this?" I asked, holding my arms up to Dr. Gray's face and trying to speak through convulsive heaves and tears.

"My dear Melody, you have been living in an abusive marriage for years, haven't you?" the doctor asked but didn't mean for me to answer. "Sometimes, when trauma is too hard for the brain to deal with, it does things to protect itself. You created Melody to survive, to keep you going, because you let yourself die figuratively in a marriage to a domestic abuser. You let Melody take your name because, to you, you were already gone. You have what we in the industry call Dissociative Identity Disorder. Some people call it Multi-Personality Disorder," she said.

"But she had Joey. How could I have invented Melody as another personality? I watched him grow up. I changed his diaper… she had a son."

Dr. Gray looked at me and pursed her lips as though she was trying to figure out carefully what her next statement was going to be.

And then, I realized Joey was my own son.

Suddenly, I remembered I'd called Jonah "Joey" when he was a baby. When he'd turned five, Peter had forbidden me from calling him Joey any longer. It had to be Jonah.

"Jonah was his given name and biblical, so we were to use that. How could I have forgotten that?"

"The amygdala is responsible for memories. Typically, we find abuse victims have memory problems..." the doctor said softly. "The brain is a tricky organ."

Dr. Gray stayed in my room for two hours, talking, asking, and answering more questions. I learned that not only had I created Melody, but she was the younger version of myself, and my brain made her to protect and preserve me. I'd created Joey to fill the void and relive Jonah's childhood before he was as alienated as his father manipulated him to be. I'd been living in a parallel universe, it seemed.

I'd found myself in bed with my own husband and tried to kill myself for the betrayal.

"You've been on suicide watch since you entered the hospital near-death and since you've been here. You've come a long way, but I must ask you how you feel now," Dr. Gray said, looking over my chart as she spoke.

"So, I'm crazy," I said, more of a statement than a question.

The doctor assured me that I was not. But it took months for me to finally accept that.

"I had been suicidal and planned to kill myself the day I met or created Melody," I said frankly. "It seemed like having her friendship had given me a reason to survive and live."

I wondered what I'd do now that I didn't have her to lean on – now that I knew she wasn't real, but I feared telling Dr. Gray this, especially since I had just learned I'd been on suicide watch.

As the weeks passed and my stay on the mental health floor lingered, I learned that Peter was likely a malignant narcissist. Dr. Gray gave me information pamphlets the day before I was discharged to a domestic abuse shelter. At first, I wasn't sure why I'd be placed here, but then I learned Peter had divorced me as I lay unconscious in the hospital bed. He had abandoned me before they had moved me up to the Baptist Memorial Mental Health floor where I had to relearn to live as Melody, the thirty-eight-year-old version. I had no home, although I don't think I would have gone home to Peter under different circumstances, either.

Once I was ready to leave Baptist Memorial Hospital, Adeline came up to say goodbye. She had been my nurse for as long as I could remember being there.

"Hey, sweety," she said, smiling brightly at me. She waited with me as discharge papers were drawn up and signed.

"Why have you been with me all this time? You were downstairs. I remember your voice and the warmth of your touch, but then you were up here on this floor with me?" I asked my nurse.

"I had a sister. She was married to a pastor for six years. He seemed like the perfect husband to all of us. My parents loved him. They looked up to him. But he was abusing her and controlling her behind closed doors. I remember her trying to tell me once that he wasn't who we all thought he was, but I'd callously waved her off. Rachel killed herself. She left a note describing the years of abuse and her inability to get anyone to believe her... I didn't believe her, Melody." Melody looked down at her hands. She didn't know what to say. Tears stung her eyes as she reached to touch Adeline's hands. "That was thirty-nine years ago. She would have been sixty-three last Thursday. When you came in, I was on duty in the ER. At first, I thought you were single. You had no ring on your finger, and no one had come in with you. Two weeks after we'd gotten you stabilized, a man named Peter came into the hospital. His mannerisms, his speech, the smirks on his face, and the way he spoke of you all brought back memories of Rachel and her husband, Steve. I knew in my gut why you'd tried to kill yourself, and I swore I'd stay by your side until you were better and well enough to go home. The hospital let me move floors with you and assigned you to me because they understood I had to do for you what I hadn't done for my sister," Adeline said through strained tears.

We hugged and told each other we were sorry. Tears streamed down our faces as we said our goodbyes and promised to stay in touch. She had purchased the outfit I wore to leave and arranged for my transportation to the shelter. She walked with me through the various empty corridors, to the elevator, and around to the front door.

The shelter had changed a lot since I'd last been there eleven years earlier.

The kitchen and bath had been remodeled, and the staff had changed. The case worker assigned to me set me up with career readiness courses and found a home for me in a converted motel. It was a single room, just like a motel, except that there was a kitchenette with a full refrigerator and stove. I started working as a housekeeper on my floor.

I'd grown angry with society, myself, and God. I felt like I'd lost so many years and more to come as I put my life back together. I didn't go to church, didn't care to read the Bible, and stopped myself short from praying each time I summoned His name. I felt as though He'd abandoned me and allowed me to suffer for too long to be a merciful God like I'd been taught and thought all my previous years.

I spent months researching narcissism, the effects of narcissism, and everything else I could get my hands on reading or watching on YouTube. As I grew in knowledge, I grew in strength and in confidence.

It took me nine months to heal and get past the anger. I came to accept the ignorance of people and their own self-preservation.

I forgave God and asked Him to forgive me. I gained confidence and decided to get certified as a teacher. I took classes every Saturday through the summer and gleefully waited for my certificate to upload on the state teaching website. I was hired in a small town to teach eighth-grade English.

For months, I battled memories and thoughts of Melody and how real she had been.

I tried to see her as my imaginary friend and wondered endlessly what a fool I'd made of myself for years.

CHAPTER 40

I was released from the Baptist Memorial Mental Health Facility the day before I turned thirty-eight years old. I became a
teacher the following year and had to pass a background check
to get hired, so I knew I wasn't crazy anymore on the official.

I moved to Woodland and started a small farm. I lived there
alone. My custody petition was still pending in the northwestern
jurisdiction of Mississippi.

Peter had kept the children from me for nearly two years. I'd
contacted friends from our church and been altogether ignored
or called 'the abuser.'

Myra was the first one to even take my call. I asked if she'd write
a letter for the judge about the type of mother I'd been during
all the years we'd gone to church together. She told me she didn't
remember what kind of mother I was and didn't want to have to
make anything up and lie.

Beth and Brian turned in the other direction if they saw me in
public.

Janice and Craig smiled and waved as they quickly ran in the
opposite direction.

It was good to live on the northeast side of the state, where I
infrequently saw anyone I knew.

I had become an outcast, seen as an abusive wife, mother, and crazy woman who tried to kill herself and thought she was killing her imaginary best friend instead.

Peter had many girlfriends living in my old house. One stayed long enough to redecorate before she was gone, and another took her place.

They were all the same. Tight clothes, dyed blonde hair, and more makeup than Bobo, the clown. They went to court with him, the one he was with at the time, and they spun their stories of how crazy I was.

There was one person who stayed in a fixed relationship with Peter even through all these floosies. He had a partner. James, the worship pastor at his church, and Peter stayed close. They took vacations together while Peter left his current girlfriend home and James left his wife behind. They'd been together for several years. They were lovers. It turned out Peter was a gay man who used women to keep his secret life in the closet.

At first, there was me. I was the marrying type and the perfect diversion.

Our family and being married made him look like a perfectly straight Christian man. Even his flirtatious and predatory gawking at Beth's breasts, and later Jane and all the others, was about playing the part of a "hedonistic straight man" – to throw everyone off from ever uncovering his greatest secret.

Now that he was not married, he instead looked like a sinner and had live-in girlfriends and went to church being called a fornicator rather than letting anyone know he was actually gay.

Jonathon, his friend since the eighth grade, had been his first lover. They'd been off and on for decades, it turned out, and he really was broken over Peter's move to the South with me. They had each married as a cover for what their families wouldn't have accepted, and Peter betrayed him by moving.

Peter's mystery disappearances had been to gay bars and hookups. It turned out he not only solicited sex with male escorts but dabbled in escorting himself when money was needed, such as with that prison van. He'd already made plans to hook up with a man he was contracted to escort when I'd intercepted and sent him to Myra and Chris' home. The man he shared the motel room with had actually paid for it, and the rental vehicle was part of what Peter included in his services.

When I had thought porn was his worst sin and the reason he couldn't find me attractive, it had really been because I wasn't a man. He'd left enough hints. I didn't know why I hadn't seen it. The thing that puzzled me most was that it was the twenty-first century. Homosexuality had come out of the closet and been celebrated. I could not understand why he went to such lengths to hide his orientation, but he wasn't my problem any longer. That alone is a relief that escalates my own healing.

It took another year before the court finally allowed me to have visitation with the two youngest boys. Jonah refused to see me. The other two had been tentative at first and still were as they left their father's work van, but as soon as we saw the vehicle leave, they came alive with endless chatter, hugs, and kisses. They spent each weekend riding our pony, driving through the fields with their go-cart, and making mud pies outside under the old cedar trees. We went out to the far-north end of our farm to fish and pick blackberries when they are in season. There were trails we'd carved through the most southern part of our farm and a tree with a trunk bent at a complete 90-degree angle. Gregory and Andrew climbed that tree and pretended it was a myriad of things from dinosaurs to airplanes.

I missed my Joey. I missed the way he used to be, but I'd accepted the alienation. It had, after all, been a long time in the making. I tried to stay in touch with him through text and Facebook, but the relationship was still basically non-existent.

We were currently involved in another custody battle. There had been Psychological Evaluations, MMPI 3's completed, and NPI's completed. Peter had been officially diagnosed with Narcissistic Personality Disorder and Anti-Social Personality Disorder, also known as being psychopathic. My therapist believed he was also likely to have the third Machiavellianism, completing what is known as the dark triad, and I had actually recovered from my Dissociative Identity Disorder.

The report read as follows: The multiple personalities of Melody Ann Timbre have been reintegrated into a single, healthy, functioning personality.

We weren't allowed to have copies of the report, but my lawyer sent me a screenshot of the line. I had it printed and prominently displayed on the dining room wall of my farmhouse above a poster of a painting of a woman from the 1950s walking her horse and dog with a banner across the bottom that read: "And She Lived Happily Ever After!"

We had a court date coming up in a week and a half. I was hoping to get custody of Gregory and Andrew. No one was sure what should happen with Jonah.

The sounds of summertime filled my ears again. I'd been awakened to how exhilarating it was to finally hear them again. The quartet of cicadas that serenaded long crescendos all throughout the days and into the nights were accented by the definitive calls of a lone whippoorwill once the sun began to fade. The intermittent prestissimo of a nearby wasp or yellow jacket added to the overture but was soon taken over by the solos of mourning doves, bluebirds, and the occasional shrill yell from a red-tailed hawk. The distant sound of dogs was hardly an interruption but more of a downbeat to the wild, orchestrated music being conducted by nature itself right outside my bedroom window. I could finally hear the sweet melody of life again.

As the newness of this symphony of nature passed through the open windows, so too did the suffocating heat of the Mid-South. Still, I'd rather endure the malaise of near-heatstroke just to hear this sweet melody than close the windows and have air conditioning. It was a tune I'd missed for over a decade. A song that my heart had longed to enjoy. But being locked away in an abusive marriage and the makings of my own mind had kept me from hearing the escapades of these beloved mistrals for too long.

It had been over two years since I began to wake from the stupor that stole approximately half of my life. Turning forty seemed to be the last ingredient I needed to escape the lasting effects of a somnolence that had confined my mind to paralysis. I finally felt alive again.

I reached over in my oversized bed and put my arm around my two sleeping sons. I'd lost so much time with my babies. My memories were still tainted with Melody and little Joey. It was hard to remember what was real and what I'd made up to survive the abuse. It was harder to live without Jonah and be unsure of how to help him after living through the brunt of abuse by his psychotic and narcissistic father.

A sense of security, peace, reverence, and piety enveloped me as a new resident of Woodland. I had achieved my dreams. I had the farm I'd always wanted, my own horses grazing outside my bedroom window, a large farm dog, and my kids tucked in beside me. I was a single mom teaching in our local school district and making great strides in many of my students' lives.

Guarded in heart and by strong fences surrounding our home, I knew I was alright. I'd survived and was now thriving and getting out of bed to start the new, glorious day.

"I will restore to you the years that the swarming locust has eaten, the hopper, the destroyer, and the cutter, my great army, which I sent among you. You shall eat in plenty and be satisfied, and praise the name of the LORD your God, who has dealt wondrously with you. And my people shall never again be put to shame." (Joel 2:25-26 ESV)

J. Kenkade
PUBLISHING

Our Services

Author Retains Royalties & Rights

100% Royalties
Professional Proofreading
Copyright Registration
Book Formatting
Cover Design
Ghostwriting
Self-Publishing Classes

For inquiries:
Website: www.jkenkadepublishing.com
Email: info@jkenkadepublishing.com
501-943-8300

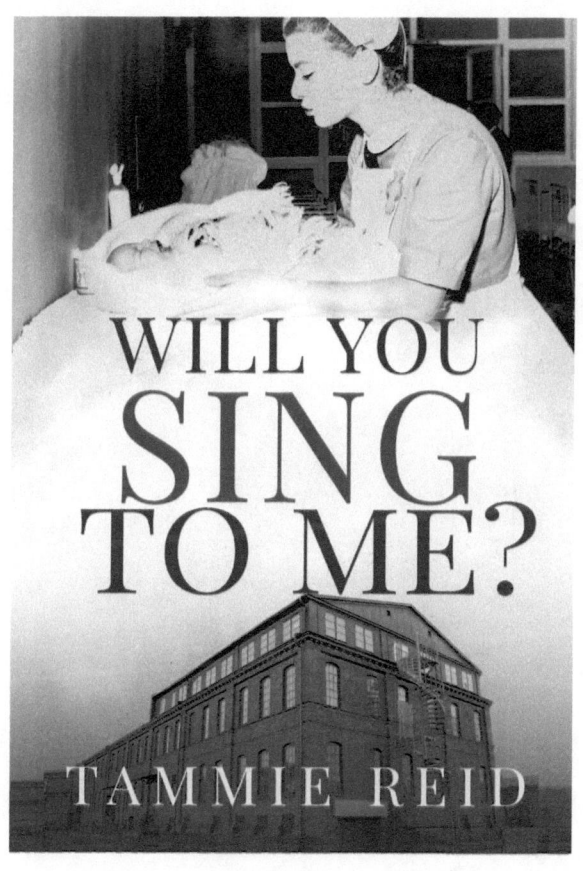

Also Available from
J. Kenkade Publishing

**Also Available from
J. Kenkade Publishing**

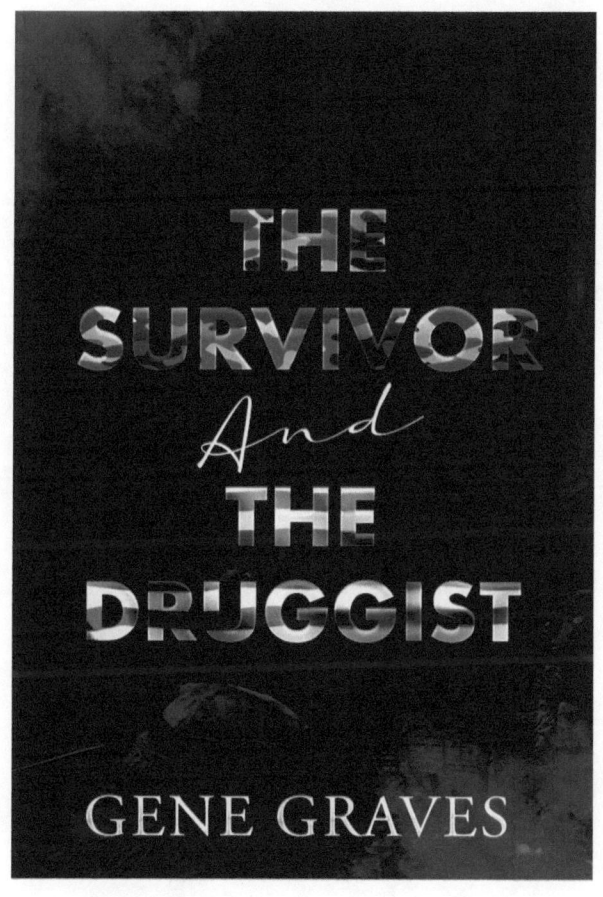

www.ingramcontent.com/pod-product-compliance
Lightning Source LLC
Chambersburg PA
CBHW022107240626
47153CB00007B/2267